For my beautiful sister,
who has finally found her happily-ever-after.

Chapter One

City of Ephesus— west coast of modern
Turkey—
Roman Empire—AD 99

There were two kinds of Roman men: the ones
who lived in search of *Gloria* and the ones who
lived in search of *bona fortuna*. Arria's father
was the second kind. No matter what family cri-
sis or holy ritual, what call of duty or act of the
gods, nothing could keep him from the fighting
pits and that was where she found him the night
he sold her freedom.

'No women allowed,' growled the guard,
standing at the entrance to the pit-viewing area.
'Unless you want to do me a favour?' He gave
himself a rude scratch, then flashed Arria a
wine-stained grin.

'Go to Hades,' she told him, and in the split

second of his astonishment she slipped past him into the rollicking crowd. There must have been two hundred men gathered on the slope before her—portly merchants and seafaring traders, oily-haired plebeians and watchful freedmen, even a smattering of patricians—all vying for position around the large gladiator training pit known as the Chasm of Death.

Arria scanned the men's torchlit faces, searching for her father. She told herself that it was possible he was not here at all. There was a chance that he had been on his way to the fighting pit that evening and been struck by a bolt of reason.

I am an honourable pater familias, Arria imagined him realising. *I should not continue risking my family's survival on the uncertainties of bets.*

Arria almost laughed. As if her father were capable of such Aristotelian logic! No, he was here, as was every other corrupt gambler in the province. The fighting pits of Ephesus were as popular as they were bloody and the Chasm of Death was the largest and bloodiest of them all. The only hope now was for Arria to find her father and seize his purse before the damage was done.

A shell horn moaned. A ringmaster's voice resounded from below. He was introducing the next set of gladiators—a Dacian and a Berber, whose heights and weights he announced first in Latin, then in Greek. Nearby, a Jewish man echoed the information in Aramaic and Arria thought she heard someone say it again in the Armenian tongue. Second only to Alexandria in influence, Ephesus was the most important commercial centre outside of Rome—a place where people from every corner of the world gathered to live and trade. They spoke different languages and worshipped different gods, though Arria doubted any kind of god was present in this bloody place.

Keeping out of the torchlight, she stalked along the edge of the crowd in search of her father's stooped form.

The fight below commenced. Arria could hear the metallic clang of weapons and the grunts of effort as the gladiators began their bloody brawl. The Chasm of Death was the training ground of Ephesus's largest gladiator school and several times a year its owner, Brutus, would invite spectators to place their bets on fights between old or unpromising gladiators in an effort to clean out his stock.

It was a twisted, bloody business and one which the idle and desperate men of Ephesus looked forward to with perverse joy. Arria calculated that her father had lost enough *denarii* at the pits over the years to equal the cost of a herd of goats, or a fine fishing vessel.

But tonight he had reached a new low. He had seized a purse full of *denarii* that did not belong to him: Arria's purse, the purse that contained the *denarii* that would see their family through the winter.

Arria pushed deeper into the crowd and nearer to the pit's perimeter. 'First blood to the Dacian!' someone shouted. Men cheered and grumbled. Coins changed hands. Someone smashed a wine flagon against a slab of stone.

'Where are you, Father?' Arria mumbled, feeling a little dizzy.

She felt a large hand push against her back. 'Move yourself, boy.' A man in a purple-trimmed toga brushed past Arria, his eyes sliding to the small bump of her bosom. He paused. 'What is this?' He yanked her braid out from beneath her tunic. 'A woman? At a fighting pit?'

Arria stared into his kohl-rimmed eyes, too stunned to speak. She knew the man's face: the bent nose, the high cheeks, the oil-soaked hair, combed into perfect rows. She had seen it carved on statues and sketched on walls from the cities of Miletus to Pergamon. 'Proconsul Governor Secundus?'

'You are under arrest, woman. Your presence

here is an affront to Mars and a disgrace to feminine honour. *Lictor!*' He motioned to a bodyguard somewhere behind her.

The governor of the province? At a fighting pit? How was it possible? More importantly, what was she to do? She needed to find her father. It was September already. *Fortuna* alone would not keep Arria's family warm and alive through the cold, bleak months to come.

She lurched her braid free from the governor's grasp and attempted to run, but he caught her by the arm. His bodyguard drew closer.

'I must go!' Arria burst out. There was no time to explain. There was no time to even think. There was only her heel slamming down atop the governor's foot and her teeth burying themselves into the flesh of his gripping hand.

'Ow!' the governor howled.

Oh, gods, what had she done? She unlocked her jaws and, as he recoiled in pain, she was able to detach herself from the most powerful man in Ephesus.

'Little asp!' he shouted behind her. *'Lictors!'*

A death bellow resonated from the pit below and the crowd erupted in celebration. Seizing on the chaos, Arria tucked her braid beneath her tunic and ducked low, losing herself in the crush of bodies.

Horror rioted through her. Had she really just bitten into the flesh of Proconsul Quintus Vibius Secundus, the venerable governor of the Roman province of Asia?

'Prepare yourselves my fellow Romans,' chimed the ringmaster, 'for in this next bout, limbs will be hewn and innards strewn. I give you the Ox of Germania versus…'

Arria was caught in a sudden rush of movement. She was pulled, then pushed, then pressed backwards. Dizzy and fumbling for balance, she turned to find herself staring down at the blood-spattered sand at a bald, muscle-bound man in a rabbit-skin kilt.

'The Beast of Britannia!' shouted the ringmaster.

The barbarian gladiator raked his gaze over the crowd and for a moment his eyes locked with Arria's. Startled, Arria stepped backwards. She had never seen such eyes. They were neither green nor brown, but some indescribable colour that seemed to change with each flicker of torchlight. Incredibly, she did not feel fear, though she was aware she was being appraised by a killer. It was something else she felt. Something strange. It was as if her breath had become stuck in her chest.

A second later, the ringmaster stepped in front of the man and the spell was broken.

'Barbarian versus barbarian!' the ringmaster cried. 'Place your bets!'

The cacophony increased as the spectators conferred, staking their fortunes on one gory outcome or the other. 'The Beast is the obvious choice,' someone near Arria pronounced.

'Agreed,' said another. 'I do not understand why Brutus has put him in the ring. He is one of the Empire's finest.'

'He is old now. His days are numbered,' said a third. 'Besides, look at the chest on the Ox. They have fattened him.'

The men might have been discussing fighting cocks, or horses for sale.

'I say the Beast will prevail!' said the first. He nudged the back of Arria's shoulder. 'What say you, man?'

'Piss off,' Arria grumbled, keeping her back to the men and feeling thankful for the low light. Besides, she had nothing to say, no opinion to profess. She did not find any of this interesting, exciting or even vaguely human.

Still, there was something about the gladiator's name that rang familiar. The Beast of Britannia. Where had she heard it before? Probably at the baths. Women were always talking about gladiators at the baths. They spent endless hours discussing the fighters' looks and conjecturing about the size of their…weapons. Even if he were not famous, a gladiator with a name like the Beast would never have been safe from their gossip.

Nor was he safe from death, for he wore no armour and was protected only by symbols— haunting blue swirls that had been painted across his chest.

His opponent was scarcely better off. The thick-chested Ox stood on the other end of the arena in a skirt of leather straps and little else.

She wondered if either of the men had any idea how thoroughly they were being mocked. The gladiators who fought and died at the circuses and amphitheatres wore at least light armour— helmets and shields and usually *manicae* for the arms, depending on the roles they played.

Gladiators skilled enough to perform at theatres were issued additional protections, including greaves to protect their shins and, depending on their assigned role, chest plates. These men did not even don sandals.

Arria gazed down at her own sandals. She had almost worn through the soles. Not that her father would have cared. When she looked up, she caught sight of him at last. He was nodding his head in conversation with a barrel-chested man just across the pit. She motioned with her arms, trying to get her father's attention, though she could tell by the tightness in his jaw that it was already too late.

The bet had been made. Arria's savings had been staked. Now there was nothing to do but pray. Arria gazed down at the two hulking barbarians standing in the arena below. But pray for whom?

Two slaves emerged from a tunnel and delivered the gladiators their swords. 'Die well, gladiators!' said the ringmaster, then followed the slaves back into the tunnel, closing an iron gate behind them.

For a moment, all was silent.

The Ox of Germania sliced the air with his sword. He danced towards the centre of the ring, feinting and jabbing to the encouragement of his supporters.

The Beast of Britannia was more circumspect. He skulked along the curved stone wall of his own side of the ring, watching the Ox with those bottomless eyes.

Arria saw her father's lips moving. He was praying to Fortuna herself, no doubt, the goddess who so often wiped her feet with his toga.

The gladiators drew closer. Taunts rained

down from the crowd along with a cascade of obscenities in a variety of tongues. The Ox lunged; the Beast dodged. A path of blood streaked across the Beast's chest. 'First blood to the Ox!' someone shouted. A smattering of cheers. The changing of coins.

The Beast was bleeding. Arria had never seen such a terrible gash. It began at the tip of his shoulder and split his muscled chest diagonally, concluding at the thick arc of muscle at the top of his hip.

Arria was not the only one stunned by the wound. The Beast himself appeared utterly perplexed by it, as if he had never suffered a single wound in all his life. He stared in wonderment as blood leaked out and began to trickle down his rippling stomach. He appeared to laugh. In that instant, the Ox charged forward. Arria saw her father nod.

The Ox, then, thought Arria. *I must pray for the Ox.*

But the Beast dived to the ground and rolled over himself and the Ox's blade missed its target. In a blur of motion, the Beast jumped to his feet and sliced off the Ox's head.

It rolled to the edge of the ring, hitting the stone wall without a sound.

'The Beast has won!' shouted the ringmaster.

The crowd roared. Arria placed her hand over her mouth, willing herself not to vomit.

The slaves emerged from the tunnel and dragged away the Ox's convulsing corpse. The Beast made no gesture of triumph. He dropped his sword into the bloodstained sand and spat, then stormed past the ringmaster back through the iron gate.

Arria braved a glance at her father. His face ashen, he reached beneath the folds of his toga and produced Arria's red-leather coin purse.

As her father handed the purse to his companion, Arria pictured its contents: seventy-six beautiful, shiny *denarii*. She had earned the precious coins from the sale of four carpets—four Herculean efforts of knots and wool, which had required an entire year and nearly all her waking hours to weave.

Her father's betting companion leaned backwards into the shadows, tucking the purse in a pouch beneath his bulging stomach. He gave her father a friendly clap on the back. *Would you like another bet?* he appeared to ask.

No, he would not, Arria thought bitterly, *for he is utterly ruined*.

But her father nodded vigorously and reached beneath his toga once again.

Impossible. Her father was perennially poor.

He was a sand scratcher, a circus rat, a man who lingered outside the arenas begging better men for loans. But a glint of gold caught the light and Arria watched in horror as her father held out her mother's golden *ichthys*.

It was the most sacred object her mother owned, a gilded fish, a symbol of her strange faith. The fish had once belonged to a Jewish man named Paul who had come to Ephesus many years before to spread something called the good news. He had secretly converted many Ephesians to his new religion, including Arria's late grandparents.

The golden fish had been her mother's inheritance and only comfort. She kept it near her bed and each evening she rubbed it lovingly as she mouthed prayers to her singular god and his son, Jesus.

Now the fat man cradled the fish in his palm, measuring its weight. Arria thought of her own mother's palms, red and chapped from having to take in other people's laundry. The man lifted the fish to his mouth and tested it with his teeth, one of which, Arria observed, was made of gold itself.

He gave a satisfied nod.

No, no, no. Arria opened her mouth to scream, then bit her tongue. Out of the corner of her eye, the governor's ghostly toga came into focus. There he was—not a dozen paces away—on the very same side of the pit where she now stood.

She sank back into the crowd. He had not noticed her, thank the gods, for his attention had been fixed on the dozens of coin purses changing hands beneath his gaze.

Arria pushed backwards against the press of bodies, determined to reach her father before the next bout.

But she was once again thrust forward as the men behind her moved towards the ringmaster's voice. 'Behold your champion,' he announced, holding the Beast's arm aloft, 'for he is also your next competitor!' The crowd howled at the unexpected change of rules. 'Will this champion survive a second bout?'

'By Jove's cock he will!' someone slurred.

'Two *denarii* says he pays the boatman.'

'I'll wager five,' shouted another. 'The man is losing blood!'

And he was. Blood was still seeping from the long diagonal wound that traversed his chest. It had mixed with his blue body paint to produce a sickening shade of green, which had smeared across his ribs like fetid mud.

Blood. There was too much blood. It pooled at the top of his loincloth and streaked across his furry kilt. It dribbled down his giant legs like paint on pillars. It had even smeared atop his bald head.

He gazed up at the crazed spectators in a kind of wonder. If he were not breathing so hard, and bleeding so terribly, he might have been a statue—some splendid, towering ode to the male form. Or he might have been the figure of an ancient god standing there in the sand. A great spirit brought low—cut down by the ugly world.

An aching sadness overtook Arria. The blood. If only she could staunch the flow of it, or somehow wash it all away.

Instinctively, she pulled her handkerchief from her belt. As if such a small piece of cloth could possibly help this man, or any of the gladiators. They were slaves, criminals, captives of war. Their deaths had not been spared, only delayed for the entertainment of the bloodthirsty mob.

'I give you the Beast's next foe,' announced the ringmaster. 'The Wrath of Syria!'

The man who emerged through the iron gate was shorter than the Beast, but twice his width, with fat arms and legs like twin logs. The Wrath held a tall trident spear, but was without the net that usually accompanied such a weapon. Across his broad forehead were the large tattooed letters of a field slave.

'Romans, place your bets.'

She watched in resignation as her father gripped the gold-toothed man's arm, sealing the next bet. Her mother's *ichthys* had been staked.

'Die well, gladiators!' said the ringmaster.

The Beast circled the Wrath, who was thrashing his trident about wildly, as if he had no idea of how to use it. In a single swing of his sword, the Beast knocked the weapon away. Incredibly, the Wrath did not even attempt to retrieve it. He simply dropped to his knees and awaited the final blow.

The Beast held his blade to the Wrath's neck and gazed up at the governor, awaiting his command of mercy. But the governor was not even watching. His head was bent over a collection of coins.

'Iugula!' someone shouted. *Kill him!*

Without looking up, the governor drew his finger across his neck. *No mercy.*

Arria turned away. She hated them—all of them—the ringmaster, the governor, the spectators, the Roman Empire itself. This was not entertainment. This was Roman conquest writ small.

There was a collective groan, and when she returned her gaze to the arena she saw that the Wrath of Syria had been granted a merciful death. He lay face down in the sand, blood pooling where his throat had been slit. She saw her father bury his head in his hands.

Which meant he had bet on the Wrath.

Her father's companion patted him on the shoulders consolingly, gently relieving him of her mother's golden fish. Her father stared down at his empty hand. When he finally looked up, his eyes locked with Arria's.

He flashed her a smile of recognition, followed by an odd frown. Arria made a gesture of departure. *Come now, Father*, she mouthed, pointing towards the exit. *It is time to go.*

But her father's attention was distracted once again by the ringmaster, who stepped forward holding the Beast's arm in the air. 'The Beast of Britannia will fight a final bout!'

The crowd cheered with fresh abandon. The exhausted Beast raised his sword and his gaze found Arria's once again. Her chest squeezed. His eyes were no longer green, but black, like the darkest part of Hades. She remembered what he had done—the cool indifference with which he had removed the German's head and the terrifying efficiency with which he had killed the Syrian.

It was no wonder she felt so weak beneath his gaze. So completely exposed. He was a killer of men—a kind of monster. She hugged her arms around her chest, feeling the heat of fear burn in her stomach. The heat could not be contained. It was spreading to her limbs. She could feel it colonising her very cheeks.

'*Gloria!*' someone shouted.

Straight away, a man half the Beast's size skipped through the gate. He wore a comical goat's tail and sandals shaped like hooves. 'Romans, prepare yourselves for a battle that only the Great Jupiter could conceive.' The ringmaster gazed reverently at the heavens, then returned his attention to the crowd and flashed a wicked grin. 'I give you the Beast of Britannia versus... Felix the Satyr!' The crowd disintegrated into laughter.

Now the mockery was complete. The goatman scuffed his hoof-like sandals in the sand, bleating and bobbing to a cacophony of jeers. Arria assumed he was mad, though his ropy muscles and fast movements suggested an ability to fight.

She returned her attention to the Beast. He was still looking at her assessingly. It was as if he were some terrible predator trying to decide if she was worth the effort to hunt. Or perhaps he had already decided. She swallowed hard.

'Romans, place your bets!'

Her father and the gold-toothed man were

speaking together fervently now and she wondered what they might be saying. Were they haggling over some promised credit? Impossible. Her father was not credit worthy and he had nothing left to bet. At length her father raised his finger. He was pointing across the ring.

At Arria.

Chapter Two

The air around Arria acquired a strange weight. It pressed down upon her so hard that she could not lift her feet, or her arms, or even her head, which slumped along with her shoulders in a reflection of her father's own miserable posture.

She watched beneath heavy lids as her father and the gold-toothed man discussed their wager. Soon they were met by a third man—a scribe. The sober old documentarian scratched hastily upon a scroll, then offered the men his quill. Her father signed the scroll and gripped the gold-toothed man's arm for a third time.

The bet had been made. Arria had been staked.

She felt tears falling unbidden down her cheeks. There were too many tears. Her handkerchief was not big enough to absorb them all.

'Die well, gladiators!' said the ringmaster.

Who was she supposed to pray for now?

Surely the Beast, for only a fool would have bet on the little man with the swinging tail. Even now, the howling Satyr was retreating from the Beast, kicking up sand and scratching at the arena walls. When the two finally engaged, the Beast quickly knocked the sword from the goat-man's hand.

'Kill the Satyr! Kill the Satyr!' the crowd chanted.

It appeared that her father was chanting along with them.

Thank the gods—he had bet on the Beast. For once he had made a sound judgement. Perhaps he even stood to regain what he had lost. Arria could only send a prayer to Fortuna to make it so.

The Beast had the Satyr pinned to the wall and Arria could already feel the weight of the air beginning to lift. She glanced at her father. His eyebrows arched hopefully and his wrinkled old mouth was bowed up into a grin.

Strangely, the gold-toothed man was smiling, too.

That was when Satyr thrust his finger into the Beast's chest wound. The Beast stumbled to the ground in howling agony and released his sword. The Satyr placed his hoof upon the Beast's bloody chest, pausing above him for the death blow.

Stunned, the spectators fell silent. The champion was about to lose, right before their eyes. Arria strained to believe her own. Something was not right. The Beast would never have lost control of his sword as he had done. Even Arria could see that he was too experienced to make such an error.

The Beast raised two fingers—the traditional entreaty for mercy.

Was it obvious to no one but her? The Beast had deliberately lost.

'*Mitte! Mitte!*' the crowd thundered. *Spare him!* All eyes turned to the governor, who gave a simple bow of the head. Mercy. His chest wound still leaking blood, the Beast lumbered to his feet and Arria found herself searching for his gaze. But he kept his head bowed as the ringmaster raised the Satyr's hand into the air. 'Romans, I give you Felix the Satyr, your winner.'

Arria should have been relieved. The Beast's life had been spared. For once this terrible night, mercy had triumphed over bloodlust. But injustice had triumphed, too, for the Beast had deliberately succumbed to the Satyr and Arria had been sold into slavery as a result.

She gazed across the ring. Her new owner was already assessing her. His eyes scraped over her: her hair, her breasts, her arms. He was regarding her physical form just as the bettors had regarded the gladiators'. *No, no, no.* This could not be.

Desperation seized her. 'The Beast deliberately relinquished the fight!' she shouted without thinking. 'Did nobody see it? The outcome was fixed before the act! You have all been cheated! Robbed!'

Now it was not just the gold-toothed man's eyes on her. It seemed that every single man gathered around the Chasm of Death had turned his attention to Arria—including the governor.

Oh, gods, what had she done? The governor gave a tight-lipped command, and soon his guards were pushing towards her from the left edge of the arena. From the right, her father and her new master were nearing, as well. The pit sprawled below her. The distance to the ground appeared to be three body lengths or more. There was only one direction in which she could flee— back into the bustling crowd.

But when she turned around she was confronted with a large guard smiling down at her through a mouthful of wine-stained teeth. It was the guard from the entry. He had pursued her, it seemed, and now he had her trapped. 'Now you *really* owe me a favour,' he growled.

She was surrounded on three sides, and there was only one option for escape. She closed her eyes, swung her legs over the edge of the pit and jumped.

'Criminal!' commanded the governor.

'Harlot!' hissed the entry guard.

'Daughter!' shouted her father.

The shouts grew fainter and she knew that she was falling through the air towards a very hard end. And then it came. *Thunk.* Her legs buckled, her arms, too, and when she looked up she half expected to find herself upon the shores of the River Styx. Instead she was wallowing in the bloodstained sand. There beside her lay the Beast's fallen *gladius*.

She commanded her hands to seize the sword and, miraculously, they obeyed. Her legs obeyed her, too, and as she struggled to her feet she became aware of the riotous crowd. 'Gladiatrix! Gladiatrix!' they chanted.

Above her, two of the governor's guards were already straddling the arena wall, preparing to jump in after her. The crowd was taunting them, daring them to take the plunge, and out of the corner of her eye Arria could see more coins changing hands. The men were making bets. On her.

The governor shouted down at the ringmaster. 'Seize her, you fool!'

The ringmaster stepped towards Arria.

'Stay back!' she hissed, slashing the heavy *gladius* through the air. The ringmaster stepped backwards. He turned to the Beast.

'You heard the governor,' the ringmaster shouted at the Beast. '*You* seize her!'

Arria waited for the towering gladiator to make his charge, but he only stood and stared, a rueful smile twisting his lips. He shook his head, and glanced above them. 'You would do well to run,' he said.

The governor's guards were perched at the rim of the pit and preparing themselves to pounce. The tunnel loomed before her: dark, terrifying and her only hope. She dropped the sword, kicked up a cloud of dust and dashed through the iron gate.

She found herself surrounded by a prison of stone. A long, dimly lit hallway stretched past several empty, iron-barred cells. There was the smell of blood and moss, and the sound of dripping water, though she could not determine whence it came.

Drip, drip, drip.

She heard a shout from the arena and a thud upon the sand. Doubtless the first guard had made his jump. Arria could hear him coughing and shouting obscenities while the crowd coaxed him on. *Think, Arria.*

She seized the nearest torch, shaking it to extinction. She did the same with the other torches until she had plunged the barracks into complete darkness.

Reaching the end of the hall, she pushed against a heavy stone door. Incredibly, it gave way. An exit. She felt a rush of fresh air and paused. The guards would expect her to escape through this door and they would come after her on legs faster than hers.

Think.

She left the door open, then stepped backwards.

She could hear the slap of the guards' sandals upon the stones now. They were moving down the dark hallway, getting closer to her by the second. They stopped suddenly, listening for her.

Drip, drip, drip.

Cal heard a splash in the large water urn outside his cell. If he had not known better, he would have thought it a drowning mouse.

'That was a remarkable show you gave us tonight,' called Felix the Satyr from the adjacent cell.

'Well, of course it was,' Cal replied. 'For I am the Empire's finest gladiator.'

'I am not talking about you, idiot,' said Felix.

'I am talking about the woman who has taken up residence in our barracks. Do you not see her there? You need only stand up and peer into the urn across from your cell.'

Cal stretched out on his bed and closed his eyes. In truth, he did not care if Venus herself had taken up residence across from his cell. All he wanted was a little rest before the arrival of his promised reward.

'I hope she knows that she will not escape this *ludus* by cowering like a kitten all night,' Felix mused. 'If she is going to escape at all, she must leave while darkness reigns.'

There was a long silence and Cal was sure he heard another splash of water.

'Why does she continue to conceal herself?' mused Felix.

Because she is a Roman woman, thought Cal. *And thus nourishes herself on the melodramatic.*

Cal rubbed his bald head. When he had first caught sight of the woman that evening, he had half believed her an illusion—some vision of divinity foreshadowing his own death. In his three years at this *ludus*, he had never once seen a woman attend the pit fights and thus naturally assumed she had come for him—his personal escort to the Otherworld.

But the fights had gone exactly as planned. He

had killed his first two opponents, then taken the fall, just as Brutus, his owner and trainer, had instructed. The governor granted mercy, just as Cal had been told he would, and the governor, Brutus and Brutus's gold-toothed brother Oppius had all made large sums of *denarii* on the outcome. It had been business as usual at Ludus Brutus that night, with no chance of a trip to the Otherworld after all.

He should have known she was not divine. When he had glanced up at her that second time, he had noticed her appearance and it was about as far from divine as a woman could get. Her tunic was tattered, her expression was pinched and worried, and a distinct spatter of blood stained her shapely lower legs.

Though it was not her appearance that had finally convinced him of her mortality, it was what happened to her cheeks when she looked at him. A dark crimson hue had spread over the twin mounds and down her neck to the notch at its base. There, a tiny relentlessly pulsing drum of skin had betrayed her racing heart. He had been able to see it even from his position in the pit.

He never tired of witnessing it—the effect he had on Roman women. First came the blush, then the shudder, and then the look of fascinated derision, as if the woman were witnessing the incarnation of her darkest, most forbidden thoughts.

He was like a strange food from a foreign land: they all wanted to try a sample. And though this particular Roman woman was one of the loveliest he had yet seen, he was not so foolish as to let her stir his lust. Roman women were all alike in his experience. They were selfish, bored creatures who used gladiators like men used whores.

Pah! He had only a few nights left upon this earth. He did not wish to waste his thoughts on a Roman woman.

'We are locked in our cells if that is what you are afraid of, sweetheart,' called Felix. 'And even if we were not locked in, you would have nothing to fear. Why not emerge from the urn where you are hiding and dry yourself? We promise not to watch. You see, we are honourable men.'

Still more silence. Then, finally, 'You are *not* honourable men.'

It was as if she had spent the last few hours sharpening the words upon a whetstone.

'We die to honour Rome, my dear,' said Felix, his tone thick.

She pulled herself from the vessel with feline grace. 'You die to honour profit.'

He craned his head and saw her shadowy figure lifting the skirt of her tunic and squeezing it back into the urn.

Felix cackled. 'You wield your tongue as well as you do a *gladius.*'

'And you wield your boasting as well as you do your deceit.'

Cal smiled to himself. Perhaps what she lacked in judgement she made up for in wit.

She jumped in place, apparently attempting to dry herself. Finally she drifted beneath the torchlight near Cal's cell and he gave her a glance.

Her efforts to squeeze herself dry had been for naught. She was still dripping wet. Her large dark eyes blinked beneath thick, water-clumped lashes that glistened in the torchlight and played off her ebony hair, which had come loose from its braid in places in small, distracting spirals. Worse, the top of her threadbare tunic was soaked through, giving a full view of her breast wrap, which was itself so thin that he could see the dark shadows of her nipples beneath it.

He had never seen anything so erotic in all his life. Her big, blinking eyes, her bouncing curls, her small, shapely breasts and thinly veiled nipples: perhaps she was divine after all. Maybe she was the very *naiad* that had been painted on the urn itself, come to kiss him with her sultry lips.

Although those sultry lips were currently

twisted into a Medusan scowl. 'You deliberately succumbed to the Satyr,' she accused Cal. She stepped forward and gripped the bars of Cal's cell gate. 'Do you deny it?'

Cal did not look her in the eye for fear he might turn to stone. 'Do you not have some escaping to do?' he asked.

'I asked you a question.' She folded her arms over her bosom and that was a shame. But he could still observe how her skirt clung tightly to the shape of her thighs. She was lovely, female and completely without defence. Did she not understand how quickly he was able to move? That he could simply jump to his feet, pull her body against the bars and have his way?

'You say nothing because you know that I speak truth,' she spat. 'You deliberately succumbed to the Satyr, though it was obvious that you were the better fighter.'

Cal grinned. 'Did you hear that, Felix?' he called. 'She said I am the better fighter.'

'Rubbish,' replied Felix.

'Your second opponent had expected to die,' she continued. 'I saw him begging you for a merciful death.'

'And I damn well gave it to him,' he grumbled.

He did not wish to think of the Syrian's death. The man had been a farmer, not a fighter. He had been purchased by Brutus only weeks ago—a field hand who had been put up for sale as a punishment for attempting an escape. He had not been a bad man—not like most of the gladiators who came in and out of Ludus Brutus. Still, the governor had decreed his death and the governor had to be obeyed.

'So you admit it?' she pressed.

'Admit what?'

'That you deceived everyone.'

Why were Roman women so unrelenting? 'I admit nothing.'

'The only true fight was the first one,' she observed. 'You relieved the Ox of his head with little effort.' She pushed her face between the bars. 'You lie there acting as if you are proud of your deception. They call you Beast, but in truth you are a snake.'

Ha! If only he *were* a snake. Then he could slither through the bars of his cell and devour her whole. Surely that would shut her up.

Her scowl deepened and he waited in dull irritation for her next accusation. Would she remind him of the gladiator's sacred oath, perhaps? Or would she explain the Roman code of honour and then recite it for him *ad nauseum* while she shook her little plebeian finger at his nose?

'You defied the gods,' she spat.

'Which gods? Whose?'

'You ruined my father.'

'Your father ruined your father.' This was almost as diverting as swordplay.

'I know that you are famous,' she said. 'I have heard your name at the baths and seen it scrawled in graffiti. Why would you deliberately destroy your own reputation by rolling beneath the Satyr's blade?'

'And what of *my* reputation?' Felix called cheerfully. 'Have you also heard it spoken at the baths?'

'And mine?' called another gladiator from down the hall.

But the woman paid the other gladiators no mind. She seemed bent on making Cal alone suffer.

'Do you think I care a wink for my reputation?' Cal asked mildly, but her scowl remained fixed, as if she had not heard him.

Typical. In his experience, Roman women never heard what they did not wish to hear, never did what they did not wish to do and rarely saw beyond their own toes.

She was staring down at her own toes now, as if they alone could tell her everything she wished to know about what had happened that night. 'By the gods, it was *all* theatre!' she exclaimed at last.

'All of it! You were told to kill the German spectacularly and that is what you did. And the Syrian knew he was going to die before he even set foot upon the sands. Those first two bouts were designed for you to win the crowd's favour so that they would call for mercy when the time came. Your *lanista* knew it. The ringmaster knew it...'

She gazed up at the stone ceiling, thinking, and Cal observed the elegant length of her neck. 'Even the *governor* knew it! And the gold-toothed merchant—he knew it, too. That is why he smiled when you had the Satyr at the tip of your blade. He already knew you were going to lose.'

Cal did not know whether to be impressed or furious. He settled for a smirk. 'You are remarkably perceptive for one so naive,' he said.

'I am not naive.'

'Your denial of your own naivety is itself naive.'

'You speak in knots. I assure you that I am quite the opposite of naive.'

'And what is that exactly?'

She paused, searching the air, and he observed the fine cut of her jaw. '*Un*-naive.'

'Your cleverness slays me.'

Her eyes narrowed. 'You are clearly trying to distract from admitting to your deception.'

Her accusations were growing tedious. Fortunately, he knew how to shut her up. 'And you are trying to distract from admitting that you wish to lie with me.'

The woman gasped. And there it was, that look of fascinated derision—though on her face it more closely resembled straightforward disgust. 'That is absurd,' she snapped, then added, 'The very thought is an abhorrence.'

An abhorrence? Well, at least she was original. 'I know you want me.'

'I want nothing to do with you. You are a mon—'

She bit her lip.

'A what?'

'Nothing.'

'I know what you are thinking.' *You think me a monster.*

'You cannot read my thoughts,' she said.

'I know you are Roman and that is all I need to know.'

'You know nothing about me.'

'Nothing about you?' His mind churned. 'Let me see. You illegally shoved your way into a house of men. Only an innocent would be so stupid. You either have no brothers to act on your behalf, or if you do have a brother, he is useless.'

A small cringe. A glance at the ground.

'Ah, so you do have a useless brother,' he continued gleefully, 'and his very mention causes you pain. Probably returned from one of Domitian's foolish campaigns? A drunkard, perhaps?'

Her pink lips pressed into a thin red line.

'Your father, too, is useless, for he is the kind of man who must be followed by his own daughter to the pits. He has plunged your family into ruin, has he not? And you pity yourself mightily for it. *Pah!* You are fortunate he has not sold you into servitude.'

Her face turned an unnatural shade of grey.

Had her father sold her into servitude?

'I curse you,' she spat suddenly. 'I curse you and this *ludus* and everyone in it, but you most of all.'

He spouted a laugh—a hearty, deep-throated laugh that nearly split his chest wound. He swung his legs to the side of his bed and stood, watching her take in the sight of him. He had not washed or changed out of his fighting kilt and the bloody paint on his chest had caked and crusted into what he imagined was some nightmarish rainbow.

She stepped backwards as he approached the bars. 'I have never had the pleasure of being cursed by a Roman woman,' he continued. He swept her body with his eyes. 'I think I rather enjoy being cursed.'

'Then I curse you a thousand times, Beast of Britannia. Whatever you long for, may it be as sand through your fingers. Whatever your dream, may it turn to dust.'

He had to grip his stomach so as not to howl. 'Such poetry! But before you go on, I am afraid I must tell you that you cannot curse me, for I am already doomed.'

'Doomed?' She glanced around his cell, then scolded him with her gaze. 'You are one of the finest gladiators in Rome. You are worth as much as twenty common slaves. Your bed is perched two cubits off the ground, by the gods! I will not hear about your supposed doom.'

'You do not believe me?'

'Why will you not admit to your wrongdoing? You wronged every single man in that crowd to-night. You wronged Rome.'

No, he had to stop her there.

'*I* wronged Rome? Rome that invaded my land and burned my fields?' He let out a savage laugh. 'Rome that raped my tribe's women and sent its men off to the Quarry of Luna?' He continued to laugh, though his wound had begun to throb. 'Do you know what it is like in the Quarry of Luna? If you cut less than ten cubits a day you are whipped. Less than five and they remove a toe.' He continued to laugh, feeling his wound begin to split. He could not seem to stop.

He lifted his foot to show her his missing digits, laughing harder. 'I dug for worms each morning to fill my stomach. My flesh baked in the sun each day and then froze in the wind each night. And I wronged Rome? Ha!' His laughter was crazed, like the laughter of a hyena, but he could not make it cease. 'Ha! Ha! Ha!' He doubled over, feeling the warmth of leaking blood down his side.

And then suddenly he was drowning.

Chapter Three

He choked and coughed as the cold water poured over his head and dribbled down his limbs. Already there was a pool of it expanding at his feet. The woman had apparently discovered the dipping pot and he watched in horror as she slung it over the lip of the urn for another filling.

'What…? Why…?' he sputtered.

'Your wound. It has not been properly cleaned.'

He peered down at the long diagonal gash across his chest and felt another assault of cold water. 'Cease!' he hissed and watched in horror as she returned to the urn for yet another potful.

She approached the bars. Mercifully, she did not give him a third dousing. Instead, she set down the pot and studied the wound. She reached out and touched the skin of his stomach.

A shiver rippled through him, followed by an uncomfortable heat. He grabbed her wrist.

'What in the name of Erebus do you think you are doing?'

'Be still,' she commanded. 'I am merely assessing the depth of the wound.' Ignoring his grip, she gently traced the skin around the gash with her other hand. Her audacity was stunning, but her fingers were like soft wax. Their touch sent an unexpected pang of sadness through him.

Fifteen years. That's how long it had been. Fifteen years since the last time a woman had touched him without the expectation of bedding him. That woman had been his yellow-haired wife.

'There is sand within the wound that will bring infection,' she explained. 'Take this in your mouth.' She pushed the thick, tasselled end of her tunic belt into his grip. 'Now bite down. This may hurt a bit.'

There was no time for protest. There was only exquisite, burning pain as he bit down and felt her fingernail razor into his soft flesh. 'Ugh,' he groaned.

'Just a little bit of sand...' she crooned.

He bit down harder, envisioning certain forms of torture.

'I fear there is some dirt lodged very deep,' she said, absently picking a tiny metal hairpin from her braid. She held the pin to her lips and bent it taut with her teeth.

It might have been her proximity. Or it might have been the unusual shapeliness of her lips. Or it might have been the fact that he had just survived an excruciating amount of pain and was savouring its absence. But watching her bend that hair clip was the most deliciously sensual thing he had ever seen a woman do.

Then she plunged the terrible instrument deep into his wound. 'Ah!' he shouted.

Across the hall, Felix was laughing. 'What? Is the Empire's greatest gladiator crying?'

'Piss off, Goat-Man!' shouted Cal.

'Not much longer now,' she assured him, probing deeper.

He twisted his body in agony. 'I did not ask for this.'

'No, but you must have it if you wish to survive.'

Survival was not exactly the plan.

'Hold this,' she said, handing him the hairpin. She lifted the pot and gave him a final dousing.

He gasped for air and for something to say: something scathing and clever, something that would burrow beneath her skin as painfully as she had just burrowed beneath his. But the words did not come and all he could do was stare as she began to dab the wound with her handkerchief.

Her face was lovely in the torchlight. Haunting brown eyes and ruddy red cheeks. Eyebrows so high up her forehead they looked painted. For all her vitriol, her appearance was bright. Cheerful, even. The colour of her skin reminded him of well-fermented beer.

'I wish I had some dried yarrow,' she said. She was dabbing his wound with a strange reverence. 'My mother used to keep some on her night shelf to help mend my father's wounds.' Her eyes searched his cell. 'Ah! I know what we can use.' She pointed over his shoulder to the distant corner of his cell. 'Do you see it?'

Cal studied the dark corner, wondering if the woman had lost her wits. 'Just there,' she said. She was nodding her head, full of certainty. 'The spider's web.'

'A spider's web?'

'You must fetch it for me.'

'Are you mad?'

'I am trying to help you.'

'I did not ask for your help,' he said.

'And I did not ask to be...' She bit her lip, stared at the floor.

Enslaved. That is what she wanted to say, but she could not find the courage to voice it. How could he deny her anything, knowing that she had been condemned to such a life?

He sighed and found himself crossing to the corner of his cell and gazing down at a fine silken temple shining beneath the torchlight. At the temple's edge, a large black weaver posed regally. 'How should I…*collect* it?' he asked.

'Just wave your palm through the web gently and gather it on your hand. Do not take it all, lest you incur Arachne's wrath.'

Cal did as instructed, giving a nod of reverence to the tiny creature whose sanctuary he had just harvested. *Reverence for all creatures big and small.* It was what the white-robed Druids had taught him in his youth.

He returned to her with the silken prize and was no less fascinated watching her ball up the strands and stuff them into his wound. Why was she helping him? He did not understand it at all. Nor did he have the heart to tell her that her effort was pointless.

'My mother used spider webs on my father's wounds, as well,' she explained. 'It is an old Greek remedy. My mother is Greek, you see.'

Pride lurked beneath her words. Cal knew that the Romans despised the Greeks in the manner of a jealous younger sibling.

'Is your father Greek?'

'No, I am afraid he is as Roman as they come. Born in Pompeii and left before Vesuvius blew. Lucky him. Though he could not escape the wounds of war…and now, I suppose, of peace.'

'Was your father often wounded?'

She nodded. 'After he returned from military service he became a *lictor* for a new *aedile* here in Ephesus. The young mayor had as many enemies as he had gold *auris* and my father was paid to protect him. I was always so worried for my father back then. *Pah!* I had no idea what worry was.'

She pursed her lips, and Cal sensed her trying to stifle her emotion. If there had been any doubt in his mind that she had been sold into servitude, it was washed away by the small tear he watched leak from her eye and trace a path down her cheek.

Without thinking, he pressed his finger to her skin and caught it.

She blinked, stared up at him.

His stomach tightened. He realised that he wanted to kiss her.

'There,' she said with finality and her deep blush told him that she had felt it, too—whatever *it* had been that had just passed between them.

Lust, he told himself. Simple, physical lust, born of the fact that he had not enjoyed a woman's company in months. But that would be remedied—and very soon, thank the god Gwydion.

The woman stepped away from him and he was glad of it. If she had not, he might have taken one of those small, coiling curls of hair and wrapped it around his finger. He might have made the mistake of reaching through the bars, catching her by the waist and pulling her close enough to drink the tiny bead of water that had lodged itself in the small crevasse of her shapely upper lip.

He might have violated one of his most important rules: never to kiss a woman.

'It will heal quickly,' the woman was saying, nodding confusedly at his wound. In truth, the gash already felt much better.

'I am in debt to you,' he said. Not that the debt would ever be repaid. Not that any of this mattered at all. A dressed wound was of no benefit to a man whose days were numbered.

'I suppose you *are* in my debt,' she said. It was just the sort of thing a Roman woman loved to say and he knew what came next. 'So tell me, how will you pay it?'

Reflexively, his eyes slid down the length of her. Curses. What was the matter with him? 'I do not know,' he said.

'Why not tell me the truth as payment?' she

asked. The woman was like a dog with a bone. 'Why did you agree to take the fall tonight? Tell me, I beg you.'

'Because of a woman.' There, he had said it. Surely it would be enough to put her off.

But she only frowned. 'I do not understand.'

He could tell that she wanted him to confess totally. But if there was one thing he held sacred in this wretched world it was the memory of his wife and he was not about to cheapen it by admitting how much he missed her, or what he planned to do to honour her memory. 'I took the fall for a woman and that is all I am going to say. I do not expect you to understand.'

'Come now, you must do better than that, Briton.'

Briton. She might as well have called him a butter eater or a beer guzzler.

'I am not a Briton,' he said through his teeth.

'Not a Briton? But you are called the Beast of Britannia, are you not?' There was the Roman arrogance again. It rankled him.

'That is what you Romans like to call me, because you know nothing about the lands you call Britannia.'

'Are you a Briton then?' she asked. His stomach twisted into a knot.

'I hail from the island that the Romans call Britannia, yes. But I am not "a Briton" as you say.'

'So what are you?'

I am a Caledonii warrior, proud and true, and I cannot trust you to ever respect that.

'Do you wish to escape this *ludus* or not?' he asked, changing the subject. 'Because if you are here arguing with me when the guards arrive, I promise that they will have you for breakfast. You are a slave now and your body is no longer your own.'

She looked at him as if he had just slapped her face. 'Yes, I know that you have been sold into slavery,' he continued, 'and by your own wretched father no less. Now listen to me. You have no more legal protection now and your security depends on the whims of men who regard you little better than a vase of flowers.' There were tears at the edges of her eyes and he knew that he had put them there.

'Do you not see that I am trying to help you? Get tough, woman. Toughness is the only thing that will serve you now.' Along with a dose of humility. 'You have one chance to escape this *ludus* and that chance will come very soon, when a group of guards will open the door to the barracks to bring us our rewards.'

'Rewards?'

'You must hide yourself behind the door as it opens and, as soon as the group passes through it completely, you must slip out the door and run, do you hear? As fast as you can. Then you must find your way back to your new master and beg his forgiveness. You must do this all in haste, lest you be caught by a slave catcher on your way.'

She shook her head and he could sense the mix of anger and panic at war inside her mind. It was illegal for a *pater familias* to sell his children into slavery, but few paid attention to such rules outside Rome. She was as doomed as he was now, though she had no idea what that meant. Yet.

She was studying the floor again. 'And do not even think about trying to escape into the wilds,' he continued. 'You cannot live for ever off wild berries and grass. Believe me, for I have tried. You will be caught eventually and your new master will be forced to pay for your return. Ask yourself if a few days of starving in the wilderness is worth your master's name tattooed across your forehead.'

That was the punishment for most escaped slaves, after all, though he could tell that she had not appreciated the reminder. 'I curse you,' she whispered.

'That again? It is the Empire of Rome you should be cursing, my dear, for it consumes us all.'

And he was done with it.

No more selling his soul for some elusive hope of escape. No more doing the bidding of his cursed *lanista*, Brutus, who valued gold and silver over flesh and bone. It was true that Brutus could control where Cal ate and lay and pissed, could decide when Cal was beaten and when he was bedded, could even control how often Cal was allowed to lift his face to the sun. But there was one thing Brutus could not control—the moment in five days' time when Cal would choose to die.

There was the sound of creaking hinges as the barracks door began to open The woman froze in terror. 'Get tough,' he told her. 'Now go!'

Chapter Four

Arria lunged behind the door just as the guard opened it, pressing herself into the corner as an entourage of women swept into the barracks on a perfumed breeze. They were followed by a cluster of guards, the ringmaster among them, along with Master Brutus himself, whom Arria recognised by his gaudy, gold-trimmed toga.

'Gladiators,' Brutus said, 'Governor Secundus sends his gratitude for your performance tonight.' He gestured to the women with a bejewelled hand. 'You have already received your allotted wine and here are your promised women. You will be rewarded similarly for a performance of equal merit at the Festival of Artemis this spring.'

One of the guards began to unlock the Beast's cell, and Brutus gestured to a blue-eyed woman with a nest of yellow hair atop her head. 'Here she is, Beast. Long blonde hair, blue eyes. Just as you requested.'

'Whence does she hail?' asked the Beast.

Brutus nudged the woman. 'You heard him. Where do you come from?'

'Germania.'

The Beast gave a nod and the guard let her into his cell.

'And the second woman?' Brutus asked the Beast.

'Do not want a second.'

'You do not want a second woman?' Brutus laughed. 'Then you are a fool.'

Arria watched the chosen woman float into the Beast's cell. She wore a flowing white-linen tunic and matching long shawl which she let fall to the floor just as the gate clanked shut. She must have been from far in the north, thought Arria, for her eyes were a startling blue and her hair was as yellow as wheat. She was beautiful.

But the Beast did not even look at her. He reached for a flagon of wine and guzzled it, then offered it to the woman without meeting her gaze.

She accepted it eagerly, taking a long draught herself.

If Arria was going to run, it had to be now, while the entourage of guards and women made its way deeper into the barracks. Unfortunately, she could not bring her legs to move.

She could only watch in quiet awe as the yellow-haired woman removed her tunic, revealing a landscape of dips and curves. She was the kind of woman Arria would never be—fleshy and abundant. Lovely as a bowl of fruit.

Arria was studying the woman so closely that she did not notice the guards turning back towards the door. 'They are yours for two hours,' announced Brutus.

Arria cowered in the shadows as Brutus and the guards exited and the door to the barracks closed with a slam.

And that was that. She had missed her chance to escape. Now she would have to wait two hours and pray that she could keep herself concealed as the men and women…as they…

From somewhere further down the hall came a long, ecstatic moan.

Oh, gods.

The Beast's cell was only steps away from where Arria squatted. Arria could see his muscular figure sitting at the end of his raised bed. His head was stooped. He was studying the floor, though the German woman stood only a breath away from him, her body exposed, her tunic in a pool at her feet. 'You are handsome, Gladiator,' she told him.

'Do not call me Gladiator.'

'Beast?'

He shook his head.

'What shall I call you, then?'

The Beast paused, looked up. 'Call me Husband.'

Call him Husband? What a strange request. Arria closed her eyes. She should not be watching this. Whatever *this* was. A ritual of some kind? A fantasy? Arria's sense of propriety was duelling mightily with her curiosity and she sensed her curiosity quickly gaining ground.

Why should she not watch? It had been a night of firsts, after all: her first pit fight, her first discussion with a gladiator and now, it seemed, her first real lesson in the act of love. She might as well watch, for this first lesson was also likely to be her last. Propriety be damned. She opened her eyes.

'It is well, ah, Husband,' the woman said. She reached up to her golden bun and pulled out a comb. Her hair tumbled on to her shoulders in a curtain of yellow silk. She shook it hard and the strands danced in the torchlight like shiny ribbons.

The Beast stared up at her, his head cocked

in contemplation. 'I shall not kiss your lips, understood?'

The woman shrugged her assent.

'May I have the comb?' he asked.

She placed the comb in his palm. He reached beneath his bed to produce a small brazier pan full of coals. He moistened a single tine of the comb with the tip of his tongue, then dipped the small instrument into the black residue of the pan.

'May I adorn your face?' he asked.

The woman nodded. He stood and touched the blackened tine to her chin, gently dabbing the coal stain into a mark of Venus. He dipped the comb into the coals once more and thickened the mark, then leaned backwards to behold his work. 'Perfect,' he said.

He returned to sitting and reached again for the jug of wine. He took a long draught, never taking his eyes off the woman's face. 'Rhiannon,' he whispered. He might have been a sculptor naming his bust—his lusty, lifelike bust that seemed to have been polished by the very hands of Venus.

'Will you not make love to me, Husband?' she asked in soft, melting Latin.

The Beast sighed, then bowed his bald head so that it came to rest against her smooth white belly. 'Ah, Rhiannon,' he said. 'Wife.' He reached to the woman's hips and pulled her closer, burying his face in the creamy white flesh of her stomach.

He sat there for a long while, his head resting against her stomach, as if she were some familiar, domestic goddess and he had come to offer his daily prayers. And then he did begin to pray, or so it seemed, for a torrent of words sprang from his lips. They were strange, tangled words—words so full of breathy desire that they might as well have been kisses themselves.

Arria had no idea what language he spoke, but she could feel what he was saying in her very bones. He was speaking of love and lust, of sweetness and yearning, of things that Arria had never known. They were words so lovely, they might have been birds, or tiny fishes swimming beneath some invisible wave of emotion that Arria could sense was about to crash.

And then it did. He rose to his feet to face the naked woman, speared his fingers through her hair, and lavished her neck with the hungriest, most passionate kiss Arria had ever witnessed.

His mouth rioted down the long column, biting and tasting and sucking in a torrent of urgency and lust. He gripped the woman by the waist and pulled her against him, and Arria had to brace her shoulder against the low wall to keep her own legs from buckling beneath her.

And then, just when she thought the wave had dissipated, just when the bruising neck kisses had subsided into soft, tender caresses, he bent to take one of the woman's breasts into his mouth.

Blessed, sweet Minerva.

A strange heat invaded Arria's bones—pleasurable, radiant, alarming. He released the woman's nipple and followed a winding path down her belly, festooning it with small kisses, until he was sitting once again on the bed before her and his lips came to a halt at the soft curly mass atop her Venus mound.

Was he going to...? Arria covered her eyes, then peeked between her fingers. Yes, he was going to. Arria watched in fascination as his tongue slipped into the woman's sacred opening.

'Oh,' the woman sighed and Arria felt another disconcerting wave of heat. The woman arched her back, gripping the Beast's naked skull as he began to move his mouth around her folds, kissing and sucking and...licking. It was the most forbidden thing Arria had ever seen in all her life. The woman began to whimper and Arria noticed her own breaths growing short.

What could it feel like to be kissed in such a way? In such a place? She strained to imagine it and found herself growing warmer still. She watched his hands slide slowly from the woman's hips to her backside, which he squeezed and caressed as he continued to pleasure her with his tongue.

Arria could not look away. She could not close her ears, even as the woman's moans transformed from soft sighs into low, rhythmic groans of the sort that Arria occasionally heard outside the baths. The woman's arms stiffened. Her body shuddered. Her moans crescendoed as her whole body convulsed and Arria felt a shiver ripple across her own skin.

Slowly, the woman's breaths subsided. She was still whimpering when he pressed his head against her stomach once more and hugged her close. He was breathing her in—deep, gulping breaths whose exhales sounded like sighs.

If the woman had been a goddess, he might have been her truest acolyte. But Arria knew she was even more than that to him. She was his beloved wife.

The cruel, hardened gladiator had disappeared. The monster that had taken life with cold efficiency had retreated to some faraway arena and in his place was a man—a gentle, loving man who seemed to overflow with tenderness.

At last he raised his head and stared up at the

woman. 'Wife,' he said. In a single motion, he stood and guided her on to the bed and Arria noticed an alarming protrusion inside his loincloth. He closed his eyes and began to speak again: husky, lilting words that made Arria's heart beat faster still.

What was he saying to the woman? What lavish words of passion were trilling off his well-used tongue? He stretched out on to the bed beside her and placed a series of small kisses down her arm. Leaning closer, he continued to whisper—a never-ending stream of small words strung together like kites.

They were words of love—Arria was sure of it. The kinds of words she imagined passing between a husband and a wife. The kinds of words, Arria realised, that she was certain never to hear.

Slowly, he arched over the woman, leaning on his arms as he kicked off his kilt and deftly untied his own loincloth. His taut, muscled form made a kind of arch above the woman's prone body, dwarfing her in size and strength. Arria tried to imagine what it would feel like to lie beneath such a titan and an unfamiliar muscle deep inside her flexed with yearning.

His loincloth dropped to the floor. Arria stared, then looked away. She looked again, blinked. She told herself to breathe. It was nothing that she had not seen before, after all. Practically every corner of Ephesus was etched with some depiction of male desire or another. The images were common as clay: they were painted on walls and chiselled above doors, not to mention their prominence in statues and mosaics. Such figures even functioned as signposts, helpfully pointing the way to bars and brothels.

Why was it, then, that she could not take her eyes off his? Perhaps it was because she had never seen one in the flesh. She had always gone early to the baths, long before the patrician matrons arrived with their male slaves. And she had never even dreamed of lingering into the 'trysting hour,' or so was called the middle of the day when the women's and men's hours overlapped.

Now she wished she had lingered at the baths, if only to observe the variety of male forms, for she was sure she had nothing by which to compare him. Were the images lying, then? Did they universally under-represent the immensity of a man's desire in its fully engorged state?

A small quake rumbled through her. She should not be watching them. It was indecent. Surely she was incurring the wrath of one god or another. But how could she not watch as he slowly settled his desire between the woman's thighs?

Arria's throat felt dry.

He took the lobe of the woman's ear in his lips and began to suck. Suddenly, the woman gasped and Arria saw her hips rock upwards. The Beast was pushing himself into her. They had joined.

Arria gulped, looked away. She felt herself flush with the shame of a spy. Or perhaps it was another kind of shame pumping so much heat into her cheeks.

She sat back against the wall and closed her eyes. Other sounds of lovemaking filled the stony barracks. They made a strange, stirring kind of music that seemed to collapse time. When the chorus of gasps and moans began to diminish, Arria dared to glance at the two lovers once again.

The Beast was posed on his side, his stony expression transformed into a wistful smile. He appeared to be playing with the woman's hair. *'Fy nghariad,'* he said, and the words were so sweet and mysterious that Arria could do nothing but sigh.

'Did you hear that?' he asked suddenly. Arria held her breath as she watched his eyes search across the darkness.

'I heard nothing,' said the woman. 'Probably a mouse.'

The woman was right, in a sense. Arria *was*

a kind of mouse. A large, skinny, lonesome mouse who lingered in the shadows relishing her crumbs.

She had been relishing crumbs all her life, in truth. The first crumb had come when she was fourteen—the usual age of marriage for a Roman woman. One evening, her father had invited a fellow *lictor* to dine with them—a handsome, ambitious young man named Marcus. When Marcus pulled her into an alcove after the meal, her heart had begun to pound. He was so very handsome and he wore his earnest goodness like a fine mantle. She remembered thinking that he would make a splendid husband. 'Arria, I want to ask you…' he had begun saying, then hesitated. 'I want to tell you that I wish to pursue marriage…' Another hesitation.

Remembering that moment still made her insides dance, then turn to stone. 'I wish to pursue marriage…' he repeated, 'with your friend Octavia. Would you counsel me, Arria? You are so amenable. How is it that I may win her affection?'

After that night, Arria had retreated into her weaving and the Greek and Latin lessons that her family had still been able to afford. 'There is time,' her mother assured her. 'But you must go out more. Join your friends at the festivals.

Come with me to the market. And hold your head high when you walk. A towering lion will never notice a cowering mouse.'

But Arria did not want a towering lion; she wanted a soft, baying sheep: a man who was gentle and kind—someone who would respect her tender heart.

The second crumb came a full year later. By then her youngest brother had returned from the army without a leg and her eldest brother not at all. Overcome with grief, Arria's father had lost his job and begun to gamble away Arria's dowry.

One day in the marketplace, a greying man spotted Arria puzzling over a tower of onions. 'They may appear wilted and old,' he chirped, 'but just beneath the skin they are young again.' Arria had been charmed and when he invited her family to break bread in his home, they went eagerly.

But the man's wealth had been modest and when he learned of the diminished size of Arria's dowry, his wrinkled grin became a wrinkled frown.

A year later, after her father lost the remaining half of her dowry to a fellow gambler called Verrucosus, the man had offered to return his winnings for a single night with Arria.

'She is a lovely woman, your daughter,' Arria

had overheard Verrucosus tell her father. 'So young and unsullied.'

It was her father's endless begging that finally convinced Arria to accept the offer. 'You can redeem me, Daughter, and thus save yourself.'

She remembered the faint smell of urine when she arrived at Verrucosus's room and the flies buzzing over the thin reed mat that was to serve as the bed where she would lose her maidenhood.

Verrucosus emerged from a corner reeking of pomegranate wine, his face decorated with warts. When he moved to embrace her with his sticky hands, she whirled out of his grasp and out the door.

As it happened, Verrucosus was the kind of man who embellished his anger with lies. 'Oh, I had her,' he bragged all around the city. 'And I can tell you that she is as cold and hard as a slab of marble.'

The gossip spread with the speed of arrows. 'He does not speak truth,' Arria assured her friends, but she could see that they did not wish to associate with a woman whose family had been brought so very low.

'Your beauty alone will attract a husband,' her mother continued to assure her. 'And your skills and education are beyond what would be expected from...'

'From a pauper?' Arria asked.

She was nineteen by that time. Most of her friends had already borne their first children. She tried to believe her mother's words. She was beautiful and worthy and as long as she believed it, the world would, too.

But she did not believe it. She was poor and without a dowry, and rumoured to be impure. How could she hold her head above so much shame and disgrace? How could she be desired by any man?

Thus she fashioned a third crumb for herself. She told herself she was, in fact, fortunate that no man wanted her. Indeed, she was blessed to be free of a husband. Men were careless and inconstant, after all—prone to gambling and drink. Her father and brother were burden enough. She could not even imagine what she would do with a *husband*.

She fed herself this crumb in moments of yearning—moments such as this one, as she observed the intertwined limbs of the Beast and the woman he had pretended to be his wife. No pleasure of the flesh could be worth the burden of matrimony, though to be fair this particular couple was not married at all. And they had shared something beautiful.

In that instant, Arria realised that she was

tired of crumbs. She wanted the whole pie and now it was too late. Somewhere in the course of her life, she had managed to miss one of its greatest pleasures. The opportunity for love and passion had passed her by.

And now she would be invisible for the rest of her life.

Chapter Five

The guard placed a bowl of barley mash on the floor of Cal's cell, then slammed the iron gate and pulled the lock into place with a clank. The ritual was wholly unnecessary, at least to Cal's mind. Even if the gate were left open wide, he would not attempt to flee.

There was no point in flight. He had learned that lesson well enough after his fourth attempt at escape—or was it fifth? They always caught you. They always won. He had the lash marks to prove it—twenty of them, or was it twenty-one?

The Roman citizenry had been divided since time immemorial—the patricians versus the plebs, Romulus versus Remus, the red charioteers versus the whites. But Roman citizens were remarkably united when it came to the control and policing of slaves.

They were especially vigilant here in Ephesus,

one of the largest slave markets in the Empire, whose number of slaves made up a full one-third of the population and whose number of professional slave catchers grew with each passing day. The Romans feared an uprising and justifiably so. A proper slave revolt would bring revenge killing, looting and, gods forbid, the loss of slave labour.

Cal himself had tried to start such a revolt once. He had the stab wounds to prove it. Five of them—or was it six?

There was no escaping the Empire of Rome. That was the lesson he had finally learned. At least not in this miserable world. Thus, in four short days, he planned to depart. He would lay himself bare before his opponent and position himself for a clean death.

And thus he would finally escape Rome for ever.

He glanced at his possessions, which he kept neatly arranged in a small cubicle in the wall. The concavity was meant to be a shrine—a place for gladiators to place their religious idols and offerings. But Cal had long ago given up on his gods and so he used the cubicle as a storage space for the few objects he called his own: a clean loincloth and lavatory sponge, a toothpick, a bottle of olive oil for washing, a shell from the beaches of his homeland. A spoon.

And now, it seemed, a hairpin. He picked up the tiny metal object. It was too small to be of use as a weapon, or as a pick for any kind of lock. It was so very delicate, in fact, that he wondered of what real use it could be in a typical woman's hair.

Though the woman whose hair it had graced had been anything but typical. And when she had bent it with her teeth before his eyes, it had seemed the most incredible object in the world. He could hardly remember the pain that had followed when she had plunged the pin into his open wound. All he could remember was the woman's lips around the pin and the quiet, savage confidence she exuded in bending it.

Strangely, it was the memory of the Roman woman that had lingered in his mind—not the German woman he had bedded. The German had been familiar; the Roman a living riddle. How perfectly appalled the Roman had been when she realised that the fights had been fixed. As if justice were a thing to be expected in this world. As if it were some kind of birthright.

Yet her birth itself was obviously quite common. Only a plebeian woman would dare thrust herself into a crowd of drunken men. And by the look of her threadbare tunic she had been low-born indeed. Not an exchange-and-trade kind of plebeian. A bread-and-circuses kind of plebeian.

Not that Cal knew very much about plebeians at all. Winning gladiators mixed almost exclusively with patricians, who frequently paid *lanistas* like Brutus to place gladiators on display at banquets. In his tenure at Brutus's *ludus*, Cal had had seen the inside of more luxurious villas than he could count. He had bedded an equal number of luxurious matrons—women willing to line Brutus's pockets for a tryst with a killer.

As a reward for his obedience, Cal was also sometimes granted the company of expensive harlots—women like last night's German. Over the years, Cal had discovered little difference between the patrician matrons whom he serviced and the expensive harlots who serviced him. Both types of women spent their days looking in mirrors and in so doing seemed to lose a good measure of their souls. Painted, bejewelled and reeking of costly perfumes, they floated from one banquet to another in search of attention and diversion.

Such women cared little about justice. What interested them most was the size of Cal's member.

The Roman woman he had met last night

was altogether different. She had been totally unadorned and by the looks of her thin limbs had not seen a banquet in all her life. She had not smelled of perfume but of musk and wool— a strange, earthy aroma that he yearned to smell again, though he could not say why. And her hands had been healing, not lustful, though her touch had nonetheless provoked him.

Even now, as he fondled her hairpin, he felt his blood getting a little warmer. Curses. There were a million pretty women in the world. Why did this one insist on lingering in his mind, distracting him from his goal of death?

Perhaps he pitied her. He had known few female slaves in his experience, but he was sensible enough to see that their lives were particularly miserable. Like all slaves, she would be expected to labour and endure hardship. She would also be required to be available for the carnal gratification of her owner, anywhere, any time.

The very thought of it sent a chill through him. He knew what it was to be made available in such a way, though at least he held the right of refusal. He never refused, however, and often cursed his own body, which was always ready to rise to the invitation lurking beneath a rich woman's silks.

Still, he knew that the act of love was different for women. It was more profound, more intimate and vastly more dangerous.

The more he considered the Roman woman's situation, the more he feared for her. She was obviously an innocent. Her shock at discovering the fights were fixed was matched only by her righteous indignation—a trait that would not serve her in her trials to come. She was as naive as a daisy and sure to wilt at her first beating. And if she did not wilt, she would inevitably be plucked.

Though he supposed she did have one weapon hidden beneath her tattered shawl: she was brave. Recklessly, stupidly brave.

When she had jumped down into the arena, he had almost believed she had been pushed. No person in his right mind—male or female—would ever make such a jump on purpose, or so he had thought until he had witnessed it with his own eyes.

He hardly believed in the gods. He believed even less in Roman women. But now he wondered if she had not been sent to him as a kind of muse—a woman to give him the courage to throw off the yoke of Rome for ever. If she could take such a terrifying plunge, then surely he could, too.

Satisfied with his assessment, he placed the hairpin on his shelf and gazed out at his cell. The rest of his possessions were on loan to him and soon would belong to someone else. The water pitcher and bedpan were standard issue, as were the brazier, bowl and cup. The raised bed he had earned after his tenth kill, as was custom. The table and chair had been issued after his defeat of Darius the Red, and the pillow and blankets in Antioch, when he slayed four Parthian warriors in a single afternoon. The wine ration was granted to every winning gladiator who did Brutus's bidding.

He poured himself a cup of wine and toasted the calling roosters. Their throaty, mournful cries seemed a just welcome to one of his final days on earth. He drained the cup and poured himself another. Now he was ready to consider his most treasured possession of all. He reached beneath a loose stone. There it was: a bundle of his wife's hair.

He ran his fingers through the thick cluster of blonde tendrils. They remained as soft and silky as the night of their wedding, when she had cut the strands and bound them with yarn. It was the traditional gift of a Caledonii bride to her husband and been followed by the even greater gift that she gave him that night.

He studied the silken bundle, imagining her long white fingers spinning the yarn that bound it. The hairs' striking golden hue had faded with the years, but the love he felt upon touching them remained.

His throat squeezed. He raised the bundle to his nose and took a long whiff, remembering how he used to bury his face in his wife's hair. Somehow, it had always smelled of smoke and earth—an intoxicating mixture of burnt oak and mint, of sunshine and the sea.

He tried to picture her face, though over time the image had changed, fading like the hair's colour, until all that remained was a vision of her heavy-lidded eyes, constant as the sky, and that irresistible black mole, taunting him from just beyond the smooth knob of her chin. He remembered her large nose, the noblest of his clan, and her thin, frowning lips that he could always coax into a grin.

The German woman who had shared his bed that night had looked nothing like Rhiannon. Her eyes had been small and guileless, her lips plump and quick to smile, and her nose of perfectly average size. The only true similarities were the mole he had painted, the azure colour of her eyes and, of course, her hair, which had been as yellow as the gilded dawn.

And thus it had all been worth it, for Cal had been able to bury his face in a yellow mane one last time. The joining itself had been unsatisfying, but had he not expected as much? There was no one in the world who could possibly replace his Rhiannon. There was only the opportunity to close his eyes and breathe deep and remember his wife when she had been alive and his own life was still worth living.

He quaffed another cup, hoping to numb the pain that had already begun to writhe in his gut. Fifteen years had passed and he had been unable to avenge her. In twelve years of hauling stones and hewing rock there had been only a single chance for freedom and he had failed to attain it.

That failure had landed him in the arena, where he had been forced to take other men's lives for the preservation of his own. With each kill, there was less of him. With each bloody blow, the image of his wife's face faded just a little more.

To take one's own life was the coward's way, or so he had been raised to believe. But to succumb to death on one's own terms—that was something different. He needed only to be brave when the moment came.

And he would. Just like the Roman woman had done when she'd jumped from that treacherous height. He would bare his neck to the blade and let come what may.

He had failed to attain his freedom. He had failed to get his revenge. But by his honour, he was not going to let the Romans win.

He kissed the bundle of hair and placed it beneath his belt. 'Forgive me, Rhiannon. I am coming home.'

Chapter Six

It was the most dismal dawn Arria had ever known. She walked with leaden feet through the Koressos Gate, trying to ignore the catcalls of the guards, which transformed in her mind into the jeers of a heartless mob.

She must accept suffering. That is what she repeated to herself as she passed the state marketplace, her stomach churning at the sight of the sausage cart and the smells of freshly baked bread.

She must do her duty. That is what she remembered as she passed the newly constructed Temple of Domitian, the Emperor who had *not* done his duty.

She must be a good daughter. That is what she knew as she turned on to Harbour Street and headed towards the cluster of crumbling tenement buildings that comprised Ephesus's Greek slum. She was almost home.

When she had finally escaped the *ludus* the previous night she had run into the forest, fully intending to flee.

She had deliberately ignored the Beast's warning against escape, for he knew nothing of the art of disappearing. How could he? He was foreign, famous and rather conspicuously bald. He could not escape his own *ludus* without being noticed.

Arria, on the other hand, was a perfectly forgettable little pleb. She knew she could survive in the wild. She would pick berries and gather olives and hunt for fish in the Roman Sea. Surely she could weave a net and though she had no practice in making fire, she could certainly steal it from somewhere, just like Prometheus from Mount Olympus.

But what would become of her *familia*?

In the end, it was the thought of her family that had convinced her to return. If she disappeared, the gold-toothed man would be within his rights to bring a lawsuit against her father. He could claim that Arria's escape was deliberate and that he had been deceived. He could seek compensation for his loss. Arria's mother would not be safe.

Arria turned a corner and her home *insula*

came into view. A crow flew into one of the shutterless windows of the top floor, and Arria watched for her mother's snapping handkerchief to emerge, gently shooing the bird out.

Every day for the past seven years, Arria had watched her mother wage daily battles against birds, sun, wind, cold and even the walls themselves, which seemed to be crumbling all around them. Though since her mother's unexpected pregnancy, Arria had noticed that she seemed to be giving up even those small battles.

Arria had told herself that she had enough determination for all of them. It did not matter that her father's gambling had only got worse, or that her brother was a wastrel. She could support them with her weaving. The proof of it had come just a week before, when she had managed to sell four carpets to a single buyer for a fine price.

She had been so thrilled by the sale that she had etched her elation on to a piece of pottery: a list of everything she planned to purchase with her earnings. She would buy honey, salt, oil and wood to see her family through the winter. With what remained, she would buy a sandal for her brother's remaining foot, wooden shutters for the window and coin to pay the midwife when her mother's time came.

And of course more wool.

Careless in her happiness, Arria had left the list beside her bed mat. She should have known that her father would find it there. Sick with the gambling disease, it had not taken him long to discover the purse itself, which Arria had hidden beneath their small clay hearth. And now their hearth would be cold and empty as a result. And so would their bellies.

A small farm was all she wished for—a place where her mother could tend a garden and worship her god in peace, where her brother could drink rain instead of wine and where her father's delusions of riches could go no further than the boundaries of a fine wheat field.

It was a fantasy she had clung to since her brother Clodius had come home from the campaigns in Britannia. After his legion had defeated a barbarian tribe called the Caledonians, he had been granted a small plot of land somewhere beyond a Roman fort called Eboracum.

But he had refused to claim the land, had said that it was made of rock, not soil, with evil winds and wicked winters and local barbarians spoiling for a fight. 'I do not care how many battles we won, the barbarian tribes still rule the north of Britannia,' he had argued.

Arria and her family had no choice but to believe him, though Arria had her doubts. Soon after her brother had returned from his service, Arria had found him lying in a puddle outside the public latrine. 'How is a man supposed to till a piece of land when he cannot even get himself to the toilet?' he had despaired.

Now she found him lying in the gutter outside their building, dozing over the mouth of his flagon.

'Hello, Brother,' she said, giving him a gentle kick.

He lurched his head forward and gave a thready grin. 'Hello, dear S-Sister. Lovely morning, is it not?' Arria no longer nagged Clodius about his reckless spending on wine, for he had come to depend on it as others did bread.

'You are drunk, Clodius,' she said. *And have managed to lose another tooth.*

His crutches lay beside him, their dented wooden grooves tracing a history of tantrums. Humiliation was an ailment that even the medicine of drink seemed unable to cure.

'Come, I will help you upstairs. Father and I have some news.'

'News? Did Father finally win some money?'

'Not quite.'

She gathered his crutches in one arm and lifted him to standing with the other.

'I know what news!' he spewed as he leaned

heavily against her. 'You found the dirty barbarian who stole my leg.'

'Not quite.'

'You found the filthy barbarians who killed our brother?'

'No.'

'You found any barbarians at all? They do not have to be the exact same dirty barbarians, you know? You can bring me any barbarians you like. I would be happy to slit their throats.'

'Not all barbarians are evil,' she said, then bit her tongue. A heedless rabbit would not have taken the bait quicker.

'What do you mean "not all barbarians are evil"? Do you not see the place below my thigh where a leg should be?'

As they hobbled past the second floor, Arria settled herself in for one of her brother's scathing lectures on barbarian culture.

'Do you know what the barbarian priests do when they want their gods' favour?'

Arria said nothing.

'They sacrifice a thousand children!'

'Unbelievable,' said Arria. Last week it had only been a hundred.

'Do you know that the barbarian women eat their babies?'

'Is that so?'

'They are like animals, Arria. Do you not remember what the barbarian did when I begged him to end my life?'

Arria nodded patiently. She had heard the story so many times she could have recited it in her sleep. 'He pissed on me! The man pissed right on the place where he had severed my leg. What kind of a monster does that?'

His eyes were fierce, indignant. It was as if he were still lying on that cold battlefield begging for someone to end his life. He leaned on her hard. 'At least they got him,' he concluded, as he always did. 'I saw him in the shackles the next day—sold away with the rest of the s-savages.'

When they arrived inside the one-room apartment, Arria's mother enveloped her in an embrace, sobbing. 'I had half hoped you had escaped to a better life,' she whispered into Arria's ear.

'The Goddess reminded me of my duty,' Arria said, touching the small rise of her mother's belly.

In the corner of the room, her father was seated on the bed mat, staring at the white stain of a bird's dropping on the wall. He shook his head, then buried his face in his hands. 'I have failed you, Daughter.' He broke into sobs. 'That barbarian Beast was not supposed to lose. The dirty, wretched fiend. If I could wring his filthy—'

'He is not a fiend.'

Her father's sobs ceased. 'What?'

'He is not a fiend. He is a man whose life has also been destroyed by gamblers.' Her father stared at her as if she had just sprouted horns. 'Do you not see it?' she snapped. 'It is the Empire of Rome you should be cursing. It consumes us, Father, and you most of all!'

Now her mother and brother were staring at her, too. She needed air. She crossed to the open window and peered out of it. Pacing towards the building was a cluster of four armed men. They flanked a short, portly man gripping a scroll. It was he! The gold-toothed victor and her new owner, already come to collect his due.

Her heart was pounding. 'How long, Father?' she asked. He would not meet her gaze. *Say a year. Or even two years.* A two-year indenture she could endure. Or even three. Or even five.

'Ten years.'

'Ten *years*?' gasped her mother.

In ten years Arria would be thirty-five years old.

'What's going on?' asked her brother, swaying against his crutch. 'What are we talking about?'

Bitterness gripped Arria's heart. 'Father wagered my freedom at the fighting pits, Brother. He also wagered the profits from the carpets I wove and Mother's golden fish. He lost all of it.

To pay his debt, I shall go now and work for a merchant for ten years—a man with a golden tooth.'

'A golden tooth?' slurred her brother, as if all the rest was only details.

There was a long silence and Arria heard the sound of footsteps in the stairwell below. Suddenly, she began to laugh. 'Yes, a golden tooth.' She laughed harder, unable to stop herself. Was that not remarkable? An entire tooth covered in gold? That was what her new owner had. Yes, indeed!

There was a loud pounding at the door and Arria doubled over with laughter. She could not stop herself, even as the guards burst into the apartment and took her by the arms. They dragged her across the room like a dog and, as she continued to laugh, a realisation struck.

This was exactly how the Beast must have felt when she had accused him of wrongdoing. It was why he had laughed so hard that he had split his wound. How could he possibly be guilty of anything when his life was not his own? It was so ridiculous as to be absurd. And now her life was no longer her own. Ha! Was that not beyond amusing? In her selfishness, she had cursed him and now she had also been cursed—by a man with a golden tooth!

Chapter Seven

On the day he was supposed to die, Cal was instead declared touched by the gods. He bowed his head before his opponent and waited for his death blow…and waited…and waited.

He had believed his opponent to be drawing out the drama of the moment. Instead, he was clutching at his chest, suffering an attack of the heart. The man fell backwards upon the sands and Cal was saved.

The crowd had been silent as Cal rose to his feet and the ringmaster puzzled up at the sky. 'Touched by the gods,' he murmured.

Now he paced inside his cell beneath Brutus's accusing gaze.

'You are not supposed to be alive!' shouted Brutus, rattling his *pugio* against the bars.

'Thank you for the reminder,' said Cal. It had

been a month since the woman had cursed him and he had already failed to die three times.

'I thought we had a deal.'

Cal spat. 'Do you think I caused that man's attack, or the omen, or had anything at all to do with the *murmillos*?'

Brutus pursed his lips. Less than a month before, Cal had gazed out at the stage of the great theatre at Miletus, fully prepared to die. It had been a good day for it, too: cool and sunny with a smattering of puffy white clouds making ethereal shapes against the crystalline sky. As he stepped out on to the stage, he had gazed up at those clouds and perceived the profile of his wife's face. She was watching him for certain, waiting for him to join her in the Otherworld.

An instant later, he had thought of the Roman woman, trying to fuel his courage. He had been paired with a *murmillo*—a gladiator playing the role of a deadly fish. As his enemy, Cal was the *retiarius*—the fisherman—equipped with a net and trident against the *murmillo*'s sword and shield. Cal gladly took the triple-pointed trident into his hand. He would make a few jabs, throw the net once or twice, then open his chest to a direct blow from the *murmillo*'s sword. It would be a clean death and Brutus the blood merchant would own him no more. He would finally, finally be free.

But just as soon as Cal and the *murmillo* had faced off, another *murmillo* stormed into the sparring ring. *Even better*, Cal had thought at first. *Two swords to finish me.* Then he heard the *murmillos* trading insults beneath their helmets. He recognised their accents. One man was Jewish, the other Nabataean: mortal enemies.

The men had practically ignored Cal. They danced about the arena to the crowd's wild cries, trading blows until the fateful moment when their swords thrust into one another's guts. Both men sprawled dead on the field and Cal was declared the winner.

'It was not my fault they fought each other instead of me,' said Cal. 'Nor was it my fault that your Jupiter disapproved of the Sardis Games.'

Days after the *murmillos*, Cal had been fully prepared to die at the theatre of Sardis, in games held in honour of the city. But the moment he stepped out into the sparring ring, a shadow had passed over the sun and day had turned to night. It was enough of an ill omen for the local mayor to call off the games entirely and Cal had exited just as he had entered: hale and maddeningly alive.

'Live or die? Which is it, Cal?' Brutus asked now. 'My purse grows emptier while you decide.'

Hoping to break his streak of ill fortune, Cal had finally confessed to Brutus his decision to die in the arena. To his credit, Brutus did not attempt to dissuade Cal from his mission. Indeed, he appeared to conclude that he could not stop Cal from seeking death, so he might as well profit from it. That very afternoon, at the Romani Games of Smyrna, Brutus had bet a heavy purse on Cal's demise.

How could Cal have known that his opponent would suffer an attack of the heart before Cal had even landed a blow? Or that the crowd would give Cal an ovation as it had, chanting that he was touched by the gods—the very spawn of Jove?

'I am a man of my word,' said Cal. Absently, he reached into his cubicle and grasped the small, bent hairpin that he had developed a habit of fondling. 'When I say I will fall, I will fall,' Cal stated. 'But I cannot control the whims of Fortuna.'

Brutus shook his jowls. 'It makes me wonder—why do the gods spare you?'

'It is not the gods who spare me,' muttered Cal. He worried the pin between his fingers.

'What did you say?'

He could see her face so clearly: her arched brows, her high cheeks, the way her shapely lips had pursed into a bud as she pronounced her curse. *'I curse you a thousand times, Beast of Britannia. Whatever you long for, may it be as sand through your fingers. Whatever your dream, may it turn to dust.'*

He had erroneously believed that she was his muse, that she had been sent to inspire him, to give him the courage he needed to bow beneath the blade. Never once did he think her a sorceress, or that her silly curse would actually take hold.

'Answer my question, Beast. Who keeps you alive, if not the gods?'

'It is a curse that keeps me alive,' Cal admitted. 'The woman from the pit fights cursed me. She is a sorceress.'

In truth he did not know if she was a sorceress. He knew very little about her, really, though she continued to occupy his thoughts. He did not even know her name.

'Why must you know my name?'

She was standing at the opposite end of his cell, pressing her back against the stone wall with such force that he feared she might break through it.

'Do not fear,' he said in his fumbling Latin. Even at this distance, he could see her lip trembling. 'I mean you no harm.'

Only a month had passed since they had met, yet she was much thinner. There were small rags tied around several of her fingers and her other fingers were as red as beets. She certainly did not look like a sorceress. She no longer looked very much like a plebeian maid, either.

'Sit down,' he said, motioning to the edge of his bed.

'I prefer to stand,' she said, eyeing the mattress with alarm.

Brutus had purchased the woman's time from Oppius after what Brutus had complained was an unnecessary negotiation. They were brothers, yet Oppius had demanded a pretty coin for this short visit, explaining that it would take precious time away from her weaving. Oppius had also made it clear that she not be touched, lest the price rise considerably.

Not that Cal required such a warning. The night they met, Cal had all but admitted that he had thrown the fight that had resulted in her enslavement. Not long after that, he had all but frightened her to tears. If she did not loathe him outright, he was certain the woman counted him among her enemies.

Still, he felt strangely reassured by the sight of her, though her once-white tunic had faded to brown and her long black braid had lost its sheen in a layer of dust. But something in her watchfulness told him she remained herself—desperate, indignant, mercifully unbroken.

'Can I offer you some wine?' He crossed to the table and poured her a cup, which he delivered with a polite bow. 'I almost expected you to be hiding in some distant forest.' He gave a good-natured laugh. 'You know—living on berries and such.'

'You summoned me here to mock me?'

He shook his head, reminding himself to tread carefully. Her freedom had been stolen from her, but she obviously still clung to her pride. 'Please, drink your wine. Relax. Perhaps you would like a honey cake?'

She stared at the honey cake sitting on the table beside him, as if calculating its worth. Finally, she looked at him. 'Why did you not summon the barbarian woman?'

'Apologies, I do not understand. What woman?'

Apparently unhappy with the specificity of the first question, the woman replaced it with a better one. 'Do women come often to your bed?'

It was the kind of question that in more

worldly circles would have stood for a proposition. 'They do, in truth, though not usually upon my request.'

'What do you mean?'

Was the woman so naive that she did not know of the private tasks of a gladiator? 'Roman matrons sometimes pay my *lanista* to lie with me,' he explained. 'I give them what they want.'

'What they want?'

'Pleasure.'

'Oh,' she said and looked away. He watched with more than the usual satisfaction as a deep crimson flush colonised her cheeks. In an effort to conceal her face from him, she turned and feigned interest in her wine cup, but her blush seemed only to grow deeper as she studied the figure painted on its side.

It was unfortunately a very naked, very aroused image of Adonis.

'I do not give them *everything* they want,' Cal blurted, though he had no idea why he felt compelled to clarify himself. 'I do not kiss the women on the lips.'

And because he had said the word *lips*, and for no other reason than that, his gaze slid to hers. And by some combination of dryness and nerves, it was at that exact moment when she chose to moisten those lips with her tongue. He felt a thunderbolt of heat split his stomach.

'Let us begin again,' he said, his knees nearly buckling. He smoothed his kilt, wishing he had thought to don his tunic. Surely she would be taking him more seriously if he were fully clothed. They both would be. 'My name is Cal. Short for Caldagius. And you are?'

'Why does it matter? Are all women not terribly similar once you have us on our backs?'

All at once it hit him—the reason for her prickly demeanour. She believed she had been summoned to lie with him.

'I did not ask you here to put you on your back.'

'You did not?'

'Of course not,' he said and he saw her eye twitch. Damnation. Now he had wounded her vanity.

'My *lanista* has purchased your presence so I may make a request of you. That is all.'

She flung a glance at the table. Was he mistaken, or did she appear to be flirting with the honey cake?

He retrieved the cake and placed it in her palm. 'I summoned you here to ask you to lift the curse you put on me.'

'Curse?' she said absently, taking a ravenous bite.

'You placed a curse on me the night we met. Do you not remember? I have suffered beneath it ever since.'

A crumb shot out of her mouth and she fumbled on the ground to retrieve it. She certainly did not *seem* like a sorceress. Then again, Ephesus was famous for its abundance of sorcerers and *maleficium* came in many forms.

'I was supposed to die in the arena just days after you cursed me,' he continued. 'I have been trying to die ever since. I believe your curse has been keeping me alive.'

She regarded him searchingly, then blanketed herself in a Stoic's calm. 'It does not sound like a very effective curse. It sounds more like the favour of the gods.'

He shook his head. This was not going well at all. 'It is not something I would expect you to understand. You do not know real suffering.'

It was the wrong thing to say. Her eyes flashed. 'You think I do not know suffering? I labour in a textile workshop with twelve other women and two windows the size of my hands. We must weave our carpets continuously, from sunrise to sundown, lest we be beaten.' She placed her hands upon her hips and peered up at him accusingly. 'I do not know suffering? Well, I certainly know that earthworms are difficult to kill. They wriggle even after being severed.'

He felt as if he had been punched in the stomach. Was her situation already so dire that she had been reduced to scratching for worms? 'I will not pity you,' he managed to say. 'Pity will not help you to survive your years of servitude.'

Besides, it was not pity he felt, it was anger. Burning, thought-splitting anger. He wanted to find the man who had done this to her and beat him senseless.

'Arria,' she said, swallowing the last morsel of cake with a sigh.

'What?'

'You said your name is Cal. I am Arria.'

'Arria,' he repeated. Such a musical name for such a troublesome woman. But at least she had introduced herself. He cleared his voice and spoke as politely as he could. 'Arria, please, I beg you to lift the curse you have placed on me.'

She shook her head, then stepped forward and held out her untouched wine cup. 'Take this. You need it more than I do.'

He dumbly accepted the cup as her eyes slid down the length of his bare chest. It felt as if she were stripping him of clothing that he was not even wearing. An unwelcome lust coiled inside his gut.

'It looks good,' she said. 'The wound, I mean.'

She stepped closer, and the scent of her hair wafted into his nostrils—a maddening blend of wool and woman. Bull's blood, why did she have to smell like that?

'The swelling has diminished,' she observed, still studying his chest. She reached up and touched just below the ball of his shoulder, where the tender scar began its long, diagonal path. Her finger was so soft that it stung.

'Do you not understand?' he said, willing the words to come. 'I wish for you to lift the curse.' Though what he wished in this moment was to draw those soft fingers to his lips and kiss them one by one. 'I wish to die.'

He thought he saw her eye twitch again, but she continued to trace the scar, leaving a forest fire of heat where her finger had touched. 'Do not do that,' he said. He felt his desire rising beneath his loincloth. By the Hound of Hades, what was she doing to him?

'Do not do what?'

He drank down the cup of wine and tossed it to the floor. 'Touch me like that. Unless you plan to *keep* touching me.'

She paused, then peered up at him. And there,

rushing between them, an invisible river, its dam breached, its waters flowing. 'I do not understand,' she said, though it was clear by the speed of her breaths that she did understand.

He stepped forward and stared into her eyes.

They stood there a long while: two opponents facing off in their small arena. *It is just lust*, he tried to tell himself. He had felt it a thousand times. His body wanted hers and nothing more. This just happened to be particularly powerful lust. Lust that pulled his body towards hers by some elemental force. Lust that made him feel as if he might burst into flame.

'I think you do understand, Arria.'

She pulled her finger from his skin and stepped backwards. 'Pink,' she blurted.

'What?'

'Your scar. It has grown pink. Pink is the colour of healing.'

'Is it?'

His scar was not the only growing pink thing. Nor did the place where she had touched him feel like it was healing any more. It felt like scorched earth. No, this was not going well at all.

Her eyes flitted about the cell, as if searching for something more to say. They seized on an empty corner. 'Look there!' She rushed to the corner of the cell and squatted low. 'Do you see? The spider has rebuilt the web.'

The heat of her nearness dissipated and he felt his wits return. 'I do see it, yes.'

'Is it not a wonder?' She flashed him a dazzling grin. 'I confess that I have never healed anyone in all my life.'

He grinned. 'But you have certainly cursed many.'

She shook her head. 'Only you. But I have healed you, as well.'

'I never asked to be healed or to be cursed,' said Cal, though he admitted that he would have paid a thousand *denarii* in that moment to feel her fingers upon his skin once again.

'You did not ask for it, but you needed it. My treatment worked well.'

'I believe it was the curse that has kept me alive and not any treatment.'

'No, I believe it was the web. And the salt.'

'What?'

'There was salt in the handkerchief I used to dry the wound.'

'Salt?'

'From my tears.'

'By the gods, you *are* a sorceress.'

She shook her head, then paused. 'Perhaps I am.' There was authority in her eyes now and no small amount of mischief. 'In any case, I cannot lift the curse.'

'Of course you can lift the curse. All you have to do is say, "I lift the curse." That is all I am asking you to do.'

She stood and folded her arms over her chest. 'How long did you labour in the quarry?'

'The quarry? Apologies, but I do not know what—'

'Twelve years. That is what you told me. Twelve years of eating grubs and losing toes and feeling the sting of the lash. If you can last in a quarry for twelve years and in the arena for three, then you can certainly stay alive for a little while longer.'

'You mean to deny me my one wish?'

'Summon me in a month and I will consider lifting the curse.' She crossed to the gate and hailed the guard.

Was this really happening? Was she really refusing him? Anger flared. 'I helped you escape the *ludus* and this is how you repay me?'

Who did she think she was to deny him his one desire? By whose authority did she trifle with his chosen fate? 'It seems you have yet to know real suffering,' he barked, 'for if you did, you would release me from my own.'

The guard grabbed her by the arm and yanked her into the hall. 'I am sorry, Cal, but if you die then you have let them win and I cannot allow you to do that,' she said. 'Get tough.'

Chapter Eight

Her first beating took place on Saturnalia. Arria had completed her carpet by the start of the mid-December festival and released it to the head guard with pride. It was her finest creation yet, or so she had believed. But when Oppius stormed into the workshop that afternoon and smacked her across the face, she knew otherwise.

'What is this?' he demanded. He held up the carpet like evidence to a crime.

'It is the carpet you commanded me to weave, Dominus.'

Oppius smashed his hand against her other cheek. 'That is not what I mean and you know it.' He dragged her out the door and she stumbled into the courtyard in a storm of dust.

'You defied me. You deliberately wove something I would not be able to sell. Get the lash,' he shouted to one of the household slaves and then to Arria: 'Remove your tunic.'

It was many days before she could lie on her back. Many more before she was able to speak. 'Do my duty,' she told herself one night, not realising she had spoken the words aloud.

'Arria speaks!' called a friendly voice from across the darkness. 'She has returned to us.' The voice belonged to the proud-faced barbarian woman they called Epona. 'You will heal in time,' she assured Arria.

More soothing words filled the workshop and though Arria tried to hear them, memories of her beating crowded her mind. The joyous sneer Oppius wore as he delivered the blows. The mind-splitting pain. The snap of the lash as it tore up the flesh of her back.

'Welcome back, Arria,' crooned an ancient voice and all the women went silent. The woman they called Grandmother rarely spoke, but when she did, everybody listened. 'You have been brave.'

'Gratitude, Grandmother,' Arria replied across the darkness, though she did not feel brave.

She rolled over on to her stomach and tried not to think about tomorrow. Or the next day. Or the next. Cal had lasted twelve years in the quarries, yet she had been enslaved for less than four months and already she felt herself fading.

'Grandmother, what are you thinking about right now?' she asked.

'I am thinking about the pigeons of Artashat.'

'Pigeons?'

'Years ago, before the Roman general Corbulo burnt the Armenian city of Artashat to the ground, my mother made frequent offerings at its great temple. I remember that thousands of pigeons roosted in its eaves. There were grey and white and brown pigeons. One day I even saw a black pigeon. Imagine that! I thought it was a crow, but it flapped its wings in that way, you know, like it was applauding the presence of the gods. It was so black that as it flew into the air I could trace the outline of its feathers against the white snow fields of Mount Ararat.'

'The augurs say that black birds are bad omens.'

'The augurs are silly fools,' said Grandmother. 'Whatever gives you hope, you must think of it now. It may be a god, or a memory, or some outlandish wish. Or perhaps it is just a vision of what your life could be. Hold on to whatever gives you hope, my dear, and a thousand lashes cannot harm you. The temple is gone, but my pigeons live on.'

Arria gazed into the darkness, trying to find her pigeons. They were not in her memories, for even the good ones seemed tinged with the consequences of her family's decline. Nor was her family itself a very hopeful thought. Her brother's drunken stupors, her father's desperation, her mother's dangerously swelling belly.

She could not even bring herself to feel hope for her new brother or sister. Even if the baby survived, how would her family feed it? It was as if they were struggling up some terrible mountain with boulders on their backs.

An image came to mind of Cal. He had struggled up mountains for years—literally. The slaves who laboured in the Quarry of Luna were criminals and captives of Rome. They were not meant to survive. They were meant to carry those boulders until they were crushed by them.

And yet, Cal had not been crushed. He had survived and had gone on to become one the Empire's finest gladiators.

If Cal was still alive, she decided, then there was hope. Plenty of it. Hope to spare. If Cal lived, then there were miracles, too. And no small helping of divine will.

Because although Arria had cursed many things in her life—her father's gambling, her brother's drinking, her family's terrible fortune—none of those curses had any effect. If her curse on Cal worked, then she was more powerful than she knew, and she could certainly endure ten years at the loom.

The thought fuelled her spirit, which slipped right through the small, slitted window and flew out flapping into the night.

The next day, by some small miracle, Arria was summoned once again to Ludus Brutus.

Arria loved her legs as they carried her down Kouretes Street. She loved the slap of her sandals against the paving blocks and the cool December air. She loved how the smoke of the eternal flame mixed with the steam from the baths: a braid of black and white against the brilliant blue sky.

When she entered the *ludus*, the winter sun shone down through small slits in its stone walls, lending something resembling cheer to the shadowy space. As the guard ushered Arria through the cell door and closed it behind her, she was further heartened by the strong, broad-shouldered man sitting in the warmth of a sunbeam: her pigeon.

'You live,' she said, feeling instantly foolish. Of course he lived. Would she be here if he did not? She searched for something more to say, but her wits were in tatters—destroyed by her exploding happiness.

'It appears I do live, yes,' he muttered. She could not guess his mood. It seemed reasonable that he would be furious with her—her curse obviously continued to shield him from the death he craved. But his expression betrayed neither fury nor happiness. His rugged, angular face appeared etched in stone.

'The curse is a potent one,' she offered.

He did not reply, but watched her closely. His gaze was too keen, his eyes too green. He reminded her of a hungry predator.

'You have been rewarded for your victories, I see.' She glanced at his tunic. The bright red garment was sleeveless and obviously new. It grazed the tops of his knees, which towered over the snaking leather straps of new sandals.

'Brutus continues to profit from my victories,' he said flatly. 'He rewards me in small ways.'

It was a shame he wore the tunic. She would have liked to have checked how his chest wound was mending. The last time they had been together, she had been unable to complete her inspection of it. She had barely been able to begin, in truth, for he had growled at her menacingly and warned that she should not touch him unless she planned to keep touching him.

She had been confused, told him she did not understand. *I think you do understand, Arria*, he had said and the words had plunged like a flock of waterbirds into the pit of her stomach.

Since then, she had thought about that moment a thousand times. She had relived it so often that it seemed very little time had passed between that moment and this one. 'It has been over two months since we last spoke,' she said. *Two long, lonely months.* He nodded, saying nothing. Perhaps he planned to berate her. That would explain his strange mood. Soon he would unleash a torrent of gladiatorial rage upon her and simply frighten her into lifting the curse.

She took a deep breath, preparing to receive his fury, and caught him glance at her breasts, which she had left unbound since her beating.

In retaliation, she stole her own peek at the tip of his scar, which jutted from beneath his very short sleeve.

That was how she found herself considering his arm. His bulging, flexing, bone-crushing arm. And then its happy twin: the *other* bulging, flexing, bone-crushing arm. And then the two arms together and the memory of how they had so easily lifted the flaxen-haired woman by the waist...

On second thought, perhaps it was fortunate that she could not inspect the scar.

She noticed that the table on the other side of the cell had been laden with wine and edibles. She drifted towards it, feeling like a deer in a forest.

She looked down at the table without seeing any of its bounty, aware that she was once again locked in a cell with one of the most deadly gladiators in the Roman Empire—a man with every reason to hate her.

'Take one,' he said at last. She nearly jumped.

'What?'

'A honey cake. The last time you were here, you seemed quite enamoured of them.' He nodded at the tower of cakes on the table beside her and she studied them suspiciously. Had he requested them just for her? If so, it was perhaps the kindest thing anyone had ever done for her.

'What mischief are you about?'

'Take one,' he repeated, nodding encouragingly.

She could not decide what to do. She wanted to take one—most desperately. Her stomach moaned with longing. But she reminded herself that the last time she had seen him she had denied his request that she lift the curse.

Thus he had good reason to be furious with

her and no reason to offer her honey cakes. If he loathed her as much as she suspected he did, then he might have been luring her into a trap. A poisoned one, perhaps. She had refused to annul the curse, so it was possible that he meant to annul her.

He rose suddenly and crossed to the table, causing her to jump backwards and shriek. He was shaking his head in bewilderment as he reached for a honey cake and stuffed it into his mouth.

'Do you see?' he said, his mouth full. 'They are perfectly safe.'

Arria watched him carefully—not because she did not believe him, but because at this angle, with the torchlight flooding the cell as it was, she understood for the first time how very handsome he was.

Not handsome in any traditional way. His eyes were a little too wide, his nose a little too large. His lips were too sensual to be considered classically masculine and his perfectly bald head shone like the beryl ball of a soothsayer.

But gods, he was handsome. Terrifyingly so. No wonder the matrons of Ephesus sought him out. It was as if some fiery furnace burned beneath his skin, illuminating his features and giving them quiet power over everything and everyone. Over her.

He swallowed his honey cake, then crushed her with his grin.

The birds. They were fluttering their wings atop the sea inside her stomach, threatening to launch. She had never been grinned at like that by a handsome man. Though handsome was not quite the right word. Perhaps it was more like grand and dashing, with a hint of ferocity. Though that, too, seemed inadequate. What was he then? She searched her mind, though it was hard to think when his body was so close.

What was she supposed to be doing? She took a quick look at her surroundings. Ah, yes! The honey cakes. She reached for one and took a large bite. When she finally recovered her wits, he was smiling still.

Curses, he was so…

'Wine?' he asked.

'Mmm,' she mumbled, quickly filling her mouth with more honey cake. She was hardly tasting it, though, for all of her attention was consumed by the sight of shoulder muscles— more specifically, the small, sinewy threads of strength that flitted and twitched as he lifted the heavy wine vessel.

He handed her a cup and took the other in his

hand. What was he doing? She forced her gaze to the ground. *Think, Arria.*

The realisation hit her like a blast of steam. 'I know what you're about!' she proclaimed. 'You are showering me with your generosity so that I will lift the curse.'

He drank from his cup, ignoring her comment. 'Drink,' he urged her. 'It is Pontic wine. Lusty and sweet…perhaps a bit naive.'

It seemed an unusual way to describe wine, but she carefully lifted the overfull cup to her lips, telling herself that this was perfectly normal—to be sharing a drink with a deadly gladiator inside his dark, locked cell. She drank deeply and warmth flooded her body.

How long had it been since she'd enjoyed a cup of wine?

Not since the earliest days of her womanhood, when she was young and desirable and life seemed to spread out before her like a grand, silken carpet.

She drank and drank until she had drained the entire cup. He was watching her closely, his eyes like twin torches pouring their heat into her limbs. She began to feel dizzy, warm, careless. 'I do not plan to stay in Ephesus for ever,' she said.

He raised a brow. 'Is that so?'

'In ten years, when my indenture is complete,

I shall go with my family north. My brother has been allotted land in one of the barbarian…' She paused. 'In one of the northern provinces. We plan to make a homestead there.' She was careful not to mention that the province was Britannia, the man's very homeland, and that the dream was hers alone, not one necessarily shared by any other member of her family. She realised that it was the first time that she had confessed the dream to anyone.

'It is a fine dream,' he said. 'I had a similar dream once.'

'Oh?'

'I had been allotted a homestead by my father on land our ancestors have farmed and grazed for generations. Until the Romans took it from us, that is.'

She closed her eyes. Of all the shadowy depths of Tartarus. She should have known better than to speak of the northern provinces. She plastered on a smile and searched for something cheerful to say. 'You are fortunate,' she said at last.

'Fortunate?'

She motioned across the cell to his raised bed, the pillows and blankets, the table full of delicacies. 'Such bounty.'

His smile disappeared. 'Brutus rewards us for

our kills. Ten kills, you get a bed. Twenty gets you a supply of wine and honey cakes.'

Arria paused. The dizziness remained, but the carelessness had been replaced with contrition.

'Apologies,' she muttered. She had not meant to remind him of his misery. She had only wanted… What *had* she wanted? To invoke a time when they both stood in well-appointed rooms enjoying wine and sweets? And when had that been, exactly? Perhaps she only wished to pretend for a moment that they were human again.

A lump of honey cake was clogging her throat. She coughed and the offending piece of cake went flying on to the floor. 'Forgive me!' she breathed in horror. She lunged to retrieve the crumb and a terrible pain seized her back. She closed her eyes, trying to breathe through it.

'What is wrong?'

'Nothing.' She felt the warmth of blood oozing beneath her tunic. *Just a wound I have managed to rip open.* She recovered her grin and stood slowly, hoping the wound would not bleed through the fabric.

'You are injured,' he said. He stepped behind her. 'You are bleeding.'

'It is nothing.' She drank down her cup. 'Please, may I have more wine?'

Ignoring her request, he pulled off his red tunic and plunged it into a pitcher of water, then straight down the back of her tunic.

'Ah!' she shrieked. The dripping water poured down her back, followed by a large, groping hand that was brushing painfully against the already leaking wound. 'Not there,' she gasped, feeling him press hard against a particularly tender spot. 'A little lower.'

He grumbled, then contorted his arm into a different position. 'Oh!' she cried.

He stopped moving and sighed. 'This would be much easier if you took off your tunic.'

Chapter Nine

She uttered not a single word of protest. She simply gathered the skirt of her tunic and lifted it, turning to reveal a confluence of deep, oozing wounds in the shape of an X across her back.

She had been beaten: there was no doubt of it. Perhaps over several days. No wonder she did not wear her breast strap.

Some of the wounds had healed. Their crusted red lines were like ancient reeds growing in a field of reddened flesh. But other wounds continued to fester, including the one currently leaking a steady stream of blood down her back.

He squeezed his tunic over the gash for a second time, then a third. 'Have you always been this enthusiastic about cleaning wounds?' she jested through the discomfort. 'Or just until I taught you?'

He smiled as he attempted to absorb the still-leaking blood. 'I have long been aware of the importance of cleaning a wound. You should count yourself fortunate that we have water.'

'And what if we did not?'

'Then I would have no choice but to flush it with my own urine,' he pronounced. Arria cringed, then laughed. She punched him softly on the arm.

'You laugh, but I have done it many times in the chaos of battle. There, I think the blood has stopped.' He stepped back and surveyed the collection of wounds.

The pattern was sickening. It was as if her punisher thought himself clever, as if he were some twisted artist and her tender back his canvas. Cal felt the familiar bubbling of rage. 'How did you receive these?'

She shook her head in shame.

'How? Tell me.'

'I fear my master does not speak in the language of rewards, only punishments.'

'This is no punishment. This is savagery.' Cal tried to imagine what possible transgression could have warranted such butchery. 'Did you attempt escape? Harm him in some way?'

'I wove a carpet that did not please him.'

'A carpet?' Cal drew a breath of air through his teeth. 'Why did the carpet displease him?'

'It was the image that I wove. It was…unusual.
May I have more wine?'

She had covered her naked breasts with one
of her arms. With the other, she held out her cup.

She looked so vulnerable standing there—her
back a bloodied wasteland, her front a hidden
temple. He had a powerful desire to gather her
into his arms.

'I would like to relieve your master of his
limbs,' Cal said.

She gave a grateful smile. 'It is of no matter.
I am weaving a new carpet now.'

'May I ask, what was the nature of the design
he so despised?'

He could see the flush of embarrassment rising in her cheeks. 'It is difficult to describe.'

He poured her another cup. 'Try.'

'It would be easier to show.'

'Then show me,' he said.

She squatted to retrieve her tunic. In one fleeting second, she reached out, giving him a view
of her naked chest. If her back was a scorched
field, then her front was a garden of loveliness.
Two mounds of tender abundance floated before
his eyes, then disappeared, and he realised that
she was speaking to him.

'In order for me to show you the design that

resulted in my beating, I must ask you to sit,' she said, pointing to the end of his bed.

Obediently, he crossed to the bed and took his seat. He expected her to produce a tiny sketch, or to find a dusty piece of floor on which to draw the offending design. Instead, she stepped towards him, moving closer and closer until the only distance between his head and her stomach was the range of his breath.

And he was breathing quite heavily now, despite the fact that she was once again clothed. *I am an honourable man*, he reminded himself as his desire bubbled. He was not going to touch her. Of course not. He liked her far too much to ever do that.

It was she who touched him, however. She reached out her hands and touched his head, gently guiding it forward until his forehead was pressing against her stomach. His bubbling desire suddenly turned to steam. It clouded his eyes, his ears, his thoughts.

He had no idea what she was doing, but curses if he did not follow willingly as she lifted his hands from his sides and guided them to her hips. 'Hold them in this position,' she told him, as if he needed prompting.

Steam. Hot and opaque. Wet and hissing. Blurring his vision. Soaking his wits.

He pretended to adjust his grip, feeling the shape of her. He laced his speech with calm un-interest. 'And then?' he asked. His palms were hot, his desire growing like a shoot. Experimentally, he pulled her closer, feeling the soft give of her stomach against his forehead. By the gods, she felt good.

She settled her soft fingers atop his head and he felt that he might die of lust. 'This is it. Do you see what I mean?'

'What?' He addressed his question to the floor. He had already forgotten what they had been discussing. He only knew he did not wish to move a single *digitus*.

'We are positioned in the shape of the image that I wove into the carpet,' she explained.

She must have been waiting for him to affirm his understanding, but all he understood was that he wanted her more than the world's most delicious honey cake.

'Here, let me trace it for you.'

Gently, she lifted his hand from her hip and guided his fingers down the length of her arm. 'This is one line of the design,' she said. Had she no idea how aroused she was making him? 'And here is the other line.' She guided his fingers up the length of her own stomach, brushing them lightly around the curve of one of her breasts.

'Oh, by the gods,' he muttered. The steam was denser now. A thick, hot cloud of it, swirling inside him. He could barely see her through it.

'You can picture it then? The image of a man's head pressing against a woman's stomach?'

'Ah…' He could picture more than that. He could see his hands cupping her breasts, his lips caressing her nipples.

She returned his hand to her hip and placed her own hands atop his head.

'It is the outline of our bodies in the position they are now. Do you see?'

'I see,' he said, though his eyes were closed and he did not wish to open them ever again.

'What is this?' said the guard, turning to discover them. Arria jumped back.

'Touching is forbidden,' the guard said. He unsheathed his *gladius* and rattled it between the bars at Cal. 'Fooling in the bushes costs more, do you hear? No touching unless your *lanista* pays first.'

May you die a thousand deaths, Cal thought, bowing his acknowledgement.

The moment was gone, the mist cleared. Arria had retreated to the other end of the cell. She had got as far away from him as she could get—and was once again studying the honey cakes.

Come back, he thought. His eyes feasted on

her shape, imagining the curves that he had touched only moments ago. The memory of her nearness made him ache.

She was shaking her head, obviously distraught. 'I admit that it was an unusual design for a carpet, though not completely novel. I have heard that in Rome such designs are sought after in patrician circles. They seek the unusual, you see...'

So she had felt it, too—that outrageous pull between their bodies—because she was chattering on as if to erase it. '...in the end I really had no choice but to weave it.'

Were they still talking about the carpet? *Come back. Let me put my hands on your hips again. Slide your soft fingers over my head.*

'Why did you have no choice?' he asked.

'The image would not leave my mind.' She was lingering beside the table, puzzling over a plate of olives. 'Weaving it was the only way to purge it.'

'Where did the image come from?' He wanted to keep her talking. The more she could distract him with her words, the less he would think about how she had just made him feel.

'It was a memory.'

'A memory of two lovers?'

'Yes.'

An unfamiliar pang of jealousy twisted in his stomach. 'A memory of you and another, then? A lost love?'

'I am afraid that would be impossible,' she said, her eyes searching for a new object to study. She absently picked up a cucumber, then set it down in apparent alarm. 'I have never had a lover.'

'A woman as lovely as you?'

Her dismissal of the compliment was so automatic that it made him wonder if she had ever been paid such a one. It was enough to confirm his suspicion that she was an innocent; her virginity worth a price. No wonder the guard had scolded them apart.

Not that he would even think of bedding her. No, his carnal indulgences were limited to women he loathed—namely, the bored patrician matrons who pursued him after his victories. They flung themselves at him like rose petals. They salivated over him like hungry dogs— tiresome, vapid women who caressed his battle-hardened chest and believed they were touching *gloria*.

He never kissed them and tried not to look them in the eye. The women used him and he was perfectly happy to use them in return. They meant nothing.

But a woman he cared for? He would never even dream of bedding a woman he cared for. That would be too much like making love. Even now he puzzled at his own desire and scolded himself for it. He would never betray the memory of his wife by making love to another. Cal had made a vow, after all—to love his wife all his life.

And that was what he intended to do.

'I have had the pleasure of *witnessing* lovers,' the woman was saying.

Cal gazed down the hallway, his breaths slowing. 'I see,' he said absently.

'I do not think you do see.'

Cal shook his head. 'I am sorry, what were we talking about?'

'About the image I wove that earned me the beating. It is an image of two lovers set in wool.'

'Did you not already explain—?'

'The image is a memory of you and the flaxen-haired woman.'

'What? But how did you—?'

'I was here the night she came to you.'

Cal stiffened. 'You were here?'

'I saw you press your head to her stomach. That is how I got the idea for the design.'

She had spied on him? She had watched him in the act? He did not know how to feel. He pictured her lurking in the shadows, watching him caress the German woman. He should have been incensed, but his curiosity reigned. Why had she spied on him? Had she done so out of curiosity? Desire, perhaps? For him?

'I thought you had escaped,' he managed to say.

'I saw little, I assure you.'

He thought back to the moment he had pressed his head against the German woman's stomach. Then he remembered the moment just after, when he had slid his tongue into her folds. 'I believe you saw quite a bit.'

She returned her attention to the olives. 'It was not my intention to intrude. It was the closest I ever believed I would get to—'

'To what exactly?'

She shook her head. 'I should go.'

Chapter Ten

She had offended him for certain. She cursed herself for telling him the truth. What man wished to learn that he had been spied on? She stepped towards the gate and prepared to call the guard.

'Stay,' Cal commanded. His expression was cool. He gestured to the chair behind her. 'We have not yet even discussed the reason I sent for you.'

He was walking towards her now. There was nowhere to retreat. Was he finally going to berate her? He certainly had cause. She had refused to lift the curse, then all but admitted to spying on him. She stepped backwards and folded herself into the chair.

The position gave her a remarkably good view of his naked chest. She tried not to stare. It was just a naked chest. It was like any other naked chest of any other fearsome gladiator or towering Greek god wandering among mortals. Just the usual massive twin planks, the predictable rows of rippling muscle, the swathes of sinewy strength. The generalised magnificence.

She almost choked. That was it—the word she had been searching for to describe him. He was...magnificent.

He stopped before the table and exhaled loudly, angling his body away from her as he lifted the wine flagon. 'I fear we have little time left and I have much to tell you, but first I will pour us more wine, for I find myself in need of it, though in truth I prefer beer. I am a barbarian after all, or so they tell me...'

Now he was the one who was chattering and he seemed to have completely dismissed her confession. 'And what I would not give for a taste of butter! Why do Romans not use butter? Have you ever tried it on bread? It is quite delicious...'

She nodded absently. It was almost as if he were trying to distract her attention. She pretended to watch him pour, but he was so close and her neck was starting to ache. She let her gaze slide down his rippling chest. That was when she discovered the reason for his chatter. It was a large bulging reason that stretched the bounds of her comprehension—along with all the threads of his loincloth.

She had seen plenty of naked male bodies in her life. The statues outside the Harbour Baths gave eye-popping lessons in the details of the male form. Inside, the mosaic that decorated the bottom of the *caldarium* pool transformed that form into something even more…enthusiastic.

But this was something altogether different. This was not an image hewn from rock or glazed in tile. This was flesh. It was a man's desire, fully discharged, larger and realer than she had ever imagined. And she had somehow awakened it.

She attempted to scold herself. She should have known better than to remove her tunic. She should not have placed his head upon her stomach and she certainly should never have made bold to trace his finger along the contours of her body as she had done.

She tried to feel regret, discomfort, shame. Instead she felt as if she could hear the blare of triumphal trumpets. She had aroused him. For the first time in her life a man wanted her. And not just a man, but a magnificent man.

She looked up at him briefly. He was gazing down at her, his expression stony. But his eyes smouldered and she saw them move slightly to take in the bumps of her breasts. Her breasts!

He was looking at them again. Perhaps he liked them. Then again, she had directed his finger across one of them only moments ago. What had she been thinking?

She had not been thinking—that was the problem. She had told him that she wished to demonstrate the image she had woven into the carpet, but that was not the whole truth. What she really wanted was to *be* the woman in that image. Just for a moment, she had wanted to feel his head pressed against her stomach and his hands upon her hips and know what it was like to be wanted.

He finished pouring the wine and popped an olive into his mouth. She thought of something clever to say, but could not keep her gaze from sliding downwards once again and quickly forgot whatever it was she had meant to say to fill the maddening silence.

Surely he despised her now—first for cursing him, then for spying on him and now, apparently, for exciting him. Men did not like to be toyed with, or was that not the lesson of every divine story she had ever been told? She tried to steady herself, for she feared the wine and honey cakes were merely the sweet before the salt.

'Here we are,' he said. He offered her one of the cups, his fingers grazing hers. Their gazes met and she felt another pang of sensation low in her body. She drew the cup away quickly and he gave an amused grunt.

Did he find what had just passed between them amusing? And what had passed between them, exactly? And why was her heart beating as if she had just run a mile?

She studied the crimson contents of her cup. Her hands were shaking and the sloshing liquid was making her dizzier still, but she feared that if she looked up, she would find herself staring squarely at...

He was handing her his own cup. 'Hold this for a moment.'

She gave an obsequious nod, now completely confused.

He was placing the wine and plate of honey cakes on the floor, along with all the other edibles. 'I can see that you are nervous,' he was saying, 'though you have no reason to fear me. And if we are going to have a conversation, I will not stand over you like Claudius at the judgement of Caractacus.' He took back his cup and patted the high table. 'You sit here.'

'On the table?'

He rolled his eyes. 'I can sit upon the cursed table if you like, but I will not continue to stand before you like this.' He glanced down at himself.

Afraid he would say more, she nearly lunged

herself up on to the slightly higher table and watched him take a seat in the chair that she had warmed for him. Now her sightline was occupied by his face, thank the gods. In the cascading daylight, his eyes sparkled like green gems.

'Do you not wish to know why I sent for you?' he asked.

'I already know why you sent for me. You wish for me to lift the curse.' There was a long silence and she watched her legs dangle from her high perch.

'It is of no consequence to me whether or not you lift the curse.'

She gulped her wine, trying to appear unmoved. 'That is well, for I do not intend to lift it.'

'Arria, it is not the curse that has kept me alive.'

'Well, of course it is,' said Arria. Perhaps he was testing her confidence in her ability as a sorceress.

'I know that you are not a sorceress. You are not even a very good liar.' Arria opened her mouth to protest, but a hiccup escaped instead.

'Even if the curse did exist once,' he continued, 'it lifted many days ago at the Ludi Plebii of Tarsus, when I faced the Titan of Perinthus.'

'The Titan of Perinthus?' She could hardly believe it. The Thracian killer was considered one of the finest gladiators in the Empire. Arria gave a smug harrumph. 'You survived the fight. Is that not proof enough that I have cursed you utterly?'

'There were many opportunities for me to die, I assure you. I simply chose not to take them.'

She shook her head dismissively, unwilling to concede.

'Have you *seen* the Titan of Perinthus?' he asked.

In truth she had not, though she had heard the rumours. It was said that he was as tall as a camel and as strong as an ox, and that his roar shook the heavens.

'I'm sure you delivered him a spectacular death.'

'On the contrary, we battled for what must have been an hour, trading blows like two men playing dice. Finally, he pinned me to the sand. I was exhausted and his sword hovered over my neck in the promise of a fast, clean death. The spectators screamed and shouted, and I closed my eyes and waited to see the face of…someone I once loved.'

'And?'

'And instead I saw your face.'

Arria choked on her wine, coughed. 'Apologies, what did you say?'

'I said that I saw your face.'

Arria frowned. In the moment before what he thought was his end, he had thought of *her*? There was the fluttering again—that flock of birds deep in her stomach. Against her wishes, they were taking flight—carrying her back to that day so long ago when she had gazed into a young man's eyes and believed she saw her future. *Take care*, Arria, she told herself. *Do not mistake friendliness for desire.*

'*Why* did you see my face?' she asked carefully.

'Because you had a message for me.'

'What was the message?'

'That if I died, then they would win.'

And there it was—the whole truth. Thank the gods she had had the wisdom to await its revelation. The breath went out of her and the birds disappeared in puffs of feathers. It was not care or desire that had motivated his vision of her, but her wise words. She was not his heart's desire, it seemed, but his mind's counsellor.

'The spectators were howling like animals, hungry to watch my blood pour out on to the sand. I could not let them win, Arria, so I rolled away from the Titan's sword.'

'Thank the gods.'

'The sword stuck in the sand and the Titan stumbled. But I refused to kill him and the crowd grew angry at me. They hissed and howled. They spat and threw rubbish. As I passed close to the stands they poured barley water on my head.'

'And you were not disheartened?'

He grinned lavishly. 'Their hatred only fuelled me. The more they howled, the stronger I became. I fought the Titan with unrelenting energy and there were many opportunities for me to strike a fatal blow. The crowd called for blood, but I refused them. Finally, the Titan threw down his sword and then so did I.'

'And what did the crowd say about that?' asked Arria.

'They were stunned at first. Many stalked out of the amphitheatre in anger. The rest fell silent. After many moments, I perceived a group of guards making their way across the arena. I was certain they had been ordered to slay us both.'

'Were you not terrified?'

'Not at all. I did not even attempt to pick up my sword. Instead, a strange peace settled over me. I gazed up at the crowd and realised that we had won. The Titan and I had beaten them. By refusing to defeat each other, we had defeated everyone else.'

Arria might have congratulated him, but the idea of Cal's death—however triumphant—made her feel ill. 'Thank the gods you were not killed.'

'I believe we would have been, had it not been for the spectators, who slowly began to applaud us. I watched them rise to their feet in the stands in sombre adulation. It was as if we had given them something they did not even know they craved.'

'Catharsis,' said Arria absently.

'Is that the name for it?' asked Cal, not waiting for an answer. 'Well, when the guards finally reached us, the crowd was shouting for mercy. The mayor delivered his decree and we were saved.' He reached up and grasped Arria's hand. 'And it is all because of you, Arria. You were the one who inspired me to beat them at their own game. If you cursed me to life once, now you have convinced me to keep it.'

They were glorious words, though she could focus on little else but the feel of his hand grasping hers and how easy her name had rolled off his tongue.

'I will go on defying them, Arria, for as long as I can. I will fight, but I will not kill. I will hold a mirror to their faces and show them how ugly they are!'

Arria squeezed his hand. The Satyr had been right. He was an honourable man—the most honourable she had ever known. But if he refused to kill, would he not eventually be overcome? An unnameable emotion plugged her throat.

'What is it, Arria? What is wrong?'

'What of your next foe? What if…?' She could not even say it.

'What if he is more difficult to subdue? Or what if I am faced with a host of foes? Cavalry? Lions, perhaps?' He flashed a ferocious grin. 'It is inevitable that I will die. It is the fate of all gladiators.'

'Not all. You could be granted a *rudius*, could you not?'

He laughed. 'The wooden sword of freedom? Do you think the governor would give one of those to a gladiator who refuses to kill? Besides, the governor himself makes too much money on my battles to ever free me. Now at least I will die in defiance of them all.'

'But you cannot die.'

'I am a gladiator, Arria. I am meant to die.'

'But…' Arria sputtered. It was of no matter that he did not want her, she realised. What mattered was that she wanted him.

'But what?'

'But you are my pigeon.'

He frowned, then laughed. 'No more wine for you!'

She squeezed his hand hard, as if the strength

contained within her fingers might alone be enough to save him. 'You do not understand,' she said. 'I need you to stay alive.'

'Do not fear.' He smirked. 'You will find some other source of wine and honey cakes.'

She blinked and a tear rolled down her cheek. 'But none so very sweet,' she whispered.

'Time is up,' shouted the guard. Arria shook her head in frustration. 'If only we could make an escape,' she said.

'And then what? We would be discovered, Arria, and punished in a way designed to break our will. There is no escape.'

'How can you be so hopeless?'

'I will show you how,' he said. Slowly, he turned around. The broad expanse of his back appeared before her, filling her vision. She saw scars—layer upon layer of them. They criss-crossed his skin like a hideous net. Arria could practically hear the lash snapping as she gazed upon the history of violence, the geography of pain.

How had she never noticed?

'People see what they wish to see,' he said, reading her thoughts, 'not what is. You wish to see a way out. For a long time I did, too. But I am telling you that for a man like me, there is only one. You, on the other hand, must learn to endure. You must be patient. Your day of freedom will come.'

The first guard had returned with a second and began unlocking the gate. Their time was running out.

'When is your next battle?'

'I will fight in the New Year Games of Pergamon in fifteen days. If I succeed, I will ask Brutus to purchase another meeting with you. Thus I can tell you the story of my defiance. If I live, I will become known as the gladiator who spurned the Roman Empire.'

Arria did not dare to voice the question that hung like a poison cloud in the air. *And if you die?*

He bent to her ear and whispered. 'When the day comes, I do not want you to mourn me. Only remember me and endure.'

He took her hands and helped her down from the table. A blade twisted inside her. She did not wish to remember Cal and endure. She wished to stay with Cal now, to wrap his arms around her and keep him whispering in her ear. But how?

Think, Arria.

How could she inspire Cal to keep himself alive? Apart from her advice, she had only one thing to offer and it seemed he did not want it, despite the…enthusiasm she had provoked in him.

Still, she had only one life and she could no longer allow the twin demons of duty and despair to prevent her from living it.

She bent to his ear and, this time, she was the one to whisper.

Chapter Eleven

Cal could see very little inside the subterranean barracks beneath the Pergamon circus, but he could feel the thunderous pounding of the hooves above and could hear the crowd roar as the chariots raced past. It had been over a year since he had fought at a circus and he had nearly forgotten how much noise a crowd of seventy thousand could make.

If only they could somehow make it warmer. He jumped up and down on the cold stone floor. The first snow of the season had fallen the night before and had blanketed every city from Ephesus to Caesarea with a layer of white.

Cal rubbed his bare limbs, wondering how Arria had endured the cold. Oppius was not the type to light braziers for slaves and Arria had likely huddled with the other slaves on some cold concrete floor, fighting the chill. The vision gave him a pain in his stomach.

Above him, the spectators chanted from the stands, their breath visible in tiny puffs of steam. The Roman New Year was a time of celebration and purging, and the throngs had braved the cold in order to witness what was traditionally the bloodiest purge of them all—the New Year Games.

Cal counted at least twenty other gladiators in the barracks—men brought in from gladiator training schools throughout the province. They clustered together according to *ludus* while their respective *lanistas* had gathered in a conspiratorial group at the back of the room.

Cal tossed Felix a sympathetic grin as his friend puzzled over the blue swirls that had been painted on his chest.

'I look like a damn barbarian,' Felix said. He gestured to the other men. 'We all do. What is the meaning of it?'

'I believe we are meant to represent the enemy.'

Felix shook his head. He was not the kind of man to show fear, but Cal could see it in his friend's eyes as he considered the ragged fur kilt he had been issued. 'Nor does Brutus give any instruction today,' Felix observed. He did not need to give voice to the truth slowly descending upon all the men. They had not been given instruction, because they were all meant to die.

The chariots rumbled past once again. When the dust finally settled, Cal caught sight of a bird circling high in the sky.

He smiled to himself, thinking of Arria. What on earth could she have meant when she'd called him her pigeon? If he resembled a bird at all, it was a hawk or a falcon—something menacing and powerful. A bird of prey. But a pigeon? He felt himself begin to smile, then pushed the thought from his mind. Why should such things matter to a man standing on the brink of death?

The hoofbeats finally ceased and outside the crowd roiled with impatience. The morning races had concluded and already Cal could hear the angry shouts of men brawling over which chariot team had won—the reds or the whites.

Soon the midday executions would commence and the spectators would continue to brawl, swilling wine and ignoring the bodies hanging on crosses and dangling from ropes before them. It was absurd—reds versus whites—like a child's game, yet more important, apparently, than life and death.

'May Fortuna favour you today, Beast,' said a young attendant, handing Cal a metal shoulder guard. He gave Cal a prolonged bow.

'Gratitude, youth,' Cal said, though he did not believe in Fortuna. Unless she came in the form of a big-eyed Roman woman who spouted curses and smelled of smoke and wool.

Why did the thought of her plague him so? For fifteen whole days he had been unable to get her voice out of his head—or rather her whisper: *'There is another thing we can do in defiance of our masters,'* she had told him just before she had departed. *'Let my innocence be yours—not some greasy Roman lecher's. Tell your master to purchase me for the night of your victory. Help me keep a small piece of my soul. Keep yourself alive. For me.'*

'Let my innocence be yours.'

The words haunted him. They kept him awake at night, teasing his desire and testing his resolve. Not that he was unaccustomed to being propositioned. If the blood of a gladiator had the power to heal, then the gladiator himself could make a woman immortal, or so Roman matrons foolishly believed. They used him like priests used white bulls—to mate, then sacrifice to the glory of the sands.

Surely Arria was no different than they, though in truth she was no longer even Roman— at least not in the eyes of the law. Her citizenship was revoked the moment her father had sold her into servitude. Nor was she a matron—quite the opposite. From her sad history, Cal guessed that Arria had spent her marriageable years taking in laundry, foraging for food and weaving at a loom, working to keep her family alive.

She seemed to be the kind of Roman woman that he did not believe existed. In other words, she was good and it made his chest squeeze to think of her bending to the will of any man, let alone the kind of corrupt, twisted man who was likely to purchase her for her innocence.

But that was not the real reason her proposition haunted him. It was how he had felt when she'd said it. As she'd whispered into his ear, the hairs on his arms had risen and his breath had caught in his throat. 'Let my innocence be yours,' she had whispered and the rush of lust that flooded his body had been almost too much to bear.

It had scared him, in truth. *She* had scared him. If the guard had not yanked her away from him after she had made her bold request, he did not know what he would have done.

And yet she was a Roman woman. The enemy. There was no past between them and there could be no future. There was only the hot, shimmering present that seemed powerful enough to obliterate everything.

Including the memory of his wife.

A loud horn signalled the last of the executions. The gladiators grumbled, loathe to begin the journey that was likely to end in their own deaths.

For Cal, it might have been the perfect day to die. The men would need to fight as a group, leaving him little opportunity to defy Rome. It was kill or be killed and Cal and Felix were clearly among the gladiators who had been marked for death.

Strangely, however, he did not wish for it. He pulled his wife's bundle of hair from the folds of his loincloth and squeezed it in his fist. He knew she was waiting for him and yet...

He tucked away his wife's hair and took out Arria's hairpin, rolling it between his fingers like the stem of a flower.

'Line up to receive your weapons,' called one of the *lanistas*.

Cal walked up the stairs and stood behind the door that led to the arena above. But it was as if he were not standing before one door, but two.

Behind the first door was everything he stood for, everything he was: husband, warrior, vengeance seeker, defier of Rome. To fulfil his destiny, all he had to do was open the door and proudly go to his doom.

Behind the second door was everything he wanted. In other words, behind the second door was Arria. She was waiting for him there in her tattered tunic, beckoning him with her big brown eyes. She *wanted* him and, by the gods, he wanted her—so badly that it made him ache. But to see her again, he had to live. He tucked her hairpin away.

The men began to take their places behind him. They spoke in hushed tones, speculating about what lay behind the door; wondering how they might survive it.

Cal should have been wondering the same. At the very least, he should have been formulating a strategy. He should have been trying to figure out how he might beat the Romans at their own bloody game.

But all he could think about was Arria and all he could feel was that strange alchemy that had him sweating and pacing and shaking his head and realising that a whisper was not going to be enough.

Not nearly enough.

Arria was shivering beneath her blanket when Oppius burst into the workshop. 'Happy New Year,' he huffed. He lifted the blanket from her limbs and promptly informed her that she would be helping him in the market stall that day.

'You, too, Epona,' he told Epona, whom he often summoned for market days. Epona closed her eyes for what seemed to Arria a little too long, then nodded.

'Now go wash yourselves. If you are not ready in a quarter of an hour, I will beat you myself.'

Oppius glanced at Arria's first carpet, which she used as a bed mat. 'And you may as well bring that godforsaken thing,' he told her. 'Perhaps someone will buy it out of pity. Now go wash.'

Arria and Epona rushed to the courtyard. They removed their tunics and poured buckets of frigid fountain water over each other's heads. Arria scrubbed the dust from her limbs with violent energy, relishing the cold, which distracted her from her racing thoughts. Today was the start of the games at the circus of Pergamon—the day Cal would either endure or die.

She squeezed her hair, then dipped her fingers into a small amphora of oil beside the fountain and coated her body with it. She found the dull *strigil* and scraped it along her shivering skin, then wordlessly handed it to Epona.

The young woman's expression was as dreary as a shroud. To be chosen to accompany Oppius to market was no boon, for he went to market to sell more than just his wares.

Arria reached over her own shoulder and touched the tip of one of her scars. She had finally healed and was now suitable for sale. She knew that Oppius would be looking for the highest bidder for her innocence.

Epona jumped in place, trying to dry herself. 'We must pray that the cold will keep the old lechers home today,' she said.

Less than an hour later, Arria was stumbling on to the concrete expanse of the marketplace, yanking on the rope tied to the metal collar around her neck.

'Pick up your feet,' Oppius called from the driver's bench of the horse cart she followed. A statue of Artemis was teetering on the edge of the cart, threatening to fall.

Arria moved to right it, but was stopped by a low hiss from Epona, who marched behind the cart just like Arria, wearing her own rope and collar.

Better to let it smash, Epona's eyes told Arria, and in that moment Arria became a conspirator in what she realised was a quiet war.

Arria's stomach rumbled as the driver brought the horse cart to a halt next to the stall. Oppius unleashed Arria first, then Epona, and the two went to work emptying the cart of its statues, carpets and blankets while Oppius wandered over to the nearby baker's stall.

Their task complete, the two women jumped in place and Arria gazed longingly at the blankets.

'He would beat you for it most certainly,' said Epona, reading Arria's mind. 'He enjoys watching us shiver.'

Arria slid a glance at Oppius, who had purchased a rather large flatbread from the baker and lounged on a bench beside his guard. Arria thought her master looked something like a grazing bull as he sat there chewing, though she could see that he was watching them closely from behind his crust.

Arria wished the sun would emerge from behind Mount Pion and warm her bones. She had never been to the commercial marketplace this early and the place was eerily empty. The statue atop the water clock at the centre of the plaza had yet to rise above the pool and the stairs to the Serapis temple were still littered with sleeping dogs.

But Arria could already smell the smoke of the sausage merchants and could see the herbalists and the spicers setting out their colourful baskets.

The sound of laughing seagulls resounded from the harbour and a faint scent of urine came up on the breeze. Arria pursed her lips.

'If you think the Ephesus market smells bad, you have clearly never been to Rome,' said Epona, putting her arms around her throat in a mock choke. Arria stole a worried glance at Oppius, who was thankfully busy speaking to his guard.

'Do not fear. I know when he is not watching us,' said Epona.

'You have developed eyes in the back of your head?'

'After all these years, I can tell you the moment that man is going to burp.'

'Hazah!' Arria giggled softly, still keeping a wary eye on Oppius. If he caught them chatting, who knew what new torture he would conjure for them to endure? 'How do you know the markets of Rome?' Arria asked.

'I lived in Rome for most of my childhood,' said Epona. 'When I was a girl, Emperor Domitian brought most of my tribe to Rome in chains. We are known as the Chatti.'

Arria sobered. 'I have heard of your people. I am sorry.'

Epona waved her hand in the air as if swatting flies. 'Why sorry? It was not your doing. I was fortunate, really, for my family was sold together. We laboured on one of the wheat plantations just outside the city.'

'How did you come to Ephesus?'

'My mother and father—and many others—attempted to escape the plantation. They were killed in the public executions at the Ludi Capitolini and I was sold to a slave merchant bound for Delos. The rest is history.'

'Mercy of Jupiter,' muttered Arria.

Epona laughed. 'I consider myself fortunate, for I am young and beautiful, or so I am told, and when I am old and ugly it will not matter, for I know how to weave.'

Epona flipped her long auburn hair behind her head and pursed her lips into the shape of a kiss. Arria laughed. Epona was indeed quite beautiful, her eyes hauntingly grey, her pale skin adorned with joyous freckles.

'Before I was sold, I was betrothed, you know,' Epona added thoughtfully.

'Really?'

'He was also a Chatti, also brought to Rome in chains, though he was much older than I. Still, I often wonder what my life would be like had we been able to marry.'

'What happened to him?'

'Oh, he was also executed,' she said.

'Great Mother Goddess.'

'Some might call it a better destiny than ours.'

'I do not think so,' said Arria.

'But you have laboured at the loom for only a few months.'

Arria nodded, though in a sense she had been at the loom much longer than that. 'My mother once had great hopes of finding me a patrician husband,' Arria said.

'Don't all mothers?'

Arria smiled. 'It is the reason she taught me to weave and also to read. She said it would make me more desirable to a well-born man. She had a fine dowry for me...'

'Until your father gambled it away?'

Arria nodded. 'I would give anything to see my mother now.'

'Be careful what you pledge before gods,' warned Epona, stealing a glance at the cold morning sky. 'I have found that they quite enjoy breaking our hearts.'

By mid-morning, the sun had finally come out from hiding and so had the people of Ephesus. Arria and Epona guarded their master's merchandise while he answered the questions of passers-by and the sprawling U-shaped plaza slowly filled with souls.

Arria was just beginning to relax when she spied a large group of uniformed men walking up Harbour Street.

'Is there an invasion I don't know about?' Epona quipped.

'It is an unusual sight,' averred Arria and she watched in alarm as the legionaries turned into the marketplace and began browsing its shops. There must have been fifty of them, each in a short red tunic covered by a chainmail shirt, a thick leather belt, a hilted *gladius*.

The soldiers were not shy and the young women passing near them cowered beneath the men's lusty gazes. Several of the soldiers stopped outside the sausage cart and watched the man turn his sausages on the grill.

'They are not allowed to enjoy meat while on duty,' Epona remarked. 'Or women, for that matter.' Her grin sparkled. 'We are off the menu.'

'Oh, thank the gods,' said Arria and the knot in her stomach loosened as a group of them approached.

'Welcome, soldiers!' greeted Oppius. 'To which campaign do you journey?'

'Not allowed to say,' said one, glancing backwards at a man whom Arria guessed to be his commander, for his cuirass was made of leather, not mail, and had been shaped to follow the general contours of his chest.

The commander stopped outside their stall. 'I was noticing the fine quality of your carpets,' he told Oppius, his eyes ranging across Epona's body, then Arria's.

'The carpets are indeed fine, Tribune,' said Oppius with a deferential bow.

'Which one requires the most beating?' the man asked. His face twisted into a malicious grin.

'This one,' Oppius said at last, pointing to Epona.

The tribune eyed Epona closely. 'How much for the night?'

'Forty *denarii*,' Oppius said. It was the same price he had set for the smaller carpets.

'And that one?' he asked, pointing to Arria.

'That one is more expensive. She is, shall I say, fresh off the loom.'

The tribune laughed wickedly. 'A carpet merchant who is also a poet! I should have known the great port of Ephesus would produce such a soul.'

'I am here to serve the Empire,' said Oppius.

'In that case wait for me a moment and I shall return with your richest client yet.'

Arria felt the seconds stretch out. She braved

a glance at Epona, whose sparkling eyes had grown dark and hollow.

In minutes the tribune had returned with a tall, white-haired man whose wrinkled face and yellowed teeth betrayed an advanced age. 'Here she is, Legate,' said the tribune. 'Pretty and unsullied, just as you like them.'

The old man tossed his red cape over his shoulder and squinted at Arria. 'How much?'

'Eighty *denarii*, Legate,' said Oppius. 'A fair price. And half of it returned if she does not bleed.'

The old man nodded thoughtfully. 'I will have her, then. And my good tribune here will take the other. We will return at sundown to fetch them.' The legate reached into a small leather purse. 'Here is proof of our good faith.'

He handed Oppius a silver coin and Oppius gave a sweeping bow. 'Officers, it is a pleasure doing business with you.'

Chapter Twelve

For Cal, the moments before he stepped into the arena were always the same: he would close his eyes and remember the day his wife died. That is what he did now as the trumpets blared and the door of Pergamon's underground barracks slowly opened.

He gazed at the stands. Instead of spectators, he pictured soldiers. He saw his Caledonii tribesmen gathered on the steepest slope of Graupius Mountain, thirty thousand strong. He saw their painted bodies, imagined their fearsome voices filling the air. How brazenly they had awaited the Roman approach, so confident in their higher ground.

Cal pictured the Roman army, that terrible iron serpent. He remembered how the Roman infantry soldiers had marched up the valley and come to a halt in its cleft, turning beneath their shields to avoid the Caledonii arrows and how he and the other Caledonii warriors had poured down from above, heedless of the danger.

He remembered watching in horror as his countrymen reached the valley and began to fall beneath Roman javelins. One man. Two men. Five. Twenty. Their slashing broadswords were useless in the close quarters of the chasm. Their wild, violent movements were overmatched by the Romans' short, precise ones and soon ten thousand Caledonii bodies littered the river, turning its water red. He remembered picking his way through the carnage, searching for survivors and finding none.

He had hurried back to his town to discover it plundered and burning, and remembered how the bodies had been piled like haystacks. He pictured the remains of his hut and the charred black figure at its centre, lying atop the remains of their wedding mat.

He opened his eyes. Moments ago, he had been thinking of Arria, yearning for her, even. But how could he ever even dream of another woman? His wife was all that existed, or ever would exist. No craving or passing fancy or pang of lust could take away his love for his wife, or the pain of that moment when he saw her burnt figure. Time could pass, memories could fade, every woman on earth could lay herself down at Cal's feet. There would never be any day other than that one, and there would never be any woman other than Rhiannon.

The crowd exploded in cheers. The gladiators marched out on to the hippodrome sands. 'Filthy barbarians!' someone shouted. The crowd hissed as the scantily armed warriors fanned out on to the empty field.

At the other end of the field, a phalanx of fifty well-armed men appeared. They were dressed as Roman soldiers.

They were not soldiers, of course—nor were they at all Roman. They were slaves and captives—'barbarians' just like Cal. But it did not matter. The Roman spectators would have their spectacle and, judging by the dull, rusted condition of the *gladius* Cal had been issued, they would also have their blood.

'We must stay together!' someone cried, but the other gladiators were already breaking ranks. One of the men bolted towards the stands and a javelin skewered his neck.

The gladiators dressed as Romans were almost upon them. If Cal wanted to die, this would be the day.

Cal stepped backwards and put up his rusty sword like a shield. Felix was standing behind him. 'By the gods, Cal, fight.' But Cal did not want to fight the Roman imposters. They were not his real enemies.

Two more men collapsed beside him, pierced by arrows, and it seemed that the corpses of his own team of gladiators were piling up beneath his feet. Soon it was as if he were not in a circus at all, but a narrow green valley, and the Romans were advancing like an army of the dead.

But instead of his wife, he thought of Arria. *'Tell your master to purchase me for the night of your victory,'* she had told him. *'Help me keep a small piece of my soul...'*

Peace be damned. He wanted to live. He began to swing his *gladius*.

'That is more like it,' said Felix.

His first kill was easy—a deep stab into a bulging gut. The collapsing body revealed a snarling man whose throat Cal slit for mercy. The next kills came harder, for their opponents had fine shields and well-honed swords. Cal had to scurry around them to gain advantage and soon found himself hacking at limbs.

He fought like the savage barbarian the crowd thought he was. With each spout of blood, they cheered. With each severed limb, they roared. Soon only himself and Felix remained. They stood atop a pile of bodies like actors atop a stage.

'Why do they not cheer for us anymore?' asked Felix.

'Because we are the enemy, remember? We are not Roman.'

'Well, it is over, so they can all just suck my—'

But it was not over. At the far end of the field, two men emerged from the barracks, donning the regalia of Roman officers. They carried mighty longswords, which they slashed through the air to the delight of the crowd. The larger officer wore a legate's red cape and an expression full of malevolent joy.

'You take the tribune,' said Cal. 'I will take the legate.'

That was when he heard the bell.

Arria hovered at the back of the stall, trying to understand what had happened. Had her innocence just been sold for the price of two carpets? She peered at Epona, who appeared to be on the verge of tears. That was when Arria heard the bell.

It was a low, mournful sound—one of tin, not bronze—and hauntingly familiar. Such bells were often rung by female beggars—destitute women who prowled the marketplaces pleading for scraps.

The bell clanked closer and Arria observed the piteous expressions of the people making wide circles around the woman. Her long dishevelled hair hung in unkempt ropes over her small hunched shoulders, which looked alarmingly familiar. Someone paused to give the woman a coin and Arria beheld the emaciated, pregnant figure of her own mother.

'Mother,' she whispered, knowing that if she took a single step forward, Oppius would have her by the hair.

Her mother wore no shoes, despite the cold, and her tunic was of such a loose weave that it was as if she had sewn it together with scrap yarn. Her only adornment was a small homemade necklace comprised of thick, garish beads.

Arria choked back her sobs. She knew the purpose of such a necklace, could practically read the tragic script etched on to its largest charm— Familia Arrius of Ephesus: Mother Livia, Father Faustus, Brother Clodius, Sister Arria.

It was a *crepundia*—the customary necklace fashioned by a mother for a baby whom she planned to abandon at the dump. The necklace was an amulet and also a badge. If by some miracle the baby was rescued, then the information written on the charms of the necklace could one day lead him home.

Her mother angled closer and Arria stepped out from the depths of the stall. She glanced at Oppius, who had become distracted by a passing cake pedlar. 'Arria, what are you doing?' hissed Epona. 'Oppius will see you. He will beat you.'

But Arria no longer cared. If she had to incur a beating for a few words of comfort with her suffering mother, then so be it. She raised her arm and opened her mouth to call her mother's name.

And in that instant a young woman in a gold-laced veil raised her arms in front of Arria and shrieked. 'Minerva's Owl, this is magnificent!'

The young woman rushed past Arria into the stall, followed by a small army of slaves.

'Mother, come look at this carpet,' the woman shouted over her shoulder, blasting Arria's ears. An older woman with an army of her own pushed past Arria and Arria stood on her toes to catch sight of her mother again. There was still time to reach her. Arria opened her mouth to shout.

'That is the shape of a man's head, is it not?' the young woman asked Arria, her face only digits away. She pulled back her veil, revealing a nest of carefully arranged braids and curls. 'Well, is it?'

Arria tried to speak, but no words came.

'Ah, yes, I see it,' said the elder, removing her own silken veil. 'A woman's figure. Or perhaps it is the figure of a goddess. What a wonder of a design. I have never seen anything like it.'

Arria caught sight of her mother's figure slowly retreating into the crowd.

'Can you not picture it in the dining chamber, Mother,' the younger woman was saying, 'just below the middle couch?'

'Gods, no!' said the elder. 'Such a carpet can only be hung on a wall.' She turned to Arria. 'Tell me, is this woven of lambswool?'

She had asked Arria a question, but Arria had not heard it.

'Excuse me, woman?' repeated the voice in annoyance. A pair of liquid black eyes bored into her. 'Is this carpet made of lambswool or not?'

'Ah, no, Domina, not lambswool.'

'Not lambswool? But it is so soft.'

Arria did not know what to say. Her mother was gone. Her heart was breaking. 'Tell me, do you know the weaver? Is she from Rome? She must be quite sought after...'

Arria shook her head. No, she did not know the weaver, for the weaver was a brave woman who loved her mother and would risk anything to help her. A woman who was clever enough to free herself from bondage and rescue her family from ruin. A woman, in other words, who was nothing like herself.

Chapter Thirteen

The sound of the bell was like the sound of death—thin and hollow. The crowd hushed as the ancient woman who rang it stepped out on to the field. She cackled with menace as the bell clanked out its foreboding.

Cal and Felix scrambled to the centre of the arena and pressed their backs together, gripping their swords.

What will it be? wondered Cal. He lifted a sword from one of the corpses and held it in his other hand. *Lions? Chariots? A rain of arrows?*

But it was something far, far worse.

It was women. Two tall, fair-haired gladiatrices who might have been his own kin. They emerged from a trapdoor not far from where the legate and tribune gladiators stood. One woman was older than the other, but their faces looked similar, as if they were mother and daughter.

Their breasts were bare and they shrieked and howled as they poked their spears at the sky. The crowd answered them with mocking cries.

'I cannot kill a woman,' Cal said.

'You *must* kill a woman,' growled Felix. 'And then another. There is no choice.'

There is a choice, thought Cal. *I could finally succumb.*

But then the memory of Arria's whispered words crowded into his mind, along with the vision of two dark moons pleading with him to fight. 'On my command, we split apart,' said Cal.

'Are you mad?'

'The only way to defeat the women and the men at once is to set them upon each other. You must trust me, Felix. Await my command.'

In moments their enemies were upon them. Cal's ears rang with the clang of swords as he traded blows with the towering legate. Beside him, Felix was fending off the small tribune and elder gladiatrix, but Cal could see his strength waning. In a surge of effort, Cal pushed the legate backwards into the younger gladiatrix, sending them both to the ground.

'Split now!' Cal shouted.

As Cal and Felix went running to opposite sides of the field, Cal could hear the crunch of bone as the legate severed the young woman's head.

A familiar loathing invaded Cal's heart as the crowd erupted in cheers. The young woman who had just died had been an innocent and Cal might as well have killed her himself.

Felix circled around, taking down the older gladiatrix with a deadly slash, and she spent her last breaths in a long, mournful howl. Felix shook his head and Cal knew that there would be no good dreams for either of them this night.

The legate lifted the young woman's head to the crowd. The man was so engaged in his own triumph that he did not see Cal's rusty sword until it was well lodged in the soft of his neck.

There were three men left—Cal, Felix and the gladiator dressed as a Roman tribune. He stood atop the pile of corpses in a state of pure agitation. Cal and Felix circled him like wolves.

'Iugula! Iugula!' chanted the crowd. Kill him.

'Let us fight him to exhaustion,' Cal called to Felix. If they spared the man's life, then Cal could at least return to Arria with part of his soul intact. 'We can still defy the crowd. There is no more need to kill. Take a rest, Felix. I will fight him first.'

Felix gave a nod of agreement and slowly lowered his sword. And in that brief, terrible instant, the maniacal tribune leaped down from the mountain of flesh.

* * *

That night, after the guard closed the door to the workshop and locked the bolt into place, Arria wept. She wept for her destitute mother and for the baby who would not survive. She wept for Epona, who had been sent off with a stranger while Arria herself had been spared. And she wept for Cal, for she feared he might be dead.

'To whom was Epona rented this time?' Grandmother asked across the darkness.

Arria could not find the words to answer. The tribune had arrived at dusk, paid Oppius in new *denarii* and taken Epona by the wrist, explaining as an afterthought that the legate was ailing and would not be requiring Arria's services after all.

And just like that, Arria had been saved.

And Epona had not.

'Do you know what is worse than being violated by a twisted man?' Arria asked bitterly. 'Knowing that your friend is enduring such a fate and there is nothing you can do about it.'

'She is stronger than you know,' Grandmother whispered, hearing Arria's sobs.

'It should have been me,' Arria sputtered.

'Do not weep for her.'

'I will weep for my mother, then.'

'More wasted tears! Mothers are the strongest people there are.'

'She is heavy with child, yet she starves.'

'Hush now. Remember your pigeon.'

Arria shook her head. 'My mother says that hope resides in the next world. And eternal salvation, too. I fear she will be there soon.'

'She follows the way of Jesus?'

Arria wiped her tears. 'She says we must endure suffering with grace, just as Jesus did on the cross.'

'Well, I would not go that far.'

'But is that not what you do—what we all do here?'

'Do you think that is what I do? Endure suffering?'

There was a long pause, then an ancient harrumph. Arria felt a wooden object being pressed into her palm. 'Be careful not to touch the tines,' Grandmother whispered. 'They are very sharp.'

Arria slid her fingers gently along a long flat surface that forked into two arched curves. She touched her finger against the tip of one of the curves. 'Ouch!'

'Did I not warn you, dear?'

'How did you forge such an object?' Arria asked. She had seen the guards gather the women's knives and scissors at the end of each day and count them carefully.

'During the day, when I see the guards are not looking, I use my carving tool.'

'But the guards are always looking.'

'I admit that it has taken some time to carve. Fortunately, time is something I have much of.'

'How much time?'

'About ten years.'

Arria could not believe what she was hearing. Ten years? The carving must have amounted to a single pass of the knife each day. 'You have the patience of Penelope,' whispered Arria.

'And the breasts of Kybele,' added Grandmother.

Arria stifled a giggle, then realised what Grandmother was trying to say. 'That is where you hide it? Beneath your breasts?'

'Clever girl,' said Grandmother.

'I think you are much cleverer than I.'

Grandmother gently took the weapon from Arria's palm. 'There are many things one may choose to do with suffering. Enduring it is just one of those things.'

'The son of my mother's god endured great suffering. Her goddess was a virgin when she bore him.'

'Ah, Mary,' said Grandmother. 'My own grandfather knew Mary when she dwelled in Ephesus with John. She has since become a worthy goddess, though there are many goddesses one may choose to worship.'

'And whom do you worship, Grandmother?'

'Well, I have my pick, do I not? Kybele, Artemis, Mary, Ephesia, the founder of our fair city. They all have roots in Ephesus and ashes, too. But I must say that I prefer Kybele. She is my kind of goddess.'

Arria nodded thoughtfully. 'Kybele the earth mother. Rome's Magna Mater. The Greeks' Rhea.'

'The very same, though I dare say that Kybele existed long before Rhea.'

'Kybele of the ancient earth.'

'Kybele of the pendulous breasts!' cackled Grandmother.

Arria laughed softly. She thought of Epona, who would have enjoyed the jest. She wondered what terrible encounter she was enduring in this moment. She would need the strength of a hundred Kybeles on this night.

'Grandmother, what goddess gives Epona her strength?'

'Is it not obvious? She looks to Ephesia.'

'Ephesia the Amazon Queen?'

'The very same.'

Arria smiled to herself. The Amazons were part-legend, part-history, part-divine story. Believed to have descended from the Greek gods

Ares and Aphrodite, the Amazons were beautiful warrior women who had come from the foothills of the distant Caucasus Mountains on the backs of magnificent horses. On their way home from a visit to Athens, they founded Ephesus and installed their mighty queen.

'Epona is a warrior,' said Grandmother. 'You must try to be one, too.'

'But I am a weaver, not a warrior,' whispered Arria.

'Rubbish,' said Grandmother.

Arria closed her eyes and thought of Cal. He was the true warrior and, though he always triumphed, each of his triumphs were in themselves defeats. There was too much war in the world, fuelled by too much greed. She imagined him now, giving up his life to the roar of a crowd.

'Do not give your heart to a gladiator,' said Grandmother. 'Too dangerous.'

'How did you know I—?'

'You wear your love like a crown of flowers, dear girl.'

'I do not love him. I hardly know him,' whispered Arria. 'Besides, Fortuna does not favour me in matters of the heart.'

'More rubbish,' said Grandmother.

'Tell me, Grandmother, what kind of weapon is it? The one that you carved?'

'It is no weapon at all, my dear. I thought you knew.'

'Not a weapon?'

'Of course not. It is a key.'

'A key?'

'To this very workshop.'

'But how can you know if it will fit in the lock?'

'I cannot. I have had glimpses of the guard's key and have done my best. When the time comes, that is when I will know.'

'And if it does not work?' asked Arria.

'My dear, do you not see? It has already worked, for it unlocks my spirit each day.'

Arria smiled. 'And thus you will not be broken.'

'Now you are learning.'

Chapter Fourteen

He hated himself for wanting her. He hated how his breath quickened at the sound of her sandals in the tunnel, how his heart hammered as the guard unlocked the gate. When she stepped into the cell, he willed his gaze to the floor, for he loathed how much he wished to see her face.

'Cal!' she exclaimed. She walked softly to the foot of his bed and stood before him, her small white feet curling in their sandals. 'Oh, Cal, you are alive! Thank the Goddess Artemis! Cal? Why will you not look at me?'

He was a bad man. A selfish man. A man who had put his earthly desires above all else. And because of that, his friend was now dead. *Remember Felix*, he told himself. *Remember Rhiannon.*

She stood before him in silence for a long while. When she spoke, her voice was hushed. 'The sun is already set, and it is so very cold outside.' She crossed to the glowing brazier on the table at the other end of the cell. She was holding her hands over the lit coals. 'These coals are such a wonder. I feel like I have not been warm in a month.'

Brutus had been just as cheerful when he had placed the brazier there an hour before. 'In honour of your unlikely victory,' he had said, revelling in his own generosity.

Cal wondered how much money Brutus had won yesterday from Cal's unlikely victory. Three hundred *denarii*? Three thousand? Enough to add a few more rooms to his seaside villa and buy his daughter a new slave? Probably even more than that, for he had placed Cal and Felix among the expected losers, thus increasing his odds. He had probably known about the gladiatrices, too. The shameless blood merchant had probably suggested them himself.

'I have also acquired your reward,' Brutus had told Cal. 'The one you requested. The weaver. She will be here soon. Eighty *denarii* for her. Can you imagine? But she will be yours for the night, to do with what you will.' He had winked conspiratorially at Cal—like a father winking to his child after sliding him a honey stick.

Cal hated himself then, because in truth he had been overjoyed by the news. It was as if he were a dog who had just hunted down a pack of lions for his owner, then absently been tossed a bone.

'I thought you had died,' Arria said quietly. She was still rubbing her hands over the brazier's smouldering coals, addressing her conversation to the wall. 'When my master informed me that your *lanista* had purchased me for the night, well, I just—'

'Felix died today.'

'What?' She turned.

'Felix the Satyr. The one who occupied that cell just down the hall. He was my friend.'

She bowed her head.

'It was my fault,' he added. 'I left him unguarded.'

And why had Cal left Felix unguarded? That was the real question. He did not wish to think about the answer, though it was standing right in front of him.

'You cannot blame yourself,' she said. 'It was not your choice to fight.'

'But it was my choice.'

'How was it your choice?' Her eyes caught the glow of the coals.

'I chose to live. I fought for all this.' He swatted at the air. 'For you.'

She crossed to the foot of his bed and stood

before him. Gods forgive him, he wanted nothing but to press his head against her stomach and lay his troubles at her feet. He breathed in, hating her smoky, woolly musk. It was too rich. Too enticing. And altogether too much like home.

She reached out and drew her thumb across his cheek.

'Please do not do that.' He pushed her hand aside and she recoiled.

'Apologies, I only wished to—'

'Two women died yesterday because of me,' he said. 'Their bodies were decorated with blue, do you understand? I could read the runes painted upon their breasts. They could have been Caledonii—my own country women.'

'You are Caledonian?'

He cringed. He had not meant to reveal it. The more she knew of him, the more power she wielded. He could not allow her to conquer him—not if it meant that he would spend the rest of his days killing for sport. Nothing was worth what he had done yesterday in the arena. Nothing.

'I cannot lie with you—not any more,' he said. 'I cannot do this any more. I just want to be with my wife. In the Otherworld.'

He watched the colour drain from her face, saw how she laboured to keep her breaths even.

She had offered him one of the most precious things she had to give and he had just refused her. He might as well have taken a blade to her gut.

Not that any of what he said had been true. He wanted her so badly that he ached. He had even dreamed about her—hot, wicked dreams that he shied to recall. Even now, he caught a glimpse of her shape and felt himself awaken. He wanted to rip off her ragged tunic and take her right there, right against the wall, with the coals of the brazier smouldering in her eyes.

But the words had been spoken. He had stacked them carefully like a wall of bricks between them and waited for her to call the guard.

Instead she crossed back to the brazier and took her seat in the chair beside it. 'Tell me about your wife,' she said softly.

'What?'

'Tell me about her. What did she look like?'

It was the most unexpected thing she could have said.

'Come now, Cal. If you are going to condemn me to lose my innocence to some old lecher, you can at least talk to me a while. What was she like?'

And there it was. No sharp words or pitiable tears. Just a simple question. Cal paused.

'Was she tall or short?'

'Ah, my wife was tall, almost my height,' he said.

'And?'

He closed his eyes. 'She had long golden hair and eyes the colour of the sky. Her nose was large and she had a mark of Venus just here.' He pointed to the side of his chin. 'She did not smile much, but when she did it was like…' He paused, flushing with the memory.

'Like what?'

'Like when the sails of a ship catch the wind.'

She grinned. 'How did you meet?'

How had they met? It had been so long since he'd thought of it. 'She was my best friend's sister. We had known each other since before we could speak. When we came of age, our hands were bound in my uncle's ash tree grove and we placed our oathing stone beneath its largest tree.'

She was nodding, encouraging him to go on. 'We moved into the small house I had built for us at the grove's edge. We had ten sheep, a cow and a large garden.'

'It sounds like heaven,' said Arria wistfully.

'We had a useless old dog that was missing a leg. When I brought the sheep home each night the pathetic creature would wag its tail and my wife would smile and say, "Look! She is so happy to see you!"'

He laughed. It was the primary way his wife had expressed her love to him—through that ridiculous dog. But it had been enough.

'My father once owned a small dog,' offered Arria. 'My mother hated the creature, but when my father left for the campaigns in Britannia, she cared for him tenderly.'

'Before he became a gambler.'

'When my eldest brother did not return from his military service, something in my father died. My younger brother did return, but my father does not see him. He sees only what he does not have.'

Cal shook his head. 'So many Romans chase after Fortuna, not knowing that they already enjoy her favour.'

Arria peered out the high slit of window and caught sight of the rising moon. 'Before I was enslaved, I was that kind of Roman,' she said. 'I did not know the world through the eyes of a slave. I pitied myself in my poverty and I condemned my father and brother for making it so. But now I understand that I cannot condemn them, for I have not seen what they have seen.'

It was perhaps the most thoughtful thing Cal

had ever heard anyone say. 'How did your eldest brother die?'

'He was ambushed by a gang of Caledonian warriors on his way back to the fort at Eboracum. He was bludgeoned to death and his head placed on a stake.'

Cal gulped. He did not know what to say. Her eldest brother had likely been killed by men he knew.

'And your wife?' she asked, filling the silence. 'How did you lose her?'

'It was Roman soldiers,' he muttered. 'They looted our town and burned it.'

'I see,' said Arria and bowed her head. 'And how did you become enslaved?'

His voice dropped to a whisper. 'I awoke the following morning, lying beside her. That's when I felt the shackles being fastened to my ankles.'

'You lay beside her all night?'

'After that I was taken to the quarry.'

'So how came you to the arena?'

'There was an uprising at the quarry,' said Cal. Twelve years of hatred pressed into a single afternoon. He had killed every Roman guard he could find, then gone in search of more.

'Why do you shake your head? Do you regret the uprising?'

'I could have escaped.'

'Why did you not?'

He had not escaped because a hundred Roman soldiers had not been enough. Nor had a thousand. After twelve years of being treated like an animal, he had quietly become one.

She was watching him carefully. 'You can tell me the truth.'

'Because I enjoyed the killing,' he admitted. 'I loved slitting their Roman throats with their Roman swords. They are monsters, your glorious Roman men. Thieves. They boast of honour, but have none. They killed my wife! They killed my wife...'

He shook his head, trying to gather his wits. How little it all mattered now. How little *he* mattered. Three years in the arena and he was finished. Beaten. He had done worse than fail, he had turned his rage on undeserving foes. Without knowing it, he had become the monster everyone believed he was.

He gazed at the floor. 'They make a desert and call it peace,' he muttered.

His anger was gone now. They had looted it from him, harvested it like gold from the graves of ancient Caledonian kings. Enough. He would no longer kill for Rome's entertainment. Nor would he hold out hope for some futile vision of revenge.

He was tired, so very tired. His head throbbed. His bones ached. His ears still rang with the clash of swords.

But it was not just battle that had tired him. It was her. She had kept him up at night. The woman with the brown eyes and shiny long braid and nothing left to lose. Since they had last met, he had thought of little else but her and had been unable to find peace. And now that she was here, his heart was at rest and suddenly all he wished for was sleep.

He lay back on the bed. 'It is your fault, Arria,' he muttered as oblivion took him. 'It is all your fault.'

'What is my fault, Cal?'

'That I am not dead.'

Chapter Fifteen

She watched in wonder as his exhaustion overtook him. In only moments, he was sprawled across his bed, lost in slumber.

Sleep well, tired warrior.

She sat back in the chair and studied him. She did not blame him for rejecting her. She finally understood how selfish she had been. Killing was not like weaving. It was not something you could do day after day, week after week, without losing some essential piece of your soul. It was no wonder he wished for death. *Defy them by staying alive*, she had begged him, trying to stoke his waning spirit. But it was not a desire for noble justice that had fuelled her words. It was greed. She had wanted him to stay alive *for her*.

Because whenever she thought of him, her fingers ached a little less, the moments passed a little more quickly and her stomach clenched with an unusual kind of hunger.

She should have never asked him to take her innocence. What an audacious fool she had been. To presume that he could ever want her in that way—it was the height of arrogance. She had witnessed the lengths to which he was willing to go to resurrect his wife's memory. Arria had been mistaken to think he would ever want anyone else. All he wished was to join his wife in the afterlife and Arria had denied him that.

She would not do it again.

The coals in the brazier had finally burned out. The only light that remained was a small torch flickering in the hallway across from the cell. Ribbons of light and shadow danced over his supine form, which rose and fell with his slow breaths. He had descended into deep slumber.

She crossed the cell and peered down at his face. She had always been good with faces, but when she had tried to imagine his, something always crowded the vision—something warm and peaceful—a feeling rather than an image.

Now she followed the craggy contours of his cheeks, studied the thick rise of his lips, watched his strong, stern nose move slightly with his breaths. She wanted to write it all into her memory before the torchlight faded.

And when it did, where would she sleep? Brutus had paid for Arria to stay with Cal all night. If she lay on the floor, she would freeze, for there was no bed mat. Already, the cell had grown cold and she shivered in dread of a night spent pacing for warmth. If she wished to rest at all, she would have to lie beside him and share his blanket.

The torch was in its final spasms. She removed her sandals and lay down beside him, gently pulling the blanket up over them both. When she was certain she had not disturbed him, she moved further beneath the blanket until she was completely covered by it. She let her head rest against his shoulder.

He radiated heat. She could feel it emanating from his skin like warmth from coals. It soaked through to her bones and filled the air around her in a toasty, blissful cocoon. For the first time in months, she was not cold.

She snuggled closer. The bed was so soft. She wondered if it had been stuffed with feathers. It hovered so high off the ground. It was as if they were suspended together above the earth.

Gently, she wrapped her arm about his chest. She did not want to let him go, though she knew she did not have a choice. He had made his wish clear and she had to honour it. He wanted to return to his wife. After tonight, she would never see him again.

The thought made her feel bleak. *Get tough*, she told herself, but imagining the world without Cal was like imagining a world without windows. *Let him go*, she told herself and gazed up at the moon.

Finally, she closed her eyes and let sleep take her.

She was awakened by the distant shriek of a cat, followed by the sound of howling wind. The room was cold and black. She must have rolled over in her sleep, for now she faced the hallway and she could hear the rhythmic snores of the other gladiators as they echoed down the hall.

They seemed so very close—as if they were breathing into her own ear.

She blinked, then realised that one of them *was* breathing in her ear. Cal. She perceived his arm was wrapped around her waist and caught her breath. It seemed that she had turned on her side in her sleep and he had turned with her.

She exhaled, delighting in how he had moulded his battle-hardened chest against the shape of her back. She felt so safe in his embrace and so fantastically warm. It was as if they were reposed together in their own private *laconicum* enjoying the dry, pulsing heat.

She smiled at the image: two pretty peacocks lounging amidst the marble and bronze. She would feed him grapes from their silver platter while he massaged her naked flanks with rose oil.

Arria had imagined such a life a thousand times, in all its gaudy detail. But she knew now that if she had been born into such wealth, she would have never appreciated it.

She appreciated everything now. A breath of fresh air, the sun on her face, the gaze of a man with eyes like green pools.

She snuggled closer. He had said that he did not wish to lie with her any more, but that meant that he had wished for it once, did it not? And he had all but admitted that she was the reason he had fought so fiercely at the circus—for the promise of this night together.

There was one last thought she clung to. When she had stood before him, he had breathed in her scent. It was a small thing and she might have believed he was simply drawing deep breaths. But she had seen him close his eyes and lean close and it was as if he were drinking her in. As if he could not get enough of her.

And now, in the depths of his slumber, he held her.

They were small actions, but they were enough to make her think that she was not all alone in her yearning. She wanted to believe that part of him *did* want her, if only because he was a man and she a woman.

She breathed in his scent—that strange, irresistible mix of sweat and sunburned sand. Even if he had refused her, she could at least pretend he had not. She could imagine that he had shown her the mysteries of love, had opened the palace of passion to her and made her its queen. And now they lay together, slumbering in a lovers' bliss.

She sighed and closed her eyes, basking in the fantasy. She was just returning to slumber when she felt his lips press against her ear.

Her heart jumped. Small, invisible feathers tickled down the length of her neck. She listened closely. The speed of his breaths had not changed. He was still asleep.

He kissed her ear again and the feathers continued to bother her skin, coaxing her body into a kind of blissful agitation. He nuzzled closer. He must have been in the midst of some beautiful dream—it was the only explanation for this cascade of affection. In that case, Arria hoped he would dream it until dawn.

But now his lips had begun to travel. They moved from the base of her ear down her neck, kissing with slow but perceptible purpose. He slid his arm to her waist and pulled her closer, and she felt something large and hard press against her buttocks.

By the thunder of Jove, what was that? But she knew exactly what it was. She knew it as surely as she knew her own heartbeat, which was getting faster by the second.

He was experiencing a *special* dream then— one that most certainly involved his wife. Even in his dreams, he yearned to unite with her, or so it seemed. And that was well, too.

Though the very thought of it made Arria's soul ache.

And now something else was aching inside her. Deep in her womanly chasm, a nagging yearning, accompanied by a strange heat. Perhaps if she closed her eyes, it would go away.

No, that just made it worse. With her eyes closed she could only think of his desire pressing against her backside.

And her heart—what was wrong with it? It was beating so loudly now. She could scarcely hear her own thoughts. And when had it become so hot? Perhaps if she gently stepped out of the bed…

But he would not release her. Instead he pulled her closer still. By the gods, he was enormous. What dark, sensual dream had inspired him to such heights? Such widths? More importantly, why was she not afraid? By rights she should have been terrified. She should have been reaching for her shoes, or the gate, or for the pitcher of water that she could pour over both of them to startle them back into their right minds.

Perhaps she should cough or clear her voice—do something that would coax him into a more gentle waking. But would that not also be a kind of cruelty? Besides, it was not as if she were uncomfortable. No, not exactly. Just very, very hot.

She angled her face over the blanket and let the night air cool her cheeks. Better to stay put. Let him have his moment of bliss. If she could play the part of his one true love, then she was happy to do so. If she could just slow her breaths, which were coming so quickly now. Perhaps if she could fold the blanket down a little…

Ah, there. Much better.

His face was still nuzzled in her braid, but at least she was cooler now. She felt his hand slide up to touch her breast. *'Rydych chi'n teimlo mor dda,'* he whispered suddenly.

Something deep inside her seemed to hurl itself from the roof of Ephesus's tallest *insula*, then go plunging into the sea.

'*Mor feddal.*'

He was speaking the tongue of wild men again, though the words themselves were gentle and sweet. Now there was no doubt in her mind. The caress, the words, the nuzzling kisses: Cal was dreaming of making love to his wife. And in his dream, Arria was she.

He exhaled, then pushed his desire more firmly against her back.

She could have stopped him right then. A loud sneeze. A gentle nudge. It would have been the decent thing to do. But she did not.

The truth was that she loved how his large hand caressed her breast. She loved his arm around her, pulling her closer. And she loved his desire pressing up against her, urgently, almost pleadingly, as if she alone held the key to his satisfaction.

Was it wrong to deceive him in such a way? To let him believe, dreamily, that she was someone else? If the situation were reversed—if she were the one who was dreaming—would she wish to be awoken? Well, that was easy enough to answer: no, not at all. Not in a thousand years.

'*Fy nghariad,*' he uttered. The words were familiar. He had said them to the flaxen-haired woman several times. *My love*, perhaps. She let the words invade her body like an elixir. This powerful, honourable, magnificent man was calling her his love.

So what if he believed she was his wife? So what if his desire for her was not real, but a product of his dream? This was the first and quite possibly the last time in her life she would ever feel a good man's arms around her and, by the gods, she was going to enjoy it.

He sighed contentedly. She imagined that in his dream he lay inside a little round hut with a fire blazing in its centre. He was curled on a fur carpet next to his wife and was whispering words of passion into her ear, telling her how much he wanted her, how much he needed her.

'Arria,' he said.

She froze. Held her breath.

'Arria,' he repeated more urgently.

What did he mean, *Arria*?

Chapter Sixteen

It was not just her nearness. Nor was it her soft, warm body, which fit inside his so perfectly. Or the smell of her, or the heat of her, or the way her breaths came in fast, lusty puffs. It was her. Just her. Arria.

'Turn towards me, Arria. Please. Let me see you.'

She paused, frozen. 'Do you not wish to imagine that I am your wife?' she asked.

Such a simple question, born of a staggering kindness. 'No, my darling, I do not. I wish to see you.'

Silence. Slowly, she rolled over to face him. 'There is nothing to see, I fear,' she said, though her tone conveyed relief. 'It is too dark.'

'Then I must imagine your face,' he said. He propped his head in his hand and stared at her across the darkness. 'I remember the first time

I saw you,' he mused. 'You stumbled against the fighting-pit wall just as they were announcing my name.'

'I remember,' she murmured. 'Your eyes startled me. They seemed to change colour in the torchlight. I did not think they were real.'

'I did not think *you* were real. When I saw you lean over the rails, I thought I was being visited by a goddess.'

She chuckled. 'As if I—' she said, but he gently ran his finger over her lower lip and she ceased to speak.

'Forgive me,' he said. He removed his finger, realising his mistake. How could he presume to touch her lips after rejecting her only hours ago? An apology was in order and at the very least an explanation. But how could he tell her what was in his heart if he did not understand it himself?

Arria, you have haunted my dreams, ruined my plans and caused me to betray the memory of my wife. I return your curse, for yours has consumed me utterly.

He could feel her uneven breaths on his face. Her departure was imminent. He could feel it in his bones. When finally she spoke, he could hardly believe his ears. 'Cal, do you wish to make love to me?'

He drew a long, incredulous breath and as he

exhaled he was no longer locked inside a dungeon. He was running across a long, grassy plain with the sun on his face, looking out over the sparkling sea.

'Yes, Arria, I do.'

He moved closer, pulling the blanket over both their shoulders, his heart full to bursting. The woman that he had shunned only hours ago had just offered herself to him again. This time, he would not be a fool.

'May I kiss you, Arria?'

'You wish to kiss me? But I thought you did not kiss—'

'I have wished to kiss you since the moment you pressed your face against the bars of my cell.'

To Hades with his rules. They did not apply to the woman who now lay by his side. She had come to know him and, by some miracle of the Fates, she wanted him anyway. And by the Hound of Hades he wanted her back.

He made bold to touch her lower lip once again. It was soft and cool, but its small quiver betrayed her excitement. 'I have thought of this moment, Arria. Dreamed of it.'

She drew a breath and held it, and the moments stretched out. 'Will you deny me a kiss?' he whispered at last, fearing her answer.

'I will not,' she muttered.

He exhaled his relief, though he could sense that her breath was still trapped inside her chest. 'Is it so hard to believe that I have wanted you?'

She paused. 'I admit that I have doubted it.'

'Atria, I am cursed with wanting you.' He slid his hand behind her neck. 'And now you will have no reason to doubt it ever again.'

There was only one first kiss and this, he sensed, would be hers. He pressed his lips to hers gently, breathing her in, coaxing her lips to move with his own. How many times had he imagined this? How many nights sitting alone in his cell, picturing how her lips might feel against his? Even then he had known that he had been vanquished, but not by Rome—by this fearless brown-eyed sorceress who had turned his will to dust.

He paused, his heart pounding. This was going to be tricky. He was already rock hard. He would not be able to control himself for long. Nor was there any time to waste. Dawn neared and soon the guard would unlock the gate and quietly whisk her away. Then she would be gone—possibly for ever.

This was unfair, unnatural, wrong. In a just world they would be lying together in a marriage bed, not locked inside some padded prison. In a just world, they would have not a single night to-gether, but the rest of their lives.

But it was not a just world and Cal knew that he had this one chance to create something beau-tiful. If he could give them something special—something that was theirs alone—then perhaps some small part of his soul would be redeemed.

He let his tongue slide softly across her lower lip, relishing her sigh. Gods, how good it felt to kiss her. How incredibly right. He pulled her lower lip into his mouth and sucked it gen-tly, coaxing another delicious sigh. He kissed her harder, feeling himself begin to pulse with want. His hips thrust forward, the tip of his de-sire finding the resistance of her legs. He kissed her harder still, because the way she was mov-ing her lips, the pulse of her breaths, her smell, her taste...

He took a breath, pulled back. It had been fifteen years since he had desired a woman in this way—with all of himself—and he feared he might swallow her whole. This was her first time, he reminded himself. He needed to take it slow.

But not too slow, lest he erupt like ancient Vesuvius.

He was bending to kiss her once again when she craned upwards and seized upon his lower lip.

His body quaked with lust as she tugged it into

her hot mouth and began to suck. Did she have any idea what she was doing to him? Clearly not, because she released him with a coy little giggle that left him panting. Dark thoughts invaded his mind.

So she wanted to play a teasing game, was that it? He coaxed her lips as far apart as he dared, then dipped his tongue into her mouth and waited.

The moments pulsed by. Had she changed her mind? Had her boldness retreated? But, no— there was her desire. He could feel it in the heat of her breaths. She flicked her tongue around his, experimentally at first, then with growing boldness.

He mirrored her movements, letting her tease and taunt to her heart's desire. If such was the nature of her lust in this, her first encounter with it, then Cal could only imagine the kind of lover she would make in time. If only they had it.

Her kisses grew hotter, wetter. He gently lifted her tunic to her waist, then over her head. He did the same with his own tunic. Now only the fabric of their loincloths remained between them, along with air so thick he could have cut it with his *gladius*.

He moved closer and felt the soft bumps of her breasts brush against his chest. Sacred suns, she felt good. Too good. Better than he had imagined, better than he ever could have hoped. He wanted to be inside of her, to pour fifteen years of buried affection on to her soft, hot core.

Slow, Cal.

'Come, lie back,' he said. He manoeuvred her beneath him and settled her head upon the pillow. 'Just rest now,' he instructed. 'I want to show you pleasure.'

Rest? He wanted her to rest? A hundred new sensations were coursing through her body and he wanted her to *rest*?

She closed her eyes and took a breath, attempting to obey his will. But as he threaded a string of soft kisses down her belly, she knew there would be no rest. There would be only this angst—this soft, aching angst that seemed only to worsen as he journeyed ever downwards, until she could feel the warmth of his breath tickling the curls of her Venus mound.

Oh, gods. It was the thing she had so often dreamed of, then scolded herself for dreaming, then dreamed of again. He was so close.

'I am not ready...' she said, though she knew she was ready. 'I—I cannot...' she stuttered, though she knew she could. 'I do not...'

The cell was growing lighter with the dawn.

Outside, she could hear the early birds chirping out their urgent tones. His green gaze travelled across the plain of her stomach and locked with hers. 'Are you afraid of this?' he asked. She felt the soft pressure of his finger pushing gently into her folds.

'Oh,' she cooed. 'Oh, no.' He held her gaze, watching her closely as his finger began to move, spreading pulses of heat wherever he touched her. She shivered, feeling exposed, yet strangely… obliging. It was as if her body were a lock being opened by his deft finger.

'You have nothing to fear,' he whispered. 'I will take care of you.'

Keeping his finger inside her, he stretched over her and pressed his lips against hers once again. His tongue pushed into her mouth just as he moved his finger deeper into her folds. She moaned at the disintegrating pleasure.

'That is it,' he whispered. His tongue and finger began to move in tandem, exploring the softest parts of her in slow, sultry circles.

His movements were exquisitely gentle, like a loving ode whispered on the breeze. Sweetness and languor. Softness and light. She felt her hips begin to move in rhythm with his finger.

'Yes. Now lie back, my darling,' he whispered

in her ear, then disappeared down the length of her once again. 'Just feel.'

She closed her eyes, for her eyelids had grown heavy, as had her limbs. Her very thoughts seemed slow and leaden. She sensed him un-ravelling her loincloth and heard the intake of his breath as he beheld her. Then all that existed was the warmth of his breath on her skin and the slow wandering strokes of his finger.

He seemed to be drawing a map, a path traced in flesh—pointing her towards an unknown des-tination. He moaned, as if he were enjoying his work, and she replied with her own soft whimper.

She wanted…more. 'Cal, please,' she said. She arched her hips, tried to coax his finger deeper. He was teasing her for certain. The higher she arched, the lighter he touched. Soon his finger was in retreat; her hips were bereft. Finally her entire lower half was suspended above the bed.

And in that instant, he slipped his tongue in-side her.

Soft wetness. Sizzling heat. A secret bond. 'Zeus,' she crooned. If his finger was a surprise, his tongue was a revelation. Soft and wet, wick-edly long, coaxing and thwarting all at once. The sensation was both sweeter and more tortuous than she had ever dreamed.

She reached down and touched his bare head,

opened her eyes. Yes, this was really happening. The man of her dreams was real and he was pleasuring her, worshipping her in the most intimate way. She could not feel any more wonderful. She could not be any closer to the heights of Olympus.

His tongue still caressing her folds, he slid his finger into her deepest part.

'Oh!' she gasped. A wave of pleasure sent her sprawling on her back. By the gods, what was that? That strange fullness? That clutching want? She gripped his skull.

His voice seemed to come from far away. 'You are so…small. And so very wet.'

'Yes,' she said mindlessly.

'No, no.' He seemed to be speaking to himself.

'Yes, yes.'

'No, no!'

'Cal?'

'Oh, by the gods,' he said, his voice tinged with alarm.

'What? What is it?'

He lifted himself off her and removed his finger. His expression was pained. 'It is just that… you are so very sweet, my darling…and I am…'

'What is it, Cal? Are you all right?'

He was squeezing his eyes shut. 'I fear that I may release.'

'What do you mean?'

What a foolish thing to ask. She was not so very innocent that she did not understand the end result of joining! What she had meant to ask was why he was resisting it so. He was taking long breaths and staring up at the ceiling. He looked utterly pained.

'It means that you drive me mad with desire,' he said.

They were words she had never believed she would hear, from a man too good to be real, but she was too distracted to revel in them properly, for the birds were growing louder now, and she thought she could hear the morning's first cart rolling down Harbour Street.

Could they not squeeze a bit more bliss from the waning night? It was all she wanted. If this was to be their only night together, then a crumb was not enough. She wanted the whole pie.

'Please, Cal,' she began. 'I must know all of it. I want it to be you.'

He was vexed. Perturbed. Chagrined. He wanted to give himself a good lashing. The art of self-control was something he had mastered long ago, or so he had erroneously believed. The problem, it seemed, was that he wanted her too much. So much that the simple act of pleasuring her was bringing him to his limit. He had never had such a problem and it troubled him to the bone. It seemed she had reduced his stamina to that of a lust-addled youth.

Time was growing short. He was determined to help her find her pleasure before he took his own. This was her first time, after all. It should belong to her.

In an act of pure will, he rolled on to his back, pulling her atop him. Her soft body pressed against his and, in the growing light of dawn, he could see the contours of her face. Ah, sweet Arria. Her luxurious arched brows, her full cheeks, her plump, curious mouth. And now he could just see her eyes: big, dark moons, half-lidded with longing.

This was well. This was good. He could study her face a while and try to forget how much he wanted the rest of her. If only there were a bucket of water she could throw on him—something to calm his renegade lust.

Then she did something utterly cruel. She sat up and straddled his waist. There she was—curvy, naked and glorious—hovering over him like a triumphant goddess. With a single rock of his hips, he could be inside her.

He held his breath as her eyes travelled down his chest. She reached out to his shoulder and touched the tip of his scar. 'It is healing,' she observed, 'but it requires tending.'

She began kissing down the length of it, following the long diagonal path across his chest. It was as if she was slowly erasing the wound, making it as though it never was.

By the time she had reached the end of the scar, his will was nearly destroyed. It lay on the floor in a heap, along with his tunic and all his wits. She returned to her position hovering over him. She was so close, so very close to him. And he was so very close to the edge once again.

He cupped both of her beautiful breasts in his palms: two ripe pears he wanted badly to consume.

'Let me kiss them,' he begged. Obligingly, she stretched over him and dipped one of her nipples between his lips.

'Oh,' she said, as he teased it with his tongue. This was the way. He would coax her desire until she was pleading with him once again. If he could just control himself until that time came. He gently took the whole of her nipple into his mouth.

Hours later, he would recall this moment as the beginning of the end, for when he began to suck, he seemed to ignite a fire within her. First she cried out, then sighed, then wriggled down and positioned herself over him.

'What are you doing?' he asked huskily.

'I do not know,' she said, though clearly her body knew, for it began to move with a purpose all its own. She moved her womanhood up and down the length of him—slowly at first, then with an increasing rhythm.

'By the gods, Arria, that feels too good,' he groaned. He had meant the words as a warning, but she seemed to take them as encouragement. Faster she went, grinding against him in slow, rhythmic sweeps.

'Arria, you must stop. Please. I will not be able to… Oh, by Jupiter,' he said. He placed his hands on her hips and pulled her more tightly against him, moving her faster up and down him until he could feel the wave begin to crash.

'Forgive me,' he gasped. His body bucked and seized, exploding into a great rolling tremor of pleasure that seemed to shake the very heavens. 'Demons,' he said, for it felt as if he had been possessed by them. He had never felt such a powerful release and, as he gazed up at Arria's fascinated smile, he knew why. 'Please forgive me,' he begged as he spilled on to his stomach. 'Please…'

'There is no need for apology.' She rolled over and lay beside him, wrapping her hands around his chest and holding him as his tremors slowly abated.

'Oh, sweet Arria,' he whimpered. 'I could not stop myself.'

'I am glad you did not stop yourself,' she said.

He could have cried. He could have torn up his mattress and poked out his eyes. 'I was selfish. I denied you your pleasure.'

'You gave me pleasure,' she said. 'I feel it still. I am satisfied.'

In that instant, he heard a rooster herald the arrival of dawn.

It was a disaster of universal proportions. Arria's initiation into the pleasures of the flesh had been no initiation at all, but an explosive exercise in his own fulfilment.

He wanted to turn back time. He wanted to find a hatchet and sever the neck of that cursed rooster—nay, of all the roosters that had ever lived since the beginning of the world.

He was a gladiator, by all that was sacred. His currency was physical control. So why had he been unable to control his own lust?

But he knew why. He had known it since the day she had gazed into his eyes and laid down her curse. This woman had control over him. Total, utter, terrifying control.

Already the other gladiators were stirring in

their cells. He could see them moving beneath their blankets in the increasing light of dawn.

She reached for her tunic and he felt a deathly hollowness overtake him. She was still in his bed, but she might as well have been gone. Their night together was over. He might never see her again.

'I must explain to you that we did not make love,' he muttered. 'You are still a virgin.'

'I know,' she said. She lay back down beside him. 'But it was still special. I am grateful.'

She was *grateful*? No, no, no. This was all wrong. She was not supposed to feel grateful. She was supposed to feel flipped and spun and lifted from the ground. She was supposed to feel as if she had blossomed into the world's most beautiful flower and all of nature was rejoicing.

'Gratitude, Cal.'

Gratitude? He pinned her with his gaze. 'I wanted to show you the meaning of bliss. I wanted to make you float on clouds of pleasure.'

'You did.'

No, he did not. She still had no idea of the true meaning of pleasure, for he had failed to show her.

He heard the clinking of a key ring, then the sound of voices in the hall.

'Send for me again,' she said, swinging off the bed. 'Then you can show me in full.'

The guard clanked his sword against the bars.

'Time is up, little goats,' he said and Cal found that he could not slow his breaths. She was leaving him. She was stepping out into the ugly world with nobody to protect her and no beautiful memory to comfort her in the long days to come.

'Mae'n ddrwg gennyf,' he told her. *I am sorry.* It was not enough. He owed her a debt and he would not rest until he paid it.

'Until next time,' he said.

Her eyes lit with joy. 'Until next time, then.'

Chapter Seventeen

Time was an inconstant thing. Sometimes it passed on the back of a turtle. Other times it fluttered by on winged feet. For Arria, the next two months passed like days. She knew that at any moment she might be summoned to Cal's cell and feel his arms around her once again.

On Oppius's orders, she had abandoned the ordinary carpet she had begun to weave and started a new one to feature a design of her choosing. 'If those imperious patrician tarts want to pay large sums for tasteless carpets, I am no one to stop them,' he had said.

Arria had no notion of what might or might not strike the fancy of a patrician woman. She could only weave what haunted her mind: a sculpted, scarred man with a shaved head and dazzling eyes.

He was always with her. In the morning when

she awoke and stretched her limbs, at midday, when she walked to the courtyard, in the evenings, when she finally set down her shuttle, closed her eyes and dreamed of pleasure.

Cal.

Every time she thought of him, she felt her heart smile. He had wanted to kiss her from the day she had pressed her face to the bars, or so he had said. She was his beautiful sorceress. Had he said that as well, or did she just dream it?

The pattern for the carpet had burst from her fingertips. She had not even sketched an image to help guide her. Each row seemed to emerge directly from her heart: a scarred warrior, rippling with strength, poised to defeat whatever foe should come his way.

On the first day of March she completed it and Oppius practically ripped it from the loom.

'It resembles me, in truth,' he said, studying the outline of Cal's muscular form. 'But what is this flaw here? This line?' Oppius traced the long diagonal scar. 'It makes no sense.'

To Arria, it made more sense than anything else ever had. The scar was special. It belonged to the man who had found her worthy enough to kiss, to hold, to touch. A man who could have virtually any woman he wished for and had for some reason chosen her.

She floated through her days, waiting for his summons, certain he would send for her soon. *This is what it feels like to be wanted*, she told herself and basked in the feeling, along with the knowledge that he would keep himself alive. He owed her a debt, after all, and she knew he would not rest until he paid it.

But when the summons finally came, it was a command from Oppius to ready herself for the market. 'Epona, you, too,' he said, and soon the two women found themselves stumbling behind the cart once again, their metal collars pinching.

'You should take great care now,' warned Epona. 'Your happiness has made you even more beautiful. Men will see you. You must try to make yourself less attractive.'

Epona hunched her shoulders and demonstrated a sneering frown. Arria chuckled softly.

'You must not get attached to him,' Epona warned.

'Of whom do you speak?'

'Come now, Arria. Since you returned from your night with that gladiator, I do not think your feet have touched the ground.'

'Is it that obvious?'

'He is a gladiator. Do you know what that

means? You must try to keep him out of your heart.'

'I fear it is too late for that,' said Arria.

'Men are beasts,' Epona said and spat.

Arria shook her head, but did not take heed. Something had changed in Epona after her night with the tribune. She had lost her tart humour and spent her days studying her spools of thread, as if trying to unravel them with her thoughts.

'Grandmother says you worship Ephesia,' said Arria. 'That she gives you strength.'

Epona smiled absently. 'I have always loved horses.'

'Do you know how to ride?'

'Of course I know how to ride. Every Chatti does. It is our birthright.'

They arrived at an open stall and unloaded their wares, and Arria watched the driver lead the horses to a hitching area.

'If only we could climb atop those horses and ride away to freedom,' Arria said. The idea swirled around them like a hot wind. 'You cannot tell me you have not thought the same.'

Arria glanced around the busy marketplace, aware that any effort to escape would be futile. If the mounted guards did not stop them, then a reward-seeking slave hunter surely would. And she did not even want to think of the punishment that would await them after.

'Such thoughts can drive a person mad,' Epona said at last.

'Must we choose, then? Whether to endure our fate or go mad resisting it?'

'Shh…' whispered Epona. 'When the time is right.'

Arria scowled. Grandmother had said the same thing. And in five years, Arria would likely be saying the same thing to another woman doomed to stand at one of Oppius's miserable looms. 'Find your pigeon,' Grandmother had told Arria, but the more she thought of Cal, the more restless she had become. He had not just given her a sense of hope, he had given her a taste of a joy.

She could hardly pass an hour without remembering the taste of his lips, the feel of his body against hers… She could not even bear the thought that those memories would be all she would ever have, or that she would live out the next ten years waiting for 'when the time is right.'

The time was now. She needed to free Cal and get her family and depart. Before her soul petrified. Before she quietly accepted her life as a slave.

A small tribe of litter bearers marched up to the stall and stopped.

'Good day to you, Master Oppius,' chimed a rarefied voice. Two familiar figures clad in pink and orange linen converged before Oppius, who gave them a sweeping bow.

'Honourable Ladies. It is a great pleasure to see you both once again.' His eyes glittered like newly minted coins. 'I hope you are enjoying your new carpet.'

'In fact, my daughter and I have returned to see if you have any more such carpets,' asked the elder.

'I do indeed, Domina,' said Oppius. He directed the women's attention to Arria's newest creation and Arria watched their expressions change from surprise, to confusion, to something resembling awe. They stood before the carpet for many long moments, their mouths agape.

'It is a work of genius,' the younger pronounced at last. 'The perfection of the man contrasted with the tragedy of his scar. I simply must have it.'

'How much do you ask for it, Oppius?' queried the elder.

'One hundred and fifty *denarii*,' stated Oppius. It was an outrageous sum, but the woman did not even flinch. She gestured to a guard, who quickly produced a large coin purse from beneath his toga. He counted out coins into Oppius's hand until the purse was half emptied.

'Tell me, Oppius,' said the elder woman conspiratorially. 'Who is the weaver? It is worth the rest of that purse if you will give me her name.'

Oppius's eyes grew as wide as plums. 'I would be happy to tell you, Domina, for such a generous offer.' He waited patiently for her guard to place all the coins into the purse, then took it in hand. 'But I fear that you will be disappointed when I tell you that the weaver is that woman standing right beside you.' He gestured to Arria.

The young woman stepped backwards in horror. 'A slave?'

'It is *you* who wove the carpets?' asked the elder.

'Yes, Domina.'

'But that cannot be,' said the younger. 'This is the work of a master of the craft. An artist.'

Arria bowed her head.

'How long have you been weaving?' demanded the elder.

'Since I was eight years old, Domina.'

'Under whom did you study?'

Arria's chest squeezed. 'My own mother taught me the basics, Domina. The rest I learned on my own.'

The young woman whispered something into her mother's ear and her mother turned to Oppius. 'I trust you know who we are?'

Oppius nodded. 'I do indeed, Domina.'

'Good. I should like you and this weaver of yours to pay a visit to our *domus* tomorrow morning for some further business.'

'Of course, Domina,' said Oppius and before he could even finish his bow, the women had boarded their litter and were floating back through the curious crowd.

'Perhaps they wish to hire you to weave a carpet for them,' said Epona after Oppius had left them. Her words were careful, but Arria could see the flicker of hope in her grey eyes.

'It is possible. Perhaps they only wish to question Oppius about my origins.'

'It is possible,' repeated Epona.

Possible. Another dangerous word. A word so bright that it might as well have been the name of the sun god himself. Neither of them would dare voice the idea that had invaded both their minds. It was possible, quite possible, that Arria might be purchased by a family of patricians.

Epona studied Arria for a long while, then gazed out at the bustling marketplace. 'Why do you think the house servants ignore us?' It was an unusual question, though Arria knew Epona better than to think that she ever spoke absently.

'I think they ignore us because they feel guilty,' Arria replied. 'They labour in relative comfort. They are allowed to eat the remains of Oppius's fine foods and the heat of his hearth warms their bones. I think they see the injustice of our lives and feel badly for us. It is out of guilt they cannot look at us.'

'Is that really what you believe?'

Arria nodded. 'Why? What do you believe?'

'I believe that they do not see us at all, that they have forgotten about us completely. We are out of their sight and out of their minds. They do not have to know us, so they can forget we exist.' Arria's mind raced. She feared that Epona was right. 'When life starts to make sense,' Epona continued, 'it is easy to forget when it did not.'

She grasped Arria's hand. 'Do not forget about me, Arria, and I promise that I will not forget about you.'

'I will not, dear friend,' whispered Arria. 'I promise.'

Chapter Eighteen

The next morning, Arria followed Oppius as he set off down Kouretes Street towards their appointment with the Fates. The spring sun shone earnestly above them, though winter's chill still gripped the city, along with Arria's very limbs. She wished she had a warm gladiator to wrap around her.

Any day now, she assured herself.

Oppius's pace slowed and he began searching the facades of the terrace houses opposite the baths. The sprawling mansions housed the oldest, richest and most powerful families of Ephesus and Arria's heart began to pound as they approached the most elegant facade of them all.

A tall, handsome man heralded them from beneath a marble archway. 'Oppius and the weaver, I presume?' He raised a well-trimmed brow, but did not await an answer. 'The honourable Nerva

Traiania and Vibia Secunda are expecting you. Follow me.'

He turned on his heel and they followed the man down a narrow corridor and into a large marble atrium bathed in sunlight.

Arria peered overhead, expecting to see sky. Instead, she saw several milky panels through which sunlight filtered. She could hardly keep herself from gaping at the expensive glass. Whoever the owner of this illustrious *domus*, he was rich enough to make it summer even when it was not.

As Arria's limbs thawed, she followed their guide past the long rectangular pool that occupied the middle of the atrium. At the bottom of the pool, a mosaic of a woman peered up at her. She must have been a goddess, for she was perfectly proportioned, and wore a flowing white *stola* that seemed to ripple in the water. Strangely, the urn she held was empty and Arria read something like a warning in her tile-black eyes.

'They are here!' shrieked a voice from the other side of the pool. 'Come, Mother!' The familiar young woman hurried along the other side of the pool, converging with Arria and Oppius outside a large, open door. 'Father, our guests are here,' she called into the room. 'The merchant and his weaver.'

'Ah, yes. Thank you, Vibia,' said a familiar voice from inside. 'Bring them in.' The group filed into a large, richly decorated *tablinium* office where a man in a purple-striped toga sat puzzling over a scroll.

Oppius stepped forward and cleared his throat. 'Greetings, Governor Secundus.'

Arria's breath caught in her throat. Had he just said *Governor Secundus*? No, it could not be. She peered at the patrician. He ran a hand through the perfect rows of his thin, greasy hair and looked up. 'Oppius, you old thief. What are you doing here?'

Oh, but it was.

Governor Quintus Vibius Secundus. His cheeks were still as full and his nose still as bent as the night he had tugged Arria's braid and called her a criminal.

Oppius crossed to the governor and bent to kiss his signet ring. Arria peered at the governor's large hand and thought she perceived the smallest of scars in the exact place where she had bitten him.

'Honourable Governor Secundus,' said Oppius. 'I am here at the behest of your good wife, Nerva Traiania. It is a pleasure to see you again.'

'Husband, you know this man?' asked the elder woman.

The governor chuckled. 'I do indeed, Nerva. We share a passion for the fighting pits. Oppius and his brother tend to pick the winners.'

The governor's wife frowned, but his daughter tittered amicably. 'In that case, Father, you will not be surprised when we tell you that Oppius also picks fine weavers.'

'Does he, now, Vibia?' the governor asked, smiling indulgently at his daughter.

'He is the master of the woman whose carpet adorns our *triclinium* wall.'

'Ah, yes, the Lovers' Carpet,' the governor said with a slight roll of the eyes. 'It is the talk of all our banquets. Well, let us have a look at this famous artist.'

Oppius grabbed Arria by the arm and yanked her forward. Arria fixed her gaze upon the ground and held her breath. 'Come now, weaver, do not be shy,' said the governor. 'Let me see your face.'

Arria lifted her eyes to the governor's and saw a flash of recognition. A wicked smile traversed his lips.

'We bought another of her carpets yesterday, Father. It is a sublime creation. Atticus, bring the carpet!' Vibia cried.

In seconds, the handsome man who had met them at the door appeared and unfurled the carpet for the governor's appraisal. 'A masterpiece indeed,' the governor proclaimed and Arria wondered if he recognised the gladiator depicted in the carpet's design. 'I believe now that I have guessed my daughter's intentions,' he said. 'Why hire the boat when you can own the boatman? Or should I say boatwoman?'

Arria bit her tongue. The master of this fine *domus* could have been anyone in the world. Why did it have to be the one man in Ephesus with cause to wish her harm?

'Am I to understand you wish to purchase her, Governor?' asked Oppius.

'Oh, Father, please?' begged Vibia. 'Will she not be a fine addition to our *domus*?'

The governor opened his arms in a gesture of defeat. He lifted a small, golden lamp sitting at the edge of his desk and shook it, filling the room with the soft jangling of coins. A few spilled out on to the desk: a half-dozen *sesterces*, two *denarii*, a gold *aureus*. It was enough money to feed a family for months—right there in the governor's change pot.

'What say you, Oppius? Will you sell me this weaver of yours?'

Arria watched Oppius put on his bargaining mask. 'I would love nothing more. However, as my finest weaver, her loss would, of course, have an impact on my business.'

The governor stood and stepped out from behind his desk. 'I am sure we can come to some agreement. Come, let us take a stroll through the *domus*. I will show you my newest fresco.'

The two men exited the *tablinium* together, followed by Vibia and her mother, and Arria found herself alone in the room with the tall, handsome slave who had met them at the door. 'I am Atticus,' he said, offering a bow. 'I admire your work.'

Arria returned the bow. 'I am Arria.' She glanced at the governor's desk.

'Do not even think of lifting one of those coins,' Atticus warned.

'I would not dare,' said Arria.

'He left them there on purpose, I mean. They are a test of our honesty.' Arria stared at the coins as if they were hot coals. 'It is well you should fear them. You must think of every temptation you behold inside this *domus* as a test, dear woman. It is the only way you will survive. Now come.'

Arria's mind raced as she and Atticus fell into position behind the two women.

'She will need a good scrubbing,' Arria heard

Nerva saying, 'and we must find her some proper clothing.'

'She will be such a joy to display at parties,' chattered Vibia. 'Will not the Memmii and the Cornelii families be fascinated to watch her at her work?'

'I can already feel their envy!' said Nerva.

On and on the women prattled, their excited banter muffling the low discussion taking place between the governor and Oppius just steps away.

'It is a small world indeed,' Arria heard the governor say. 'How fares your brother, Oppius?'

'My brother Brutus is well, Dominus.'

'When is the next pit night?'

'Not until after the *kalends* of April, I fear. Only after the Artemisia Games would Brutus even dream of purging his stock.'

'How go your brother's…predictions for those games, Oppius?' asked the governor.

Oppius smirked. 'Quite well, or so I have heard.'

The governor bent to Oppius's ear and whispered something Arria could not hear. They stopped outside a doorway and the governor turned to address his women. 'It seems Oppius is willing to part with his most valuable slave after all.'

Vibia clapped her hands together. 'Oh, Father, thank you!'

'Do not thank me yet, my sweet,' he said. 'First we must see if she accepts the rules.' The governor stepped before Arria and stared down his crooked nose at her. 'As a member of our *domus*, you must obey the commands you are given, conduct yourself with *dignitas* at all times and never attempt escape. Do you think you can do that, Arria?'

Arria cast her eyes to the floor and nodded. A cold, thick finger lifted her chin. 'Is that any way to address your new Dominus?'

She braced herself for a blow that did not come. 'No, Dominus.'

'Now tell me, do you agree to the rules?'

Arria felt sweat streaming down her brow. When had the house become so warm? It was as if the fires of Hades themselves were warming it.

'Yes, Dominus,' she said.

'Then it is done,' pronounced the governor. 'The weaver is ours!'

'Hazah!' shouted Vibia.

The governor grinned, then opened the door and motioned everyone inside.

Arria nearly gasped as she beheld the huge painting. It occupied the whole of the far wall, which in truth did not seem a wall at all, but a gateway to another world. At the far end of the painting, two snowy-robed women lingered cheerfully amidst a field of flowers so bright and real that Arria could almost smell their perfume.

But a kind of horror was taking place just beyond them. A chasm had opened up in the earth. A crumbling fissure of rock led into a dark realm, where a giant naked man wearing an expression of fevered lust reached upwards. A third snowy-robed woman was falling towards him, terrified.

'The Rape of Persephone,' the governor pronounced in Greek. He slid Arria a look and she felt a knot tie itself up in her throat. This was no mere display of art. This was a warning.

'It is wondrous,' remarked Oppius. 'A masterpiece.'

'In this *domus*, we appreciate works of art,' said the governor.

'Arria is well placed with you, in that case,' said Oppius. 'She will weave you very fine carpets.'

'I am sure she will. And we will ensure her well-being in exchange for her efforts.' Still smiling, the governor gripped Arria by the arm so hard that she nearly shrieked. 'Follow the rules, Arria,' he said sweetly, his fingers bruising her flesh. His black eyes flickered. 'Lest you be cast into Hades!' He released her arm and laughed, and everyone else in the room laughed, too—everyone except Arria.

Chapter Nineteen

Many days later, Arria discovered the source of the heat that permeated the governor's house. She was just finishing the hundredth row of her newest carpet when Atticus burst into the weaving room.

'Tonight there will be a banquet,' he announced. He began to pace, shaking his head and worrying his thick brown hair. 'The governor says he wishes to make an announcement, so there will have to be plenty of wine. He wants boiled ostrich with mint, though the Goddess Diana only knows how I will procure fresh mint after last night's freeze. There must also be pomegranates, though they will stain everything in sight, and pickled dormice and those damned Amarna figs...'

'What kind of an announcement?' asked Arria. He waved his hands distractedly. 'Oh, something about the future of the Empire. The real problem is where I will find musicians. And dancers! Snows of Olympus, the governor will want dancers…'

Arria blinked, held her breath. The future of the Empire? Had the Emperor been murdered, then? Overthrown? Had there been an invasion? A slave rebellion? Atticus ceased his pacing and cut her a look. 'What is the matter, Arria? You look as if you have seen a ghost.'

'The future of the Empire?'

Atticus smiled dismissively. 'I am sure it will just be announcement of the next war, dear. The governor's wife is Emperor Trajan's sister, after all. She tends to be the first to know these things.'

Oh, just the next war.

Arria remembered the soldiers who had arrived in the marketplace so many months ago. They had not been allowed to say where they were going, though they had not seemed to be in a hurry. Soldiering was a profession in Rome and Roman soldiers had to fight in order to receive their pay. The Roman beast needed to feed, lest it wither and die.

Arria sighed. 'Shall I plan to help in the kitchen, then?'

'Oh, no!' Atticus cried. 'The governor wishes for you to be put on display.' His eyes studied the rug hanging from Arria's upright loom. Arria was weaving the figure of a woman this time, but had completed only the head and shoulders so far. The face that had emerged from the threads was familiar, yet mysterious. Her almond eyes were set wide, her cheeks long, her lips large with the fullness of youth. And yet she was neither young nor old, neither Roman nor Greek. There was something eternal in her otherworldly face, as if she had existed since the beginning of time.

'Cleopatra?'

Arria shook her head. 'I will give you a hint—she is the most beautiful woman living in the world.'

'And that is…?'

'My mistress, Vibia Secunda, of course.'

Atticus grinned. 'Of course!' He gave her a conspiratorial wink. 'Now I remember why I like you.' He studied the bruises that lingered on Arria's arm. 'I am sorry for those. We must think of a way to hide them.'

Atticus disappeared and in moments returned with a dusty black tunic and matching shawl which he tossed in her direction. 'The tunic is fine linen and will make you presentable and the shawl will cover the bruises. Go to the boiler room and get them washed. I will retrieve you in the third hour so that we may set up your loom. Hurry. There is little time to waste.' And then he was gone.

Arria had only a vague idea where the boiler room was, for she spent most of her days inside the weaving room alone. She took her meals in the kitchen, where busy cooks treated her kindly, but paid her little mind. When she needed to relieve herself, she simply visited the house's latrine, which was served by running water piped in directly from the city's aqueduct.

In the short time she had served in the governor's household, life had been remarkably easy. Almost suspiciously so. There was no one to tell her to work faster and no one to slap her head when she paused to take a rest. There was no one at all really, unless she counted Atticus's busy comings and goings.

The only real visit she had received was on her second day, when Vibia had brought Arria a parchment image of the goddess Artemis, whom Vibia called Diana. 'Do you see the almond-shaped eyes?' Vibia had asked, batting her lashes. 'Is it not a perfect likeness of me?'

'Yes, Domina,' Arria lied. In truth Vibia had small, bead-like eyes and an unfortunately large, bent nose that resembled her father's.

'You must not tell me what you are weaving,'

she had said, though she had all but commanded it. 'I want to be surprised.'

In the mornings, Arria presented herself in the kitchen and was offered barley with milk. She worked all day in a warm room with a high glass window through which sun shone down on her face. In the evenings, she was given bread with fried onions and chickpeas. Sometimes even eggs.

It was as if Fortuna had smiled upon Arria at last. Life in the governor's household was warmer, more peaceful and more comfortable than anything she had experienced before, even as a free woman.

And yet Arria was miserable. She felt the bars of an invisible prison closing around her: the prison of forgetting.

While she sat in her warm room, she tried to picture Grandmother, Epona and all the women in Oppius's workshop labouring in the bitter cold. She had vowed not to forget them, but she feared that with each passing day their misery faded just a little in her mind.

Mostly, she longed for Cal. Sometimes after dinner, she wandered through the *domus*'s vast gardens, seeing him everywhere. His hands were the feathery ferns that tickled her thighs, his arms the gnarled oak boughs, his legs the pillars of stone.

And his heart was the dark garden pool into which she stared, unable to discern the bottom. She could not let herself believe that she would never see him again, though each day it seemed more likely. Did he even know where she was? Did anyone? She imagined the months passing and then the years, until all that remained was the memory of his smouldering eyes and the knowledge that a magnificent, honourable man had wanted her once.

She concocted elaborate plans of escape. In her fantasies, she pillaged the governor's lamp for its loose change, then slipped past the door guards like a ghost. With her newfound riches, she purchased a horse and cart and sent her family on their way to a new life. She somehow managed to free Cal and his fellow gladiators, along with all of Oppius's women, and they rode off together towards freedom.

It was a beautiful dream: if only she had the courage to make it real. Any day now, her new brother or sister would be born and her mother would make the long, terrible trek to the rubbish heaps outside Ephesus. Meanwhile, Arria laboured in her warm, sunny room, where the world outside seemed like some very bad dream. She was like a fly caught in honey.

'Some of the cooks do not like going to the furnace, but I do not mind it,' said a young woman, inspecting the clothes Arria had been given to wash. 'Come, I will take you there. The fire is due for a feeding.'

They crossed the garden and arrived at the top of a dark staircase. 'Careful now,' the young woman said and, as they descended the stairs and stepped into the dimly lit room, Arria instantly understood why many avoided it. A small hole in the ceiling let in a little bit of daylight, but most of the shadowy space was lit by an eerie red glow emanating from a large metal door.

'Welcome to Hades,' said the woman. As Arria's eyes adjusted to the light, she noticed that the metal door sealed the entrance to an oven-like structure flanked on one side by a tall stack of wood. On the other side there was a large metal container that appeared to be full of boiling water.

The woman lifted several dripping garments from the container with a long wooden pole and wrung them, then placed them in a basket that she handed to Arria. Lifting a large pitcher, the woman poured more water into the laundry container and dropped Arria's clothing in.

With the same wooden pole she slowly opened the metal door and tossed in a piece of wood from the stack. 'Feeding the beast,' the woman said grimly. Arria peered into the furnace and beheld its dancing flames. Just beyond them, she saw a large open space populated by a forest of brick columns.

'Some call that place the hypocaust, but I call it the Elysian Fields,' said the woman with a mischievous grin. 'Is that not very poetic?'

Arria smiled. 'You mean the part of Hades where heroic souls pass eternity?'

'The very same,' she said, then lowered her voice. 'But there is a deeper meaning to the name. This is where Dominus sends disrespectful slaves to be punished. They arrive with heroic souls and depart with obedient ones.'

The woman was smiling at her own wit, making Arria think that she had not yet endured such a punishment herself. 'And how far do the Elysian Fields stretch?' Arria asked.

'Why, beneath every room in the house. The heat seeps through the floors. It is how the house stays so warm.'

Arria could only nod her head in wonder. The boiler room was a gateway to the *domus*'s smoky underworld and also its source of heat. Arria pictured Persephone falling into the dark, hot pit.

'Let us depart,' said the young woman, shutting the metal gate. 'Lest we become ghosts ourselves…or raisins!'

By that afternoon, Arria had washed and ironed her clothes and been judged by Atticus to be a fine representative of the governor's *domus*. 'Just think of yourself as a conversation piece,' he reminded her.

Her loom had been set up in a corner of the atrium slightly removed from the main hall and she had been positioned with her back to the pool, giving passers-by a direct view of her work. She did not have to look at anyone, thank the gods. She only had to stand tall and work steadily as the guests observed her as they might a new piece of furniture, or a freshly carved statue.

'After the Vesta prayer, you should retire to the servants' quarters,' Atticus explained. 'We can move the loom tomorrow.'

Thus, at the evening hour, Arria took up her shuttle and began her hundred and first row. Soon the most important people in Ephesus were passing her by in waves of cloying perfume.

'This is the weaver of the beautiful carpets,' she heard Vibia remark several times. 'She is ours.'

Arria wondered if she was supposed to be content. She had become a member of the most distinguished *domus* in all of Ephesus, after all. She had warmth in her limbs and food in her belly and even a small measure of status. She was no longer just a faceless slave shivering in a crowded workshop. She was a 'conversation piece,' an artist.

So why did it feel like the gods were punishing her? Why did it feel like they had dangled the carrot of happiness in front of her and then snatched it away, laughing? She loathed this painted prison. She feared that she had stolen the only little bit of life she would ever have—the only bit of love—and now she would slowly forget it.

Chapter Twenty

'Do not respond,' Cal whispered in her ear, then plunged himself into a shadowy alcove.

'Cal?' she said, her voice cracking. He watched her turn.

'Do not look at me! Face your loom. Do it now.'

Arria returned to her position, facing the array of taut vertical threads. He could see her chest rising and falling with her breaths. 'You must not draw attention to us,' he explained. 'If Brutus sees me here it will be ten lashes.'

Nor could he even dream about the consequences if the governor caught them together. The man was twisted, or so Cal had learned by observing his dealings with Brutus. Though the governor rewarded the gladiators for obeying his commands, resistance was met with torturous punishment. His only softness, it seemed, was the love he had for his daughter. Cal prayed that softness translated to Arria, his daughter's newest acquisition, though he feared the worst.

Arria was moving her fingers over the vertical warp strings as if testing a harp. She paused, stared at her hands, whispered, 'Is it really you, Cal?'

He murmured a yes, scarcely believing it himself. When Brutus had announced that Cal and several other gladiators had been requested at the governor's *domus* that evening, he had been overcome with joy. 'It is I.'

He watched her body convulse with a sob. He wanted to throw his arms around her and hold her close. He wanted to crush his lips down on hers and tell her how much he had missed her. But she was not his any longer, not even for a kiss.

'By what miracle did the gods send you here? On this night?' She addressed the question to her strings. Her voice was low, incredulous.

'I am often summoned to such gatherings— especially before games. The Artemisia Games begin in ten days, as you know.'

'Are you alone?'

'I came with several of my brethren. We are called "conversation pieces."'

She emitted a small noise, then kicked her thread basket behind her and scolded herself audibly for the mistake. Clever woman. The 'mistake' gave her an excuse to turn around and she stole a long look at him.

It was the worst thing she could have done, because when he looked into her flickering brown eyes, the temple of resolve that he had spent hours building began to crumble.

'I fear that I may be dreaming,' she said. He wished she would not look at him like that. Like she wanted him still. Did she not realise they could never be together again? That even this stolen moment risked both their lives?

'I feared I would never see you again,' she said. 'I feared...'

A couple arrived at the door, and Cal retreated to the shadows as the doorman directed them past Arria towards the dining hall. Cal noticed that Arria's hands were trembling as she wove.

When the couple was finally out of earshot, Cal continued. 'I have not fought since the New Year and Brutus refused to bring you to me without a victory to reward. When I learned that you had been sold to the governor, I—' He stopped himself and remembered his resolve. 'I was very happy for you.'

'Happy for me?' She twisted once again, craning to see him.

'Do not turn to look at me!' he snapped. She

hung her head and returned to her loom. Anguish gripped him. 'Yes, I am happy for you. To have a place in such a fine *domus*, plenty of food and rest. Heat. It is more than many could ever hope for. It will be a good life for you.'

'Cal—'

'Shh, do not say it. Return to your work.' He feared her words: they had the power to unleash the creature of desire that was twisting and writhing beneath his skin.

'Have you not missed me?' she whispered.

An older woman draped in fine linen sauntered up behind her. 'What is it that you are weaving, dear?'

Arria realigned her shuttle. 'It is an image of the most beautiful woman in the world, Domina,' she said.

'And who might that be?' asked the woman.

'My mistress, Domina. The beautiful Vibia Secunda.'

The woman smiled. 'What a good little slave you are,' she said and patted Arria on the head before sauntering away.

Arria could sense Cal step closer. 'Why did you just lie to that woman?' he asked.

'I did not lie.'

'You did, for I have met the most beautiful

woman in the world and I can tell you it is not Vibia Secunda.'

'Indeed? Then who is it?'

'It is you.'

Arria's shuttle slipped from her fingers and he knew she smiled. 'You are the most beautiful woman I have ever seen,' he added. 'You are a goddess.' He heard her suck in a breath. He had failed to show her the pleasures of the flesh, but at least she would know how beautiful she was before they parted for ever.

'You did not answer my question,' she said. Her voice was so soft he could barely hear it.

'What question?'

'Have you missed me?'

Cal paused. He had missed her more than the grass missed the rain. He had missed her in seconds that passed like hours and hours that passed like days. He had missed her with every *cubit* of his body and all that was left of his soul. But to tell her such a thing would only increase both their misery.

'I see,' she said after a long silence and he caught sight of a tear running down her cheek.

Curses on his very soul. He would have given anything to take her in his arms and wipe away her tear and tell her the truth: that he loved her, that he would always love her. That she was the most divine miracle to have ever graced his miserable life.

But that was not what she needed now. She needed strength, armour, a strategy. She needed to get tough, to face the coming years like a warrior. And he would help her to become that warrior, no matter how badly it hurt him. He would give her what he had failed to give his wife: a way to survive.

'You must understand that although there are no bars or locks in your new home, it is still a prison,' he said.

'You think I do not understand that?' she asked. 'Do you know how many times I have wondered how I might get myself past the guards?'

'Cease!' he hissed. He lowered his voice. 'Clearly you do not understand, or you would not be saying such things! The consequences of escape are worse than a simple beating. You are a member of the most noble *domus* in Ephesus now. If you attempt escape, you will shame your new *familia*. Do you know what the punishment is for such a thing? Execution—torturous and humiliating. Do you understand now?'

She said nothing, though he could hear in her shallow breaths that he had frightened her. 'What I am trying to tell you is that such a fate need not be yours. If you remain in your *familia*'s good favour, you will be warm and safe for the rest of your days.'

'This is not my *familia*. And I do not wish to be warm and safe while my heart slowly turns to stone. I wish… I wish…'

'I know what you wish.' *It is what I wish, too.* 'But you must accept the fate you have been delivered.'

She squeezed the warps of her loom between her fists. He lowered his voice. 'If you fight against it, your anger will destroy you, Arria. I fought against my own fate and all I earned was pain. You must forget me.'

'I will never forget you.'

An elderly man draped in an elegant toga wandered behind Arria and paused to watch her work. As Arria moved her thread through the shuttle, her shawl slipped off her shoulders to reveal the stains of two large bruises.

A fire exploded inside Cal. *Gods, no. Please not that.* He held his breath until the old patrician moved on.

'Who did that to you, Arria?'

'Did what?'

'Who gave you those bruises?'

She pulled the shawl back over her shoulder. 'The governor,' she whispered. 'But he did not harm me. It was just a warning.'

A warning. So she had already fallen out of the governor's good favour, if she had ever enjoyed it at all. Arria had no idea the danger she was in.

'I would do anything to get you out of here,' he said. He should not have said such a thing. Such words were dangerous to a slave's soul.

'Then tell me how we do it,' she said.

'It is impossible. Even if we could somehow make it past the door guards, we would be pursued on horseback. Fugitive slaves cannot hide in Ephesus. We would be immediately captured and returned for a reward.'

'It is worth the risk.'

'You do not know what you are saying. You do not know the governor.'

'I think I have an idea,' Arria said, rubbing her arm.

'He colludes with Brutus and Oppius on the fights and games. He demands torturous and unnatural kills. He is a depraved man. You must never cross him, Arria. Your future here depends on it.'

'It is no future worth having.'

'I will not be a part of anything that causes you harm.'

'Being without you causes me harm.'

He shook his head and felt another brick of his

resolve go tumbling. She was still his Arria—despite the fine shawl and matching tunic. Her wit was still as quick, her spirit as fiery, her arguments still as convincing as any academic's. It would be a long while before they broke her down, if they ever did at all. 'You will be safe here,' he said without conviction.

'Freedom is more important than safety.'

Damn her. She had no idea what she was saying, what she was doing to him, to her own future.

And yet somehow he loved her for it.

'Meet me in the garden at the first morning hour,' she said, 'when the moon is high and the music is loud and the guests are deep in their goblets. Then we can plan our escape.'

More bricks were tumbling now. He struggled to retrieve them. 'Arria, you do not understand. There is no escape.'

'If we cannot escape, then we can at least steal some time together now. Some life.'

He was shaking his head. Another brick. A dozen. 'I have not agreed.'

'In the garden, then,' she said and he thought he saw the edge of a smile. 'I will see you soon.'

Chapter Twenty-One

The patricians were praying. Cal stood at the edge of the atrium and watched them out of the corner of his eye. They had gathered around the pool to honour Vesta, the one goddess in the Roman pantheon without an earthly form. At the far end of the pool, the governor's wife stood behind Vesta's flaming hearth. She lifted a bowl of pigs' blood to the heavens.

'We offer you this sacrifice, Sacred Vesta...'

Pitiable pig. Its death squeal had nearly shattered Cal's ears. Soon it would be dressed and cooked and would be basking in the dining room surrounded by exotic fruits.

He wondered how his own corpse would look in such a display. The thought might have been laughable, if he were not a gladiator considering whether to defy a Roman governor. If he indulged Arria's wish, there was a chance they would be discovered together and a distinct possibility of leaving this banquet with his head on a spike.

Not that he would mind. He would gladly give his head for one last night with her. It was *her* head for which he feared. It was much prettier and more intelligent than his, and she very much deserved to keep it.

He glanced at her now, standing tall beside her loom, bowing reverently. Her black clothing was meant to dissolve her into the shadows, but was having the opposite effect. She appeared elegant and stark behind the painted matrons, who clustered around the pool in their pinks and creams and blues, watching their own reflections. She hovered behind them like some dark, magnificent spirit. An ageless goddess among fatuous girls. A phoenix among peacocks.

He could not meet her in the garden.

The risk to her future was simply too great, no matter how much he ached to touch her one last time, to blanket her with his kisses. The thought of Arria stung by the governor's lash ached worse.

Not that she could not endure such a fate. She had proven herself stronger than any woman he had ever known—Roman or otherwise. Labouring in the cold workshop without rest had not defeated her, nor had her beating, nor the knowledge that she faced ten long years of misery until her indenture was over.

He wondered what secret source of hope kept her going. It was as if she had been forged in fire, then polished by hardship and fate, and had somehow come out gleaming.

She was gleaming now in the torchlight. Her bowed head was tilted slightly, revealing the place where her neck met the back of her ear. It fascinated him, that shadowy borderland of flesh. He had failed to kiss her there in their night together and regretted it mightily. It had not been the only place he had failed to kiss.

He had tried to forget her. He had enumerated her faults in his mind: that she was Roman, that she could never be his, that every step he took towards her drew him further from the memory of his wife. It had been an exercise in frustration.

Everywhere was Arria. Arria with her hairpin. Arria touching his chest. Arria telling him that he could not die, as if simply saying the words would make them so. He wanted her too much to ever leave her and he loved her too much to ever stay.

Love. It was a strange word to come to mind, but its rightness warmed him like secret sunlight. He loved her and in another life he would have wooed her and wed her and worshipped her for the rest of his days. He loved her and he would do anything to keep her safe.

He could not meet her in the garden.

He could not put her at risk. If he did, then he was no better than the young, foolish man who'd put his own wife at risk so many years ago. The world was cruel and he needed to protect Arria from it—by protecting her from impossible wishes.

He could not meet her in the garden, not there in the shadows, where he could run his fingers over her face one last time, memorising its contours. He could not meet her and finally taste the skin of her neck or follow its long sinews to the other places he yearned to kiss. He could not meet her and caress her one last time, feel the weight of her breasts, to cradle them as he traced the taut field of her stomach and then down to the place where he knew she ached for him.

What had she said exactly? That being without him harmed her more than whatever harm could come of being with him. A clever turn of phrase. A handy argument. She had no idea the danger she invited by harbouring such a belief.

Though the idea was not senseless. He had clung to the memory of his wife for years because it was the only thing that brought him joy. If one did not find a source of joy, then the hours became endless and forgettable, like a vast, scorched field. Was that not what life was? Moments of joy and pain connected by miles of forgetting? The key was to focus on the joy, was it not?

Meet me in the garden, she had said.

'Goddess of Earth, Keeper of the Family, Vesta the Pure...'

Later that evening, the Honourable Nerva Traiania Secunda would meet the gladiator they called the Dalmatian Dragon in her private chamber and whisper sweet things in his ear.

'Vesta the Clear, Vesta the Clean, Vesta the Chaste...'

Later that evening, many of the white-robed men currently lost in prayer would do much the same, stealing away with the lovely young dancers already assembled at the edges of the room.

'Virgin Mother, Keeper of the Flame...'

Virgin mother? How was that possible? By the gods, the Romans were strange.

Though Cal could not judge them too harshly, for soon he would be among them. Later that evening, he, too, would be sneaking in the shadows, stealing a bit of life where he could get it.

A bit of Arria.

Meet me in the garden, she had commanded and all he could do was obey.

The last trickle of blood sizzled on to the flames and Vesta hissed her gratitude. Freedom was more important than safety—that's what she had told him. What she had really meant was that desire was more powerful than doubt. And love? Love, he feared, was the most powerful of all.

Would he come? She could not be certain. He had been so hesitant to agree to her request. Did he desire her still? That was the real question— one whose answer she could not divine. When he had called her the most beautiful woman in the world, he had stolen her very breath. Now as she passed another hour shivering amidst the ferns, she was beginning to think that he might not have meant it.

You are the most beautiful woman in the world, but...

She was not so inexperienced that she did not recognise a placation. Was that not what Zeus told Hera when she caught him with the lovely Io?

'You are the most beautiful woman in the world, dear Hera. And this woman? She is but a cow!'

There were many such divine 'cows' at this banquet: splendid patrician goddesses who painted malachite on their eyes and dabbed wine dregs on their lips. They sought to conquer gladiators like Roman soldiers sought to conquer soil. They were probably circling him right now, jockeying for position around their magnificent divine bull.

Arria pressed her back against an old oak and stared up at the sky. He had to come. He was her pigeon after all. He had kissed her on the lips, had called her by her name. Had *wanted* her. But she had been waiting in this garden so long now that she had begun to grow roots.

And if he did not come, what then? Would she simply go on? Spend her days working diligently at her loom—warm, well fed and grateful for the life she had been given?

She knew that she could not. He had given her a taste of what it meant really to live and she knew she would not rest until she got herself free.

She believed her chance was coming soon. That evening after the Vestal prayer, the governor had announced that he had received communication from his brother-in-law, the bellicose Emperor Trajan. The new emperor would be paying a visit to Ephesus as part of his tour of the provinces. He would arrive in time to preside over the Festival of Artemis, including the gladiatorial bouts scheduled for the opening day.

Hosting the Emperor would be a great honour

and a staggering responsibility. His large military escort would need to be provisioned and its officers wined and dined. There would be chaos—wild, wonderful chaos—and in it, Arria vowed to find a way out.

Arria heard voices somewhere close. Panicked, she scrambled up the trunk of the oak as a man and woman passed beneath its branches, then quietly moved on.

Arria had hardly begun to breathe again when a silent figure stepped near, the moonlight shining on his smooth round head.

'Cal?'

'Arria? Where are you?'

She edged down the tree trunk, taking the last few *cubits* in a jump.

'You must be a goddess,' he whispered, shaking his head and catching her by the waist. 'You are always falling out of the sky.'

'I do not always fall out of the sky.' She pouted, joy flooding her heart. 'Sometimes I emerge from watery places, like urns for example.'

'That you do,' he said, his voice husky. 'You are my Venus from the foam.'

She conjured a clever reply, but when she opened her mouth to make it she discovered his lips on hers. And then he was kissing her hungrily, his breath hot, his hands stealing over her body like thieves.

It was everything she wanted, everything she had dreamed of since last they met, and all the threads of herself seemed to curl into perfect knots and the world seemed bright, despite the darkness, familiar, despite the strangeness, and somehow complete.

'I feared you had abandoned me.'

'As long as I live, I will not abandon you,' whispered Cal.

'You must always live, for you are my pigeon.'

'Your what?'

'My hope, my wings.'

'And you are the home towards which I fly,' he said.

There was no light by which to see, but as they kissed, she remembered him. Not in the simple ways one person remembered another—not just the shape of his body, the scent of his breath, the tenor of his voice. This was a deeper, more elemental remembering. Like the memory of fresh air, or sunshine, or laughter. She remembered him like she remembered happiness.

He kissed her more fiercely, his tongue growing bolder, plundering her mouth, taking what it wished.

'Do you see what you have done to me?' he asked.

Did he not know what he had done to her? Heat radiated through her body, along with a relentless, bubbling joy. It was as if she were a pot of barley mash and he the dancing flames beneath it.

He squeezed her closer, crushing her breasts against his chest and curling himself around her. 'I fear this moment's end,' he said. 'I fear that I may never see you again.'

'Then our fears are the same,' said Arria. 'But let us seize our happiness now, for it strikes where it pleases.'

'You are a sorceress,' he intoned. He was kissing her behind her ear—soft, wicked kisses that were melting her bones.

'How do you expect me to stand when you are doing such a thing?' she whispered.

'I do not expect you to stand at all,' he answered, then whisked her up into his arms.

'Cal!'

'Shush, my sweet,' he said, cradling her like a babe, 'lest they come after us with their golden goblets.'

'Am I not heavy?'

'You are exactly the same weight as the lightest boulder I ever hewed from the Quarry of

Luna,' he said and she could almost see his wry smile. She gave his arm a playful punch, then nuzzled against his chest. He smelled of wine and incense, and that delicious, dusty maleness that was all his own.

'Did anyone see you leave?' she asked.

'I do not think so, but it was difficult to get away. Vibia Secunda pulled me on to her couch.'

Arria gasped. 'Did you...?' Jealousy flared.

'Of course not!' replied Cal. 'I flattered her incessantly, gave her a massage and kept her cup full of opium wine. She stayed awake as long as she could, but finally lay back and closed her eyes.'

Arria exhaled, although the thought of Cal massaging the shoulders of Vibia Secunda had made the blood roar in her ears. 'Vibia may not stay asleep for long,' said Arria. 'When she awakes she will surely come looking for you.'

Cal sighed. 'I fear that you speak truth.'

'Why is there never enough time?'

'It is not the quantity of time, but the quality of it that matters,' he said. He kissed her forehead softly. 'Or so we must believe so that we do not despair.'

She heartily disagreed. The quantity of time mattered, too, by the gods, and she would not allow him to convince her otherwise. The real problem was how to get more of it and there was only one solution to that problem: freedom.

'Is it not auspicious that the Emperor will preside over your next games?' she said carefully. 'Perhaps he will grant you the *rudius*.'

'Arria,' he said. 'In another life...'

'In this life, Cal.'

Arria tried to picture Cal bowing to some purple-robed sovereign. She gave a resigned sigh. 'Well, you could just jump out of the theatre and run.'

He stifled a laugh. 'Do you really think I could run faster than the Praetorian cavalry?'

'You could lose yourself in the streets,' she offered.

'With this head? And this scar?' He guided her hand to the tip of his scar and he feigned a gasp. 'Stop doing that.'

Arria giggled softly. 'But I am doing nothing.'

He traced her hand slowly down his chest. 'No, really. I mean really you must stop touching me like that,' he teased. He had manoeuvred her body so that her back lay against his strong forearms and her folded legs squeezed against his chest.

'Put your legs over my shoulders,' he commanded.

'What are you—?'

'Do as I say, my little nymph,' he protested. 'The time for talk is over.'

Surely she could not contradict him, what with the time so short and his voice so urgent. Not that she would ever dream of resisting such a request. He cradled her backside as she lifted her legs over his shoulders.

'Are you a madman?' she whispered.

'Shush.' She braced an arm against the tree for balance. Her legs were now draped over his shoulders. The only thing between her womanhood and his mouth was the thin fabric of her loincloth. 'Come here, *fy nghariad*,' he said, nosing into the cloth. 'Let me taste you.'

And in that moment the all-powerful gods, who had so far been indifferent and even kind to the two lovers, decided to unleash their wrath. A woman's voice shrieked, 'Guards!'

Something hit Cal over the head and he stumbled backwards. Losing the support of the tree, Arria slid from his shoulders and tumbled to the ground.

After that, the blows landed like stones. First a kick to her stomach, then a punch to her face. 'You have given my father no choice, Arria,' said a cool, female voice. Arria gasped, sucking the air. 'You have betrayed our family's *dignitas*.'

Arria opened her eyes to behold Vibia Secunda standing beside the governor. 'I gave you everything and this is how you repay me?'

'Arria!' cried Cal. She could see his shadow only paces away, struggling against the figures of guards.

'Do not harm the gladiator!' commanded the governor. 'Stand him up. I want him to watch.'

Arria felt a strong hand grip her arm. A knee thrust up against her stomach, then something hard collided with her cheek. Blood. Pain. Blows. More blows. To her legs. To her arms. To her middle and back. No part of her was safe. How long did the beating last? Minutes? Hours? Cal's voice faded in and out of her mind. She was being dragged through the dirt, then pushed down a flight of stairs. She collapsed on to a hard floor and lay there sucking the air.

Dread infested her belly. Soon the sound of footsteps filled her ears. *No, not more punishment*. She sat up, but could not get herself to her feet. A pair of blood-red sandals appeared in her line of sight, lit by the boiler's rosy glow.

'Three simple rules, Arria,' said the governor. 'But why did I expect such a bestial woman to follow rules?' He held his hand out before her eyes and she perceived the white of a small scar in the shape of a smile. 'Do you know how long your little bite took to heal?'

The same hand gave her a sharp slap. 'A month! I had to tell my wife and daughter that I was bitten by a dog. I suppose in a sense I was.'

She tried to respond, but no words came.

'Oppius told me about your trysts with the Beast. I knew what would happen if I brought him here. Love is a powerful thing, is it not? Though I fear that in your case it is fleeting, for that barbarian scum is not long for this world. Why do you wince, Little Asp? You caused this yourself.'

The governor squatted down and grabbed her by the face. He placed his lips on hers and kissed her, his wet, sour mouth possessing hers, bruising it. 'Let us have an accord,' he said, still gripping her mouth. 'Let us say that I will not release you from this dungeon until you come to me on your knees and beg me to have you…in the carnal fashion, I mean.' He took her lower lip in his teeth and bit down hard.

She cried out in pain, but still he bit her and soon she felt the warmth of blood pooling in her mouth. Her eyes filled with tears.

Finally, he released her. He stood and smoothed his toga. 'I have no doubt you will learn, Little Asp, and you will come to me on your knees. It will just take time. And that is something I have in abundance.'

Chapter Twenty-Two

Arria opened an eye. The sun was shining overhead, casting its pale light through the small hole in the ceiling. She spied a small grey mouse. It watched her for a long while, as if pitying her, then scurried back into the wood pile whence it came.

Her fingers found a charred piece of wood. She rubbed it hard against the tile until she could see a single black mark:

Day One.

She must have fallen asleep again, for when she opened her eyes, she was screaming. In her nightmare, she and Cal had been lying beneath a warm blanket, locked in a lovers' embrace. Suddenly the governor had appeared and yanked away the blanket to reveal their naked bodies covered in blood.

* * *

When she opened her eyes once again, a small patch of sunlight filtered in from above. Her stomach burned and her limbs ached. At the edge of her face, she could feel the jagged crust of dried blood.

She scratched her second mark on to the floor:

Day Two.

Her throat was dry and tight. Water. She needed water. She pulled herself up, feeling a sharp pain behind her ribs. She crawled next to the large clay pitcher lying beside the boiler. She did not have the strength to lift it, so she bent over it like a dog.

Lap, lap, lap. She could not seem to get enough. She was still drinking when a man burst into the room, carrying an armload of wood. He dumped the wood on to the pile without giving Arria a second glance. 'Will you help me?' she asked him. He reached for two of the logs and tossed them into the fire, shutting the metal door with the same long wooden stick that the cook had used to retrieve the laundry the day before. The man departed without giving her a glance.

Did she even exist? She had to be alive, or the room would not feel so blisteringly hot. She continued to lap from the pitcher until her tongue could no longer reach the water. She wrapped her arms and legs around its large round middle and rocked backwards, letting the water pour down her throat. She closed her eyes.

Day Three.

The sun god stretched his arm through the opening in the ceiling and poked Arria in the eye. She opened it to discover that she was still embracing the pitcher. She turned her head to discover the mouse staring at her placidly.

'Are you waiting for me to die?' she asked the small creature, but he gave no reply. 'I could kill you, you know,' she said and he seemed to shake his head in disbelief. 'Are you calling me a liar?'

Well, she was a liar. She would never try to kill the mouse. She was a lover of small things now—things like the shape of her mother's smile, fresh, clean air, the sound of Cal's voice when he said her name. Small, big things. She understood now that they were all that mattered.

Day Four.

The boiler man came and went thrice a day. 'Please, bring me food,' she begged, but he paid her no mind. 'Please bring me water.' Nothing.

'Please bring me a gladiator with eyes of green, that he may rescue me.' The pitcher of water was almost empty.

Day Five.

On his evening visit, the boiler man was merciful. He fed the furnace with half the normal amount of wood. Soon after he'd departed the key wobbled once again inside the lock. *He is bringing more wood,* she thought miserably. But it was not the boiler man who entered. It was the governor, accompanied by two very angry-looking guards.

'Food,' pleaded Arria. 'Please.'

The governor smiled. 'Are you begging me to have you, then? If so, I require you be on your knees.'

Arria shrank back into the shadows, shivering despite the heat.

'I did not think so,' said the governor. 'But come with me now. We have a small errand to complete.'

Arria was ushered into a large, horse-drawn *carpentum* and settled between the two guards, who held her withered arms as if they expected her to flee. She scarcely had the strength to lift an amphora, let alone wrestle herself free of two men, but she made a show of struggle so that the governor would not think her beaten.

She promised herself she would not be beaten—not as the carriage rattled down the stone streets towards the Greek ghetto, not as they pulled up outside Arria's own *insula* and not as the governor dangled the carrot before her, willing her to bite.

'You wish to see them, do you not? Your miserable family? Will you beg me right now, then? To have you? Give me what I want and I will allow you to visit your mother.'

Arria felt the seams of her will fraying. Could she do it? Could she exchange her body for a reunion with the ones she loved? She felt her assent bubbling, the terrible, inevitable *yes* forming on her lips, but the governor had no patience. 'I did not think so,' he stated. 'Lucius, why not go fetch the Little Asp's father instead?'

Arria's heart leaped. Her father? She was going to see her father? In minutes the guard reappeared with Arria's father in his grasp. 'Father!' Arria exclaimed, reaching for him, but the guard held her back.

'Arria!' her father shouted. The second guard held a small *pugio* blade to her father's throat.

'Please, Dominus. Do not harm him,' Arria begged, struggling to her knees. 'I will have you! I will have you!'

The governor scoffed. 'Well, that is the most insincere declaration of desire I have ever heard,' he said. 'No, Arria, you will have to do better than that.' The governor nodded to the guard, who pulled Arria's father into the carriage and settled him next to Arria.

'Father!' Arria shouted. She struggled against the guard, who kept her arms pinned in her lap. 'Oh, Father!'

'Arria, I have missed—'

'Silence!' shouted the governor and Arria heard the sharp clap of a slap across her father's face. 'If you say one more word, Faustus Arrius, I will have my guard draw his blade straight across your throat. No more talking. That is a rule. Arria will avow that I make no exceptions for broken rules. Do you understand?' Her father nodded warily. The governor reached out of the carriage and rang a bell, and the driver snapped the reins.

Arria peered at her father across the darkness, trying to speak to him without words. *Are you well? And Mother? Has the baby been born? What have you eaten?* She rested her head against her father's shoulder and he began to sob. 'I love you, Father,' she dared to whisper and soon felt his own head resting atop hers.

They came to a stop outside a familiar iron gate. Two guards stood watch beside it and Arria recognised their faces in the flicker of a nearby torch. They had arrived outside the *ludus*. Arria's heart began to pound. *Cal.*

Arria and her father were yanked from the carriage into the light of a torch that burned outside the entrance. The governor's sour breath filled Arria's ear. 'Listen closely, Little Asp, for here are the instructions for the first part of your errand—you are going to go inside the gladiator barracks and tell the Beast that the Artemisia Games are to be his last. In five days, when he meets his first opponent in the Theatre of Ephesus, he is to take the fall, do you understand? He is to allow himself to be slain.'

Arria choked. 'I will do no such thing.'

The governor exhaled. He motioned to the guard who held her father. 'Go ahead, Lucius.'

The guard lifted his knife and cut a gash across her father's cheek. Arria lunged for him, but the other guard easily kept her restrained. Her father howled as a thin curtain of crimson seeped down his cheek.

The governor gave Arria a petulant look. 'Lucius would be happy to cut a matching scar on your father's other cheek if you would like to defy me again.' Arria bit her lip. 'Now here is the second part of your errand—you must tell your barbarian lover that you do not want him any more and that you want me instead. Tell him he can go ahead and return to his wife in the Otherworld or whatever it is the dirty Picts call Hades.'

Arria blinked, and the governor smiled wickedly. 'Yes, I know all about his little death wish, along with your silly curse and everything else.'

'But...how?'

'Oppius and Brutus are brothers. Did you not know? I protect their interests and they protect mine, and everybody becomes a little richer. Do not look so surprised, Little Asp. Such arrangements make the world go round. Or did you stupidly think it was honour that makes a man rich?'

Arria heard her father gasp as he realised what Arria had understood months ago—that the fights were fixed and that Oppius, Brutus and the governor conspired together.

'I do not expect you to comprehend the ways of your betters,' the governor continued. 'You must tell the Beast of Britannia that you have fallen in love with me and that you wish to serve me for the rest of your days. You must make him believe in your sincerity. If you say or even suggest that you have been forced, your father will die. Do you understand?'

Arria nodded, then felt the metal of his signet ring slam against her cheek. 'Do. You. Understand?' the governor repeated.

'Yes, Dominus.'

'And we will be here listening to ensure you do exactly as you have been told.' The governor nodded at the guard and he tugged her through the gate. 'Oh, and one last thing, Arria,' said the governor, using her true name. 'If you are unsuccessful, if you cannot convince the Beast to take the fall, then your father will meet his end. Do you understand?' Arria watched as the guard held his blade at her father's throat. The torch's flames cast eerie shadows across the governor's face.

'Do. You. Understand?'

Perhaps it was the rhythm of her breaths, or the space between her steps, but he knew she was there before he could actually see her, and when she finally crossed into the torchlight he nearly jumped out of his skin.

'Arr—'

He caught his breath, bludgeoned by the sight of her. In the place of the strong, lusty woman he had left in the garden there was a dull, trembling shell. She was thinner, though less than a week had passed since they had been parted. Her pale cheeks bore stains of sweat and ash, and a constellation of bruises decorated her limbs. She was dirty, bent, limping, and when she finally lifted her gaze to his, he saw that her once-bright eyes had been invaded by fear.

But she was alive. Alive. And here. Cal slammed his body against the bars of his door, reaching for her. 'Arria, my darling.'

She stood frozen in her sandals. What had they done to her? And why, why had he not been able to stop them?

'Cal,' she said at last. She stole a glance down the tunnel and stepped backwards. A tear cut a lonely path down her cheek. 'Cal, I have come to tell you that—'

'Will you not come to me?' he pleaded. 'Will you not let me touch you?'

Another glance down the hall. 'I do not wish for you to touch me ever again.'

The words landed like blows. Cal stepped backwards, shaking his head. He refused to believe her. She was not herself. 'Why are you here?' he asked. 'Who brought you?'

'It does not matter. I have come to tell you that I am lifting the curse.'

'What?'

'I am lifting the curse that protects your life. You can die now. You may join your wife in the afterlife.'

'Arria, I do not understand.'

More tears were flowing down her cheeks

now. A terrible army of them. They meant to defeat his heart.

'I… I have fallen in love with…with the governor,' she sputtered. 'I want him now instead of you. I wish to serve him for the rest of my days.'

'I do not believe you.'

'You must believe me!' She glanced over her shoulder, then pinned him with a lifeless stare. 'I love him and I command that you take the fall.'

'I do not understand.'

But suddenly, he did understand. She had not escaped. That is what she was really telling him. She was deeper inside a prison than she had ever been.

'In five days, at the games to honour Artemis. You must take the fall when you face your first opponent. Tell me you will do it!'

'What has he done to you, Arria?'

It was the wrong question. What Cal should have been asking was what he himself had done to her. And he already knew the answer. He had failed her.

He could still picture her shadowy form—how the guards had kicked her as she lay upon the ground. The governor himself had soon joined in, and then, to Cal's amazement, the governor's daughter. She had spat in Cal's face before landing a formidable kick directly in Arria's stomach.

And Cal had been made to watch it all. He had kicked, bucked and screamed, but had been useless against the guards who had restrained him. As if he had ever been able to come to her aid. He had failed her, just as he had failed his wife so many years ago. He was a useless man and he deserved to die.

'Tell me you will take the fall at the Artemesia Games. Please,' she begged.

'I will.'

'You will?'

He had failed her in every way that a man could fail a woman, but die for her? That he could do. 'I will. I promise.'

He had granted her wish, yet she looked defeated, boneless. She was shaking her head, studying the floor. Finally, she stiffened, fashioning her words into cold stones. 'Cal, I do not love you any more. Do you understand?'

He had just promised to do her bidding, had he not? He was not expecting gratitude, but he sure as Hades was not expecting another blow. He shook his head. No, he did not understand.

'I do not think you heard me, Cal,' she said loudly, though he had obviously heard her. 'I am trying to tell you that I no longer love you.'

His confusion deepened. How could she be taking back her declaration of love, if she had never before made it? Her trickle of tears had become a flood. She cast a glance down the hall and it finally occurred to him that they were not alone. 'Do you understand?' she repeated.

As an experiment, this time, he nodded his head.

'I beg you to answer me,' she said, as if he had given her no answer. Slowly, he began to understand the strange code in which she seemed to be speaking. She continued to repeat the phrase, her words echoing off the walls until they were transformed. *I love you*, she was trying to tell him. *Forgive me*.

'Tell me you understand that I do not love you.'

'I understand,' he said at last. 'I no longer love you, either.'

And he would go on not loving her until the moment five days from now when he met his death.

Chapter Twenty-Three

Outside the *ludus*, the governor clapped Arria hard across her backside. 'Well done, my Little Asp. Now that was not so very difficult, was it?'

'I hate you,' said Arria.

'We are going to have to work hard on that attitude, though.'

Arria searched her father's eyes. She had done it for him, after all. In order to save her father's life, she had just condemned the man she loved to death.

The man she loved. It felt so natural to describe him that way, as if she were describing a member of her own family. There was her father, her mother, her brother and, ah, yes, Cal, the man she loved.

And she did love him, though she had not realised it until moments ago, when she had strained to declare her love for the odious governor. Being forced to say the words aloud had made her think about the man to whom the sentiment truly applied.

And that was Cal. It had always been Cal. As a young woman, she had dreamed of a strong, magnificent champion such as he—someone to protect her and to love her fiercely. As she grew older, she had dreamed of a caring, loyal husband who would never grow tired of her kisses. And as her marriageable years passed, she had pictured a secret companion—someone who stood beside her at her loom and told her not to despair, that hope remained, that it was as real as honey cakes.

And then—suddenly—the man of her dreams had become real. She had discovered him inside a gladiator barracks on the worst night of her life. He was everything she had ever wanted: not a monster, but a man—a loyal, incorruptible, caring man who had made her feel like she was walking on air and not simply falling through it.

She loved him, despite Epona's warning, despite logic, despite his useless attempts to protect her from him. Her heart belonged to him. It had always belonged to him. And when, moments ago, she had finally recognised that fact, it had seemed the most important thing in the world to let him know.

Though she could not tell if she had got through

to him at all. And even if she had, the effort was pointless. Soon he would be going on the final journey—a journey that she had commanded him to make. And as for her heart, it was broken for ever.

Now she truly understood what it meant to be commanded to kill. Her father had done it and so had her brother, and it had broken them. It had come close to breaking Cal, too.

And now, by the gods, it was breaking her.

Where was her father? She needed him now, for she had just done something unforgivable. She tried to catch his gaze, but his eyes were darting about, doing that thing they did just before he made a bet. But there were no bets to be made.

Father, look at me. Tell me that Mother is well, that Brother is mending and that you will do your duty to them both.

But her father did not look at her. Instead, he turned to the governor. 'Honourable Governor, I would like to propose a bet. If the Beast of Britannia dies early at the Artemisia Games, you may have my daughter for ten more years, but if he is the last man standing, you must set her free.'

No, Father!

The governor's eyes blazed. 'What did you say?'

'I said that I would like to propose a bet. That the Beast is the last man standing.'

'But you just broke the rule,' said the governor.

'What rule, Governor?'

'The rule that I explained when you entered the carriage.' Her father cocked his head in confusion and the governor sighed. 'No talking.'

Arria's father nodded. 'Apologies, Governor Secundus,' he said. He bowed silently.

'Do you recall the punishment for breaking that particular rule?'

Arria's father shut his mouth, but it was too late. He had made his last bet. Time slowed. She saw the governor nod to the guard he called Lucius. Lucius lifted his sword and drew a long, bloody necklace across her father's throat. Her father's body collapsed to the ground.

Day Six.

Blackness.

There was nothing but blackness. No sound. No light. Only a hard floor, a menacing heat and the memory of her father beneath the guard's small blade. Perhaps she dreamed—dark, terrible dreams of her father's demise. Over and over she watched him die. The look of fear. The attempt to flee. The blood—everywhere the blood. It flooded the streets of Ephesus and everybody cheered.

Day Seven.

Sadness, weight. A terrible weight. It crushed her body against the boiler room floor. The boiler attendant came and went. He kept the boiler fed and Arria clung to the ground, where the cooler air lingered. Though not always. Sometimes after his visits, the heat would explode into the room, devouring her strength, cooking her in place, until she found herself wishing for death.

She scratched the eighth black mark upon the floor.

Thirst. There was only thirst now—a strange, withering thirst, along with the slow, terrifying realisation that she had not lost one beloved man, but two.

Cal.

He came to her in a dream.

You must drink, he told her, *or you let him win.*

There is no winning, she argued. *There is only giving myself to him or to death. I choose death.*

Get up, Arria!

She rose. The pitcher was empty. She dipped her hand into the dirty laundry water. *Drink it,* said Cal and she obeyed.

Day Nine.

She did not scratch her mark upon the floor. What was the point? The laundry water was almost gone. Tomorrow Cal would die. A few days longer in this room and so would Arria.

Cal was whispering in her ear again.

Think, Arria!

I cannot think.

There was music in the governor's garden above—the herald of a trumpet, followed by the jingle of tiny cymbals and the propulsive thump of a drum. Emperor Trajan had arrived with the dusk.

The door swung open. The boiler man glared through the blurry waves of heat. His muddy voice sounded strange in her ears. 'The governor wants to know if you have anything to tell him.'

She shook her head, saying nothing. One more night. She could last one more night.

The man sighed, opened the furnace with the long wooden pole and threw the logs in. Arria waited for the heat to descend.

When she awoke again, the sky was dark. The music had ceased and all the world was quiet. The boiler fire had dissipated, but it was still strong enough to cast a menacing glow about the room. Red shadows blanketed the wood pile and Arria watched in wonder as a small, furry creature emerged from beneath it.

The mouse! He lived still. He endured. He padded softly across the concrete floor and came to a halt just beside Arria's cheek. His whiskers twitched and when he spoke, his voice was like Cal's.

Why do you linger on the floor? he asked.

The heat keeps me here. I cannot move beneath it.

Rubbish.

Arria opened her eye. The mouse was watching her steadily.

You must try to escape, he said.

There is no escape. The prison is not the boiler room. It is the Roman Empire itself.

Who told you that?

You did.

I lied. There are limits even to Rome's reach. What did Grandmother tell you?

That there is always hope.

That is right. Now think.

I cannot. My mind is mash.

That is not the Arria I know, the Arria I love.

Do you love me, Cal? Do you really?

There was no answer. Arria opened her eyes. The mouse was gone.

She blinked. In a handful of hours Cal would be bowing before some garishly costumed foe, giving up his life.

She could not let Cal die. If he did, then the last honourable man in the Roman Empire would be gone and along with him, Arria's very soul.

Arria sat up, cast her eyes about the room. Woodpile. Boiler grate. Water pitcher. Pole. The door to the boiler room was heavily bolted and there was certain to be a guard posted at the top of the stairs. There was no way out save the concrete hole in the ceiling, which was too small to accommodate anything more than a leg.

Think. She closed her eyes, trying to picture freedom.

She imagined a large pool of cool, clear water. She was swimming in it. It flowed over her limbs, washing them clean, and into her mouth, filling her with energy. In her vision, a mosaic stretched beneath her: a goddess holding a large empty urn.

Arria floated slowly over the mosaic, marvelling at the urn's clever lip, which surely doubled as a drain for the pool.

A drain.

She opened her eyes.

The energy of hope surging through her, she poked the pole through the grate's metal loop and pulled it open. Scalding air burned her face, but soon she was able to see into the boiler's long throat.

The fire inside the passageway was in embers, thank the gods. Beyond it, Arria could see the vast, empty space that stretched beneath the house. *The Elysian Fields.* That was what the cook had called the hypocaust, though to Arria's mind it was more like a giant living creature, like a whale.

She would need light to navigate the sprawling space. She searched through the woodpile and found a piece of wood to use as a torch. She had no real weapon—nothing to defend herself against the guards who would be positioned above. She glanced at the tall, thin pole she held in her hand. It was no spear, but it would have to do.

She used the pole to clear the fire chamber of the embers, pushing them forward into the space beyond, then took a deep breath. The iron throat might have been clear of fuel, but it was still going to burn. She slapped her cheeks and counted to three, then dived through the fire chamber and into the sprawling hypocaust—the whale's hot belly.

There was so much smoke. It stung her eyes and filled her lungs with its acrid stench. Coughing, she found her makeshift torch and touched it to one of the glowing coals. Her pole in one hand and her torch in the other, she stepped forward into the infernal space.

It was not long before she had discovered a perfectly round plug held in place by hinges. It had to be the drain to the atrium pool above. Holding the plug in place with her hands, she undid each of the hinges and then released it.

The water cascaded down on to the floor with a soft sizzle and Arria's heart began to throb. She prayed that there was no one above to witness the slow retreat of the pool's water. Impulsively, she stepped beneath the steady stream and opened her mouth.

She had never tasted water so sweet.

The cascade became a trickle and she pulled herself through the drain hole, emerging from the goddess's urn cleansed, energised and dripping wet. She had done it! She had escaped from the smouldering hell. Now she had only to escape from the lockless prison.

She stepped into the atrium. The full moon shone through the cloudy glass and she peered around the shadowy hall in fear of witnesses. Eerie laughter resonated from the dining room at the far end of the pool, along with the soft chords of a lute. She needed to get out of this *domus* right now, while no one was watching and there was still enough night left to get her family out of Ephesus.

But she knew they would not get far without money.

The governor's office was empty and, save for a small candle burning on a table at the far end of the room, mercifully dark. There was just enough light for Arria to glean the outline of the governor's oil lamp, which sat at the corner of his desk just where she had hoped it would be.

She tore off a piece of her soaked gown and tipped the lamp forward, pouring out the coins from its wide nozzle. She gathered the heavy purse into her fist and was turning to leave when she heard a deep, growling voice.

'Burglar.'

Arria froze. Squinting into the darkness, she made out a large figure reclining upon a couch near a flickering candle: a terrible, languorous dragon basking in the dark.

She took a step backwards, her heart beating in her throat. *He is too far away to catch me*, she told herself.

'Do you really think you can escape, Burglar?' croaked the dragon.

'I do not have a choice but to attempt it,' she

answered honestly. She took another tentative step backwards.

He reached for the candle and lifted it to his face—his long-nosed, long-cheeked, utterly familiar face. He raised a brow. 'Do you know who I am?' he asked. The candlelight flashed on his deep purple tunic.

Arria closed her eyes. Yes, she knew who he was. He was the leader of armies, the defeater of kings, the enslaver of men. He was not a dragon, but an eagle: the proud, divine leader of the Empire of Rome itself. 'I do, Divine Emperor Trajan.'

His expression was a mixture of derision and surprise, as if he were beholding a demon of his own making. 'You know who I am, yet you continue to attempt escape?'

Arria took another step backwards. Her whole body was shaking. 'I do, Emperor Trajan.'

'Do you not fear me, Burglar? Do you not fear the death I can deliver you with a simple command?'

'I do not fear the death of my body, Emperor. I fear the death of my soul.'

The Emperor paused. 'An unexpected reply.' He reached out an arm and worried the blanket hanging over him. 'She is quite clever, Atticus, is she not?'

A head appeared from beneath the drape of fabric. 'She is indeed, Emperor.'

Atticus? She watched Atticus bend close to the Emperor's ear and whisper something she could not hear.

'My lover tells me that you are a fine weaver,' said Trajan.

'Yes, Emperor.'

'He says that Secundus has been torturing you for many days and that he means to break your will. Do you know what we do with wilful soldiers in the Roman army?'

'You flog them,' said Arria.

'Indeed we do, for there is no room for wilfulness in the finest army the world has ever seen. Do you know how it feels to be flogged?'

'I do, Emperor.'

He flashed a look of bemusement. 'And yet you persist. Why?'

Arria paused. Why did she persist, really? 'Because I am in love.'

Something in the Emperor's expression softened. 'Well, are you not full of surprises? Tell me, Burglar, how did you manage to escape your dreary dungeon?'

'I faced a trial of fire, then entered the belly of a whale.'

The Emperor laughed. 'And how did you emerge?'

'I emerged... I emerged through its very blow-hole.'

The Emperor gave Atticus a playful shove. 'You did not tell me this burglar was also a bard, Atticus.' He returned the candle to the table and Arria spied the shadows of two thick-chested guards standing behind the couch.

The Emperor reached for a goblet of wine and took a long drink. 'You amuse me, Burglar. But you will not make it past the governor's door guards. There are dozens of them on duty to-night and they're armed with spears as well as swords. If they do not kill you, they will appre-hend you, then Secundus will continue his tor-ture with fresh delight. The man is a worm.'

Arria did not know how to respond, so she simply agreed. 'Yes, Emperor.'

He laughed again—a wicked, delighted laugh that seemed to echo to the heavens—and it oc-curred to Arria that Rome would never be as great or as terrible as it was beneath the rule of this man.

'Perhaps the guards will not apprehend you,' he continued cheerfully. 'Perhaps the gods mean for you to find your lost love. If that is the case, then I certainly will not be the one to stop you.'

He appeared to pull Atticus closer. 'What say you, Atticus?'

'I say there is no woman in Ephesus who is more worthy of your mercy,' said Atticus, sending her a wink.

'In that case, my guards will show you out, Burglar,' said Trajan. 'All I ask is that if you are successful in your campaign, you remember me. I am Trajan the Merciful.'

Chapter Twenty-Four

As promised, one of Trajan's guards saw Arria past the door guards and well on her way, dismissing her with a Roman salute. Soon she was standing outside her *insula*, her heart swelling.

And there, right where he had been the morning she had left, was her brother. His head lurched backwards. 'Artemis?' he cooed, his eyes squinting. 'Have you come to take me hunting, Goddess? Let me just get my bow…' His head fell forward and he appeared to resume his slumber. She poked him again.

'Be gone, vermin!' he howled at her.

'It is I, Brother. It is your sister, Arria. It is time for you to wake up.'

He gazed at her in wonder. 'Arria? You look so very…wretched.' He lifted an amphora to his lips.

'There will be no more of that.' She wrenched

the large jug from his arms, tipped it to her lips and took a long, fortifying drink. Then she smashed the clay vessel upon the ground. The wine splashed everywhere, staining her legs red. It was quite possibly the most satisfying thing she had ever done.

'You dirty cow!' her brother shrieked. 'That was my week's ration!' He lunged forward, grasping for her ankle.

Arria stepped backwards. 'If you dare try to harm me, Brother, I will crush your wine-addled head right here upon the cold concrete.'

Her brother recoiled. He peered up at her warily. 'You have changed, Sister?'

'I bring sad news,' Arria said. 'Father is... He is dead.'

'What?'

Arria paused, letting her brother absorb the news. 'He was murdered by a very bad man. That man wants to kill me, too. He will come looking for me. If you and Mother are here, he will kill you instead.'

Her brother steadied his head. 'Father is dead?'

Arria nodded and watched her brother put his face in his hands. He did not howl or weep. He only sighed and, when he looked up at Arria, his expression had sobered.

'You are the *pater familias* now,' she said.

'Me? *Pater familias?*'

'You have a choice—you can help me get Mother to safety, or you can stay here in this filthy gutter waiting to die.' She held out her hand. 'What is your choice?'

The trip up the stairs went faster than Arria thought possible. Her brother insisted on ascending without Arria's aid and she was amazed at how quickly he moved on his crutches.

When she stepped inside her family's small room, she nearly collapsed in relief. There was her mother lying on the bed, her belly ready to burst. She was emaciated, anguished and blessedly alive.

'Mother!' Arria bent and embraced her mother, joyous tears streaming down her face.

'Arria, you have returned to me. Thank Jesus!'

'Mother, you must listen to me now. You are in grave danger. Take this purse.'

Arria quickly explained her plan. Her mother and brother would follow the aqueduct out of town, making their way towards the mountain village of Serenus. There they would use some of the purse money to purchase food and lodging for the night.

'If I do not arrive the day after tomorrow, then you must move on and do not wait for me. You must get as far away from Ephesus as you can.

The governor will be searching for you. You must not let yourselves be found.'

Her mother and brother spoke as one. 'The governor?'

'I will explain later. All that matters now is that you escape his reach.'

'Will you not come with us, Arria?'

'There are others—people whom I must not forget.'

'And your father?' her mother asked. 'He will meet us somewhere?' Arria glanced at her brother.

'Clodius will tell you about Father. Just get yourselves to Serenus. All right? Now let us get you both packed.'

A short while later, Arria was watching the two lumber off up Harbour Street—a pregnant woman and a crippled man trying to escape the Fates. She sent a prayer to the goddesses Kybele, then Artemis, then Mary, hoping to blanket the two travellers in grace.

For herself, she only begged the goddess Ephesia to send her strength. *Get tough*, she told herself. *Be a warrior.*

When she arrived outside Oppius's villa, the light of dawn was already growing in the sky.

She knew where each of the guards were stationed: the first outside the front door, the second outside the entrance to the workshop and the third walking the perimeter of the villa throughout the night. She waited for the third guard to pass around the back of the workshop, then threw a handful of pebbles at one of the small windows.

Many long moments passed, but Arria soon heard the soft thud of an object in the dust. The key.

'You must first distract the guards,' whispered Grandmother's voice through the open window.

'How?' Arria called back.

'The horses.'

Arria ducked into the stables and found both of Oppius's horses standing in their stalls. It was not difficult to untie them and lead them into the courtyard, where she opened the exit gate and sent them running. Soon, all three guards were shouting and rushing after them.

Arria dashed to the entrance of the workshop and felt for the bolt-release holes. She lined up the points of the key with the holes and then yelped in horror. They did not fit the lock. The forks had been carved just a little too far apart.

'What is it, Arria?' Grandmother asked from the other side of the door.

'Just one moment.'

Think, Arria.

The door was made of thick oak. If she had an axe she might be able to tear it down. But where to find an axe? On a whim, she put her hands on the bolt handle and pulled. Miraculously the door opened. It had never even been locked! Arria pushed open the door and blinked in wonder as she gazed out at the dusty prison in which she had unquestioningly remained for months. It was a prison without a lock. A prison of their own minds.

Arria felt the eyes of a dozen women staring at her across the darkness. 'I have come to free you,' she announced. 'The guards have gone after the horses. We must flee now.'

Arria expected a stampede of women, but only Grandmother and Epona hurried through the door. 'Will you not come with us now?' Arria begged the rest. 'You will face danger, but your lives will be your own. Is that not worth the risk?'

It seemed that it was not. The ten other women stared at her with expressionless eyes. Perhaps they had been inside this cage for so long that they had forgotten what freedom looked like. Perhaps Oppius had promised them freedom upon the occasion of his death, as so many masters did. Or perhaps they knew exactly what freedom looked like, but had only forgotten their desire for it.

Arria felt a shadow pass over her. She realised that if she had never defied the governor, if she had followed his rules and woven his carpets and languished in his warm rooms, she would have eventually become like these women. She would have slowly forgotten her family, her freedom, her love of an honourable gladiator and her desire to save his life. The days would have slipped by, then the years. Life would have become... forgettable. Slowly, her spirit would have died.

'It is not good enough!' she shouted, though the sound she emitted was more like a sob. Leaving the door open, Arria dashed down the stairs and joined Grandmother. 'Where is Epona?'

'I do not know,' said Grandmother, looking about desperately. 'She went running through the gate.'

In the distance, Arria heard a horse's whinny and a woman's loud shriek. Soon Epona was galloping towards them, her long auburn hair flying behind her like a horse's mane.

Epona brought the horse to a halt before Arria and Grandmother and smiled. It was the first real smile Arria had ever seen grace Epona's face.

'Give Grandmother a lift up!' she commanded, holding out her arm. Arria wove her fingers together into a foothold and soon Grandmother was gripping Epona's waist, her grin matching Epona's. 'Come,' said Epona, motioning to the back of the horse. 'There is room for a third.'

Arria shook her head. 'I cannot go with you.'

'You are mad if you think you can save him,' said Epona, stretching her arm down to Arria. 'Come.'

Arria stepped backwards. 'I must try.'

There was the sound of hoofbeats, and soon Oppius's second horse came galloping into view. Atop him sat Oppius's largest guard, his sword drawn.

'Go to Serenus and find my mother and brother,' Arria told Epona. 'I beg you. My brother is lame and my mother is heavy with child. They need your help.'

The rider was almost upon them. 'We will find them,' promised Epona, snapping her reins. 'But, Arria, you must run!'

And that is what Arria did. She sprinted into the field behind Oppius's villa, her only thought to evade the mounted guard. She did not know where she was going. She only kept running, changing direction as often as she could, seeking the thickest, most overgrown paths. Soon she found herself in a swampy area crowded with broadleaved trees.

She had lost her pursuer, thank the gods, but she had also lost her way. She struggled forward, feeling exhaustion overtake her. She had not eaten in many days and did not know how much longer she would be able to go on. Perhaps Grandmother had been mistaken. Perhaps she could not be a warrior after all. How did she expect to save Cal's life when she could not even make her way out of a forest?

Then she spied a bright white column amidst the tangle of trees. She stepped into a clearing and froze, struck with awe. The Temple of Artemis rose up before her in the pale light of dawn, still aglow with the memory of moonlight.

It was several moments before Arria caught her breath. Several more before she could move her legs again. The gargantuan white-columned building floated above the swampy forest like a great ship. The building dwarfed even the tallest of trees, its size and grandeur rivalled only by Egypt's great pyramids, or so Arria had heard. And that was well, for the Temple of Artemis at Ephesus was not only the Empire's most magnificent temple, it was, according to many, greatest of the world's seven wonders.

Her heart beating, Arria ascended the marble steps into a new kind of forest—one of bone-white columns. The torches had long been extinguished and daylight cascaded into the temple from the large rectangular opening in the roof. It illuminated the colourful, swirling frescoes that danced on every ceiling and surface, and brightened the elaborate reliefs that trimmed the walls and columns.

And yet she was bathed in space. Before her, the blue marble floor spread out like a placid lake. The statue of the sacred goddess stood waiting upon its distant shore, her arms outstretched, beckoning.

Arria began to walk towards the goddess, scanning the temple for a *hierodoule* or other servant of the goddess. It occurred to Arria that today was the *kalends* of April—the first day of the Festival of Artemis. This very evening, the goddess would be ushered from her dais and paraded through Ephesus by the light of the rising moon to the music of trumpets and drums.

Though now all was silent. Arria thought she saw the flap of a skirt disappear behind a column. A priestess, perhaps? 'May peace be with you,' Arria said by way of greeting, but there was no answer.

The goddess's mysterious figure took shape as Arria approached. Strange, bulbous adornments hung in white marble rows across her chest, making her appear unlike any Greek or Roman goddess that Arria had ever seen.

It was said that when the Amazons founded Ephesus, they discovered the ancient goddess Kybele in the exact place where Artemis now stood. Kybele had been adorned with similar bulbous ornaments—the severed testicles of the divine bulls that had been sacrificed in her honour.

Arria felt her palms becoming moist as she arrived at the base of the dais to behold Artemis, the Roman Diana, Queen of the Wildland, Mistress of Animals, Goddess of Birth and of the Hunt.

The Goddess's almond eyes were set wide, her cheeks long, her lips large with the fullness of youth. And yet she was neither young nor old, neither Roman nor Greek. There was something eternal in her otherworldly face, as if she had existed since the beginning of time. It was, Arria realised, just like the face she had been weaving into her latest carpet.

Arria closed her eyes and the world began to spin. Suddenly, she was not kneeling on fine marble, but soft, ancient earth. And in that moment, it was as if all of her own worldly woes were as ephemeral as grass, the only thing that endured was the sky scattered with stars.

A breath of wind softened into the temple,

cooling Arria's cheeks. The sun moved higher in the sky. In only hours, Cal would step out into the arena to face his own death. And what could Arria do about it?

Nothing. She was a weaver, not a warrior. She could not simply dive into the arena and place herself at Cal's side. Could she?

She placed her wooden pole before her. 'Blessed Goddess,' Arria whispered. 'I beg you, send me your counsel.'

The Goddess stood silent.

If only Arria had something to offer—some small token of her reverence. She reached beneath her belt and discovered her tear-stained handkerchief, still tinted with the memory of Cal's blood. She laid the handkerchief before the goddess. Blood and tears. It would have to be enough.

Arria closed her eyes. When she opened them again, the handkerchief had disappeared. She blinked. She had placed it not an arm's length away, at the foot of Artemis's high pedestal. Where had it gone?

Had the breeze blown it away? Arria glanced about the temple and strained her ears, listening for a thief. But there was no one, or any sign of the handkerchief. Had the goddess somehow *accepted* the humble gift?

She glanced down again. Arria's pole was gone, too. In its place was a mighty spear.

She dared a glance at the Goddess. There she remained, cool and distant. Beautiful and strange. Just behind her, Arria thought she heard the shuffle of footsteps.

Though perhaps her mind was just playing tricks. The spear was not really a spear, after all. It was still her pole, only now she could finally see that it was not merely a tool. And Arria was no longer a simple weaver.

'Gratitude, great Goddess,' she whispered, and kissed the floor.

When she reached the temple steps she saw that the world remained. Everything was the same. The only thing that had changed was Arria. She had been gifted a mighty spear by the Goddess Artemis herself.

There was nothing left to do now but go and use it.

Chapter Twenty-Five

Cal stood inside the stage house at the great theatre of Ephesus and stared out at the silent crowd. In the *venatio* hunt that morning, a man with a gleaming sword had killed a lion and stood atop its chest while the Ephesians found their seats. Soon after, when the same hunter had been disembowelled by an angry bear, they laughed and cheered. And in the midday executions, when three escaped slaves had been decapitated by a single stroke of an executioner's blade, they had chatted and drunk their honeyed wine.

But now they were silent, reverent, as their great Emperor Trajan stepped out on to the stage and bowed. He wore a general's purple cape and white tunic trimmed with gold, and his large chest was encompassed by a decorated muscle cuirass made of gleaming silver. He was flanked by a cluster of similarly dressed, red-caped officers and a swarm of stony-faced guards, who stared up at the hushed crowd of twenty-five thousand with the indifference of warriors.

Outside, thousands more men and women had filled the streets. If Trajan succeeded with his intended conquests of Dacia and Parthia, he would be responsible for stretching Roman borders to their greatest extent in history. No wonder the people sat on the edges of their seats. The Emperor who stood before them was not only the most powerful man in all the world, he was quite possibly the most powerful man in all of history, an illustrious peer of Alexander the Great himself.

Now Trajan held up both his hands. 'Citizens of Ephesus, to honour the great goddess Artemis, I give you these humble games,' he said simply. 'Bring forth the gladiators!'

There was a long silence and, when it became clear that Trajan had nothing more to say, someone shouted, 'Long live Emperor Trajan!' The crowd erupted in cheers as the great man took his seat beside the governor, who was already lounging beside his wife and daughter in the booth of honour at the centre of the theatre.

Sitting beside Trajan, the governor looked small and rather conniving. His black-rimmed eyes squinted against the afternoon sun and he sipped delicately at the contents of a golden goblet as if treating an overindulgence of wine.

Cal remembered how the governor had smiled as he kicked Arria to the ground, how his squinting eyes had twinkled as he commanded that Cal be made to watch. Where had the governor sent her after her beating? What unthinkable punishment had Arria been made to endure because Cal had been unable to resist meeting her in the garden that night?

He could never forgive himself. When she had begged him to give up his life that night in the barracks, she had already become a shadow of herself. What terrible combination of thirst and hunger had the governor made her endure? What amount of fire and smoke? Seeing her trembling before him had shaken him to his bones. She had finally been broken and whatever remained of his soul had softly broken, too.

Now his body would follow his soul and it was high time. No more pretending that he could defy them, or that his life had any meaning at all. The governor had won and so had the Empire of Rome. Cal's time had come.

He tightened the leather belt holding up his loincloth and checked the buckles on his armour. He had been given a greave to protect his left leg, a *manica* to shield his right arm, a small breastplate to protect his middle, along with a helmet and even a shield. He was better protected than he had ever been before and he had never needed it less.

The ringmaster stood in the middle of the stage and welcomed the crowd, then motioned to the opponents. Cal felt a shove and headed across the stage towards the ringmaster. His opponent marched towards him from the other side of the stage, a man who appeared equally matched to Cal in both size and strength.

The two met on either side of the ringmaster, who raised both men's arms and shouted to the crowd. 'Good citizens of Ephesus, your Magnificent Emperor gives you the Destroyer of Didyma versus the Beast of Britannia!' The crowd cheered as the gladiators stepped down from the stage to the large sparring ring just below it.

These are the last moments of my life, Cal thought.

He did not wish to spend them inside a helmet. He cast the heavy metal hood to the side and the audience exploded with cheers. He rewarded them with a mighty sneer. Come to think of it, he did not need the damned breastplate, either. If he was going to die, he wanted a clean, unimpeded death. He pulled off the plate and tossed it against the wall of the ring. More cheers. He continued to throw off his armour until the only thing he wore was his loincloth and the only thing he held was his *gladius* sword.

He met his opponent at the centre of the ring and the two traded dozens of blows. As he fought, Cal knew he should be remembering his wife. He would be joining her soon, after all. But all he could think of was Arria. His heart ached as he envisioned her scowling at him from between the bars of his cell, adorable in her fury. He imagined the softness of her fingers against his skin, the wisdom of her words in his ears, the music of her laugh, the smell of her, the taste of her. Overcome by the sweetness of his memories, his will to fight faded.

He threw aside his sword and collapsed to his knees before his opponent.

The crowd gasped. Out of the corner of his eye, Cal saw the Emperor rise to his feet. With a gesture of his hand, he called off Cal's opponent. 'Beast of Britannia, I command you to stand,' shouted Trajan. 'Why do you not fight?'

'I was commanded not to fight,' said Cal, rising to his feet.

'By whom?'

Cal shook his head, saying nothing. Trajan glanced at the governor, who was staring into his goblet, pretending ignorance. Cal wondered how much money the governor had staked on Cal's demise. He sensed that Trajan was wondering the same.

'As Emperor of the Roman Empire, I command you to fight. Whatever orders you have received,' Trajan said, cutting the governor a look, 'they are overruled by my own. I command you to fight, Beast of Britannia, and if you live, you shall have whatever you wish as your reward.' Trajan raised his voice for the benefit of the crowd. 'This is the Roman Empire, by the gods. We fight!'

He might have said more. He might have given a damned speech for all Cal knew. All Cal could hear was the deafening roar of the crowd and above it, nine small words repeating inside his mind like a chant: *If you live, you shall have whatever you wish.*

Whatever he wished? It was not hard to think of what that was. He wished for Arria to be set free. He had failed his wife, he had failed himself, but if he could somehow secure Arria's freedom before he died, then it would have all been worth it.

This was more than a *rudius* to set him free. It was the one thing that Cal could not refuse. What Trajan had offered him was nothing less than a chance at redemption.

'What say you, Beast?' asked Trajan.

Cal gave Trajan a deep bow, then picked up his sword and lifted it to the sky. Yes, he would fight. Whatever the Destroyer gave him, Cal would give him worse. Cal could practically picture the expression on Arria's face when she learned she had been freed, that it had been the last wish of a broken old gladiator with nothing left to lose. Satisfied, Trajan nodded and took his seat. The audience quieted, rippling with anticipation.

Cal felt light, energised. He danced around his side of the arena in a show of ease, thrashing his sword through the air. The Destroyer stalked towards Cal, then broke into a run as Cal dug his feet deep into the sand. Bracing himself, Cal held up his sword to deflect the Destroyer's blow.

But he never got the chance, for in that instant, a long wooden pole came flying through the air. It clipped the Destroyer on the shoulder, then tumbled to the ground. The Destroyer stumbled and the object rolled to Cal's feet.

Cal assumed that it had come from the crowd—tossed by some drunken troublemaker. The Destroyer was returning to his side of the arena already, visibly angered by the nuisance.

High up in the women's section, there was a collective gasp. Before Cal's eyes, a woman dressed in black was swinging her legs over the marble barrier to the ring. She pulled the shawl from her head to reveal a long black braid, though he would have known her even if she had been covered in feathers. 'Arria!' he cried.

'Cal!'

She had come for him. His beautiful, brave, foolish woman had come. She rushed to his side and he caught her in his arms. 'Have you lost your mind?'

'I have come to rescue you!' she shouted. She bent to retrieve her weapon.

'With a pole?'

'It is not a pole. It is a spear.'

Curses, she *had* lost her mind.

'Guards, seize her!' shouted the governor. Six Praetorian guards came running on to the stage and Cal had a sudden sense that he had lived this scene before. This time, there was nowhere for Arria to run. He had to keep her safe.

He gripped his sword. 'Arria whatever you do, you must stay behind me,' he ordered.

The governor's guards were as large and fearsome as the Destroyer and much better equipped. They jumped down from the stage and unsheathed their swords. 'Do you hear me? Stay behind me, Arria. That is an order.'

He felled the first guard with a ferocious blow to the thigh, but the next did not succumb so quickly. As they fought, Cal noticed one of the other guards moving behind them. Arria had lifted her pole and appeared to be using it as a defence against the stalking guard.

Cal could not let her die, whatever he did. He thrust his blade hard and caught the second guard in the side, sending him to the ground at last. A third guard quickly took the second's place. Cal was trading blows with him when he heard the sound of metal on wood.

'Arria!' he shouted. He plunged his blade into the third guard's arm, sending him to the ground, and turned to discover the stalking guard now dragging Arria away. Cal raised his blade and severed the guard's arm, freeing Arria.

The cheers were so loud that he could barely hear the clanging of the blades as he felled the fifth guard and then the sixth.

The theatre quieted and it was just the two of them standing in the middle of the arena amidst a collection of writhing bodies. But they were not done. The Destroyer remained. He was standing on the other side of the theatre, looking like a bull about to charge. Meanwhile, another set of guards was running down the stairs of the theatre, their swords drawn.

'Cal?'

'What, my darling?'

'It is never going to end, is it?'

'No, we cannot beat them. Not ever.'

'But we can still run, can we not?'

Cal paused. He had tried to run. They always found him; they always won. Why would now be any different? Perhaps because this time he would not be alone. 'We can,' he said. He grabbed her hand. 'And we must.'

They had not taken two steps towards the stage when the Destroyer made his charge. Cal pushed Arria ahead of him and told her to run, then waited until the last moment to turn and slice his blade cleanly across the gladiator's muscled neck.

The Destroyer's head rolled to the edge of the sparring ring and came to a halt at the foot of the Emperor's box. The crowd howled with excitement as the Emperor took to his feet.

'Governor, call off your guards,' commanded Trajan. Cal's pursuers stopped in their tracks and Trajan gave Cal an admiring nod. 'You have fought off more foes than Caesar at Alesia, Gladiator. What say you?'

'There may be *gloria* in taking life, Emperor,' Cal said, 'but there is no joy in it.' The crowd grumbled and booed, but the Emperor nodded thoughtfully.

'I would offer you the *rudius*, but it seems your

woman has beat me to it.' The Emperor nodded at Arria's wooden pole. 'Hello, Burglar,' he said. There was a spate of laughter and the Emperor grinned gamely. 'So tell me, Beast of Britannia, what is your wish?'

Cal could hardly believe what he had just heard. He gave a humble bow. 'I wish that the woman by my side be set free.' He felt an elbow in his ribs, then watched in horror as Arria stepped forward.

'What he means, Divine Emperor, is that he wishes for us *both* to be set free.'

Was there no end to this woman's boldness? Had she no idea that such a show of greed could just as quickly be punished as rewarded? Cal stepped forward. 'Forgive her impertinence, Emperor. She is Greek.'

He had no idea of the jest he had just made and he watched in wonder as the crowd exploded into a cacophony of laughter. When he dared look up, he saw that the Emperor was laughing, too.

'By the gods, I free you both!' shouted the Emperor, 'lest these games collapse into a comedic drama! Go now and forge your paths, and let no one in Ephesus stop you!'

And just like that, Cal and Arria were free.

Chapter Twenty-Six

There had been no room at the inn. Serenus, a small village to begin with, had been overrun by citizens on pilgrimage to the Artemisia Festival and even the villagers' homes were filled with travellers. Mercifully, a local farmer had granted Arria's mother and brother shelter in his barn and Epona and Grandmother had found them there.

'You go in first,' said Cal, who wrapped his cloak around himself against the cool of the evening. A patrician man had gifted him the garment as they had exited the arena that afternoon. He had draped it over Cal's shoulders and counselled him to hide from the gods. 'For your performance has surely made them jealous!' the man had said.

Cal had nodded his gratitude, but moments later he had muttered, 'It is the performance that lies ahead that truly matters.'

'They will love you,' Arria had assured him.

'I would settle for acceptance,' Cal had said.

When they had arrived outside the barn, Cal was trailing behind her. 'I will go in first if you wish,' she said.

When Arria opened the door, she beheld her mother's enlarged figure reclining on a bed of straw.

'Arria! Oh, thank God!' she cried. 'I prayed for you. I feared for your safety.'

Arria could not help but smile. '*My* safety?'

The farmer's wife had been kind enough to provide her mother and brother with blankets and there was a bowl of uneaten soup beside her mother's bed. 'We have been so very fortunate,' her mother said through shivering, weather-chapped lips.

Arria tucked the blanket over her mother's arms and shoulders. She looked so pale and sickly. It seemed doubtful she would survive the next few days, let alone the birth, which was already overdue.

'I am so sorry, Mother.' Arria searched her mother's eyes, so red and sunken with mourning. 'It is all my fault.'

Her mother shook her head. 'Your father chased his own demise.'

'He remains inside my heart nonetheless,' said

Arria and it was true. The damn, foolhardy gambler was a part of her and always would be.

The two embraced and, for the first time in the seven months since she had been sold, Arria breathed. Free air was different, she decided at once. It was sharper, somehow, and almost suspiciously sweet.

'We will survive this,' said her brother. He stepped from the shadows and wrapped a blanket around Arria's shoulders. In a voice so clear and certain that Arria scarcely recognised it, he said, 'We shall make a new life.'

Epona and Grandmother stepped forward and embraced Arria in turn and Arria smiled when Epona's horse whinnied out a greeting from the corner of the barn. 'I have named her Ephesia,' Epona said.

'A perfect name,' said Arria, beaming. 'I am happy to make her acquaintance.'

In that moment Cal stepped into the barn carrying an armful of wood.

'And this is Cal,' said Arria, feeling a swell of pride.

Cal set the bundle down upon the floor and in his effort his cloak came open.

Arria watched in amusement as her mother's expression progressed from confusion to fear to silent awe as she beheld the thick leather belt and blood-spattered loincloth that comprised Cal's gladiator costume.

'Cal, this is my mother and my brother, Clodius, and Epona and Grandmother, the women I told you about from the workshop. Family, this is Cal.'

The women tossed Cal friendly nods, but Arria's brother wore a suspicious frown. 'How did you meet this man?' he asked, swinging forward on his crutches.

'He defended my life,' Arria said. 'And…he made me wish for it in the first place.' Her gaze locked with Cal's and an invisible current of tenderness passed between them.

'You have a familiar face, Cal,' said Clodius. 'Whence do I know it?'

'Cal is a famous gladiator, Brother,' Arria cut in. 'You may know him as the Beast of Britannia.' Her brother was studying Cal carefully. Too carefully.

'I have heard of him,' said her brother through tightening lips. 'Do you really hail from Britannia, man?'

'He hails from—'

'Please, Arria,' her brother interrupted. 'I am sure the man can answer for himself.' Clodius fixed his gaze on Cal.

'Not Britannia,' answered Cal. 'I come from the land that Romans call Britannia.'

'What part of Britannia?' her brother asked. There was a storm stirring beneath his words. Arria could almost feel its winds.

'The north.'

'Brigante territory? Iceni, perhaps?'

'The far north.'

Clodius cleared his throat. 'Caledonia?'

Cal said nothing.

Clodius's features turned to stone. 'That is funny, a Caledonian man took my leg at the Battle of Graupius Mountain.'

'I know,' said Cal. The air between them seemed to develop edges.

Arria's voice was barely a whisper. 'How do you know, Cal?' she asked.

'I know because I am he,' said Cal, not taking his eyes off Clodius. 'I am the man who took your brother's leg.'

Arria froze. 'You must be mistaken.'

'I am not mistaken.' There was a kind of sadness in his voice. Or was it a kind of defeat? 'I cut off this man's leg in the chaos of battle. He was going to kill my captain, so I stopped him with my longsword.'

Arria heard a gasp. Perhaps it was her own gasp. Or maybe it was the soft, wicked cackle of one of the three Fates. Surely the vexatious old crones were spinning their threads somewhere near and having themselves a good laugh. Arria stared at the sunken part of her brother's tunic where his leg used to be, then glanced at Cal's strong arm, currently squeezing the hilt of his *gladius*.

'Why did you not kill me?' snarled Clodius. He gripped his *pugio*.

'Because it was not necessary.'

'I begged you for death and you pissed on me.'

'I cleaned the wound. I gave you a chance.'

'I did not ask for a chance.' Clodius lifted his blade to Cal's throat.

'Clodius!' Arria gasped. 'Please stop! It is in the past—'

'Shut up, Arria!' Clodius shouted. He gestured to the stump of his leg. 'Does this look like it is in the past?'

For so many months Arria had battled against forgetting. She believed it a kind of illness— something that would invade her mind and make her forget her desire to be free.

But now she realised that forgetting could also be a kind of cure. Each day, Clodius woke up and gazed at his leg and relived the worst day of his life. He was a prisoner of his memory, a slave to it. Forgetting was the only way he would ever be free.

Forget, Clodius, Arria thought. *Just let it all go.*

'You will need me on the journey to come,' offered Cal. He glanced at the blade Clodius held a hairsbreadth from his throat. 'I can hunt and I can fight.'

'We do not need you,' said Clodius. 'We only need our bag of coins and my good name in our journey to Eboracum.'

Cal stiffened. 'Your journey to Eboracum?'

Clodius gave an angry nod. 'The town belongs to Rome now, with a proper Roman fort. My name is on the Distributions List there.'

'Distributions List?'

'A list of Caledonii lands allotted to Roman soldiers. The Romans did win the Battle of Grau-pius Mountain, or did you not hear?'

'Those are not your lands,' Cal growled. 'They belong to my people.'

'Your people?' hissed Clodius. 'There are very few of your people left now, I'm afraid. The men are dead and the women have taken up with Roman soldiers.'

Pools of rage gathered in Cal's eyes. 'My tribe's women were ravaged by Roman soldiers and murdered. My own wife was—'

'Raped? Killed?' Clodius offered viciously. It was as if Cal was the one who had lost a leg and now Clodius was the one pissing on it. 'Clearly you care little for your late wife, or you would not have found someone to take her place.' He glanced at Arria.

'I love my wife, and no one will *ever* take her place,' Call hissed. He slid his *gladius* from its hilt and held it at Clodius's stomach. It was Arria who shrieked, however, for it was as if he had already plunged the blade into Arria's own heart.

'Stop!' she cried. She lunged between the two men. 'This is madness!'

That was when they heard the wail. It started softly, crescendoing into something so loud and heartbreaking that it might have been the wail of every suffering woman in every bloody battle from the beginning of time. Arria's mother was holding her stomach. Her face was engraved with agony.

'Her labour begins,' Grandmother pronounced. She shook her white head with impatience, then crossed the room and plucked the dagger from Clodius's hands. 'We shall need this to cut the birth cord of your new brother or sister.'

Clodius started to protest, but Grandmother was already crossing to Arria's mother, barking out orders as she went. 'Epona, I need you to gather as many pots as you can find and fill them with water. Arria, go ask the farmer's wife for whatever cloth she can spare.' Grandmother pointed at the pile of kindling. 'And will someone *please* start a fire?'

The moment of danger had passed and Arria exhaled her relief. She scanned the barn for Cal's tall figure. 'Cal?' she called, but there was no answer. He was gone.

At dawn, Arria's mother gave birth to a healthy baby boy. His hair was thick and black, and his tiny wail was as sweet and clear as a lamb's bleat. Grandmother swaddled him in her own shawl and presented him to Arria's mother with a joyous shout. 'Hail Goddess Kybele, Ancient Mother!'

'Hail Ephesia, Warrior Queen!' added Epona.

'Hail Mary, Virgin Mother,' said her mother.

'Hail Artemis, Goddess of Childbirth,' said Arria, though the exaltation sounded hollow and joyless. Epona slid Arria a sympathetic look, then diverted the family's attention with a thunderous howl.

That night they feasted on a deer that had miraculously appeared outside the door of the barn.

'The people of this village have been so good to us,' commented Arria's mother.

As *pater familias*, Clodius was duty-bound to carve the beast and sample the first bite. Instead, he carved off a piece and offered it to Arria. 'You need this more than I do,' he said.

Arria had not eaten in days, but when she placed the warm meat on her tongue she did not taste it. She could only taste the salt of her own tears.

'Why do you weep, Sister?'

'I weep for joy,' she said, though it was a lie. She wept for the anguish she had felt when Cal had spoken the truth: *I love my wife, and no one will ever take her place.* It was as Arria had always feared. He was not hers and never had been. Whatever bond she and Cal shared, it was but a handful of threads compared to the deeply woven love he would always have for his wife.

'I am happy for your joy, Sister,' said Clodius. He carved another piece of meat and offered it to Epona. The fire crackled and the two exchanged a tender smile. Arria recognised that tenderness, though she would never know it again. She would never love another. It was Cal. It had always been Cal and it always would be. And so she continued to weep quietly—not for joy, but for her broken heart.

Chapter Twenty-Seven

Cal peered out of the shadows at the woman he loved. She was sitting around a campfire talking with the other women about baby Faustus, who lay cradled in his mother's arms. The women spoke in hushed tones, but he could tell by their gestures that they were doting over the infant. When they gathered together each night, they spoke of little else.

Cal had been following them for many days now. They had stayed in Serenus only long enough to feast on the deer he had secretly delivered them and prepare for their journey. Only days after Faustus had been born, they had started out for Britannia.

Cal had followed them relentlessly, marvelling at their speed. Epona's sturdy grey mare was undaunted by the mountainous route they travelled and she bore Clodius, Arria's mother and the baby with gentle agility. Arria, Grandmother and Epona walked beside the large horse and guided its path during the day, stopping in towns to purchase food and clarify the route as they made their way steadily northward towards the Strait of Hellespont.

There, Cal knew they would cross from the senatorial province of Asia into the imperial province of Thracia, heading ever westward towards the wilds of Germania and Britannia. Cal wondered if they understood that the further they got from Ephesus, the more dangerous their travel became—especially a group such as theirs, comprised as it was of a newborn baby, a lame man and four women.

Cal worried for their safety, though he was careful not to underestimate their strength. He had recently learned that women could be as fearsome as men when they wished to be, especially when equipped with wooden poles. Or if not quite as fearsome as men, then at least twice as brave.

In truth, he simply could not bring himself to leave her.

Not even after her brother had threatened to kill him and he had realised that there was no place for him in Arria's small, fragile tribe. Watching the six of them together over the past twenty days had convinced him that he had done the right thing. With her family finally at peace, Arria was safe, needed and loved. He could never do anything to threaten that.

He could only see that she arrived safely in Britannia and that she and her loved ones found a place they could call home. He knew in time she would forget him, though the thought gave him a pain in his stomach.

In the meantime, he followed her as closely as he dared. He watched her in the mornings, when she sat up on her mat and her honey skin caught the first rays of light. Some mornings she woke up in tears, and it was all he could do not to burst out of his hiding place to wipe them.

He followed far behind them during the day, but when they stopped to rest he sometimes neared, if just to see her touch her lips to the waters of a stream. How he missed those lips. How he would always miss them.

Strangely, it was not Arria but Epona who seemed to suspect Cal's presence. She sometimes turned abruptly, as if she wished to catch him following behind the group. She often gazed into the brush wherever they made camp. Once Cal had even caught her studying one of his footprints.

Cal knew he should keep himself better hidden,

but his body was drawn to Arria's as if through some invisible force—especially on evenings like these, when he sat in the shadows watching the firelight flicker in her eyes.

'Arria, will you not tell us how you escaped the governor's *domus*?' Epona asked suddenly. 'We still have not heard the tale.'

Cal saw Arria flush. 'It is a lengthy tale,' said Arria, 'and one that you may find difficult to believe.'

'Please tell it,' urged Arria's mother. 'I, too, have longed to hear it.'

Arria gazed into the fire. 'Very well then,' she said, then began the story of her escape from a place she called Hades. She spoke in hushed tones, describing a terrible monster called the governor who locked her inside a dark, sweltering dungeon.

Cal could sense her pain as she described a battle with three demons—Heat, Thirst and Hunger, and how she had defeated them with the aid of a talking mouse.

Flames danced upon her cheeks as she painted a picture of smoke and fire, water and steam. Her voice grew softer still as she recalled encounters with a magic lamp, a benevolent dragon and a whale's hot belly.

Cal watched Clodius sit back in disbelief as

Arria described her miraculous arrival at the Temple of Artemis. He saw Arria's mother shake her head with something resembling pity as Arria explained how the goddess had transformed Arria's pole into a divine spear.

'And I bounded into the arena and sent the spear flying in defence of the man I love.'

Cal sat up. The leaves rustled beneath him and he saw Epona's eyes grow alert.

'The man you love?' Arria's mother asked.

'The gladiator, Mother. The man you met the night I arrived in Serenus. He is the man I love— the only man I will ever love.'

'The man who robbed me of my leg,' Clodius clarified and Arria stared at the ground.

Epona levelled her gaze on Clodius. 'I am afraid that the heart cannot choose what it loves, or whom.' Epona's gaze remained locked with Clodius's for a long while, as if engaged in some silent discussion. When finally Epona looked away, she gazed into the forest where Cal was hiding.

'Do go on, Arria. Finish your story,' said Grandmother and Epona returned her attention to Arria.

'Cal and I fought side by side,' Arria continued. 'We raged and battled against the governor's guards—Cal with his *gladius* and I with my spear—but they continued to pour down from the stands, the crowd cheering them on. We realised that our only choice was escape. We had just begun to run away when the Emperor himself stopped us.'

Arria's mother gasped. 'The *Emperor*?'

'Yes, Emperor Trajan himself. He congratulated us for our performance and told us to name our wish. We asked for freedom.'

Grandmother clapped her hands together. 'A marvellous story! The gods were with us that night, were they not?'

'Or perhaps they were *within* us,' mused Arria.

'What do you mean?' asked Arria's mother.

'That night, Epona was Ephesia, the Amazon queen, Grandmother was Kybele, the divine midwife, and you, Mother, might have been Mary herself on her bed of straw.'

'And you, dear Arria, were Artemis, virgin huntress, ready with your spear,' added Grandmother.

'In times of difficulty, the gods give us strength…' mused Epona.

'And in times of *great* difficulty, we become them,' Arria finished.

There was a long silence and it seemed to Cal as if Arria had just spoken some ancient truth.

'The tale stretches the bounds of reason,' grumbled Clodius.

'It is quite miraculous,' added Arria's mother.

Cal wished he could jump from the shadows and proclaim that it was all true. He wished he could shout to the entire universe that it did not matter how fantastic, that *he* believed Arria's story.

But if he truly believed all of it, then he had to believe the part in which she had called him the only man she would ever love. And if that was true, then he knew he could no longer simply watch her from the shadows, listening to her stories. He needed to find a way to make himself a part of them for ever.

Chapter Twenty-Eight

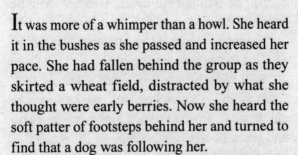

It was more of a whimper than a howl. She heard it in the bushes as she passed and increased her pace. She had fallen behind the group as they skirted a wheat field, distracted by what she thought were early berries. Now she heard the soft patter of footsteps behind her and turned to find that a dog was following her.

He was one of the shepherding breeds, his long brown hair interrupted with patches of white. She could tell by the enthusiastic swing of his tail that he was not dangerous and by the deep contours of his ribs that he was on his own.

Arria tried to shoo him away, gesturing with her arms and emitting a series of harsh hisses which had absolutely no effect. Soon he was rolling on his back at her feet and she was squatting to scratch his stomach. He gave a joyous moan, then righted himself and licked beneath her chin. He cocked his head as if to say, 'Well?'

That night, they were sitting shoulder to shoulder around the fire, watching a rabbit roast on a spit.

'We cannot keep him, Arria,' Clodius was saying. 'We are halfway through our funds already. We do not need another belly to fill.'

'But he will not eat much, Brother. And he could help keep us safe.'

'She is right,' added Grandmother. 'He can be of great use as a guard at night.'

'Will nobody take my side?' Clodius said, sending Epona a pleading look, but he found no aid. Instead, Epona flashed him a crooked grin and gestured to Clodius's lap.

'I fear that the choice has already been made, Clodius.' The dog's head had come to rest against the stump of Clodius's thigh. The creature was peering up at Clodius with unabashed longing.

Clodius masked the grin that seemed to threaten at the edges of his lips. 'He knows that I shall carve the rabbit, that is all. He thinks that if he shows his deference he will earn a piece of meat.'

'Is he right?' Epona challenged, her eyes twinkling.

If Arria had not seen what happened next with her own eyes, she would never have believed it. Her brother carved off a piece of meat and offered it to the dog. Cautiously, the dog accepted the bite, his whole body wriggling with delight. Arria knew exactly how the hungry beast felt.

So did her brother, apparently, for he quickly cut off another piece and gave it over to the grateful pup. It was not long before the dog had curled himself up between her brother's legs and began to doze. Her brother patted his head affectionately.

'Brother, I fear you are in danger of falling in love,' said Arria.

Clodius glanced briefly at Epona, then smiled. 'I suppose I am.'

'What shall we call him?' asked Arria's mother, cuddling baby Faustus in her lap. 'How about Cerberus, the Hound of Hades?' She made a scary face at little Faustus, who emitted a tiny coo.

'Or Argus, Odysseus's loyal beast,' said Grandmother.

'I vote for Romulus…or Remus,' said Epona with a wicked grin. 'I think that would be quite poetic.'

'Apologies, *Familia*,' said Arria. 'But I may have already given him a name.'

Clodius threw up his hands. 'I was beaten

before I even began!' He stroked the dog's fur.
'Well, what is it?'

'First you must promise not to laugh,' Arria
said. She scanned the faces around the fire and
took a breath. 'His name is Trajan. Trajan the
Merciful.'

Grandmother was the first to break her promise, though her laugh was more of a deep groan,
beginning in her belly and ending in her nose,
which emitted a sudden, loud snort. Soon the
whole group had descended into laughter, and
even Trajan added his howl to the chorus.

Trajan proved a worthy companion. He guarded
them day and night, keeping them together as
they trekked and patrolling their camp when they
stopped. Whenever Arria went off to hunt or for-
age for food, Trajan would follow behind, and
the two would always return with a prize. In the
night, Trajan would spread his protective presence
amidst his flock, but every morning he awoke at
Arria's side.

On the *kalends* of May, they hired a boat across
the Hellespont Strait and crossed into the Roman
province of Thracia.

The first stage of their journey complete, they
made an early camp outside a small town and

determined to rest a few days and celebrate their success.

The next day, Arria was gathering firewood when she discovered her brother standing at the edge of the glade, watching Epona groom Ephesia.

'She is a beautiful creature, is she not?' asked Arria.

'Indeed she is,' said Clodius.

'So sure-footed.'

'I was not speaking of the horse,' said Clodius.

'Clodius, Arria, there you are!' cried Epona, hailing the two. 'Watch this!'

Arria and Clodius watched as Epona took several steps away from the horse and then made a large circular gesture with her arms. Obediently, Ephesia turned around, making a full circle in the grass. Epona gave a proud bow.

'Brava!' Arria exclaimed, clapping. Ephesia whinnied, then reared back on her legs.

'Whoa there,' said Epona, calming the excited horse. Epona grabbed the mare by the mane, swung on to her back and the two broke into the forest at a gallop.

'She will never be tamed,' Arria said, chuckling.

'Epona has been working with her. She grows tamer by the day,' said Clodius.

'I am not speaking of the horse,' said Arria with a wink.

A crimson blush coloured his cheeks. 'Your perception is matched only by your wit, dear Sister.'

'Happiness strikes where it pleases, does it not, dear Brother?'

There was a long silence. 'Sister, I fear I have wronged you,' Clodius said at last. 'And now I intend to make things right.'

In that instant, Arria heard Epona's voice. She was galloping back towards them. 'Arria, you must come!' she called breathlessly. 'It is Trajan. He is in trouble.'

Chapter Twenty-Nine

It was a rather devious lie, but it could not have been helped. It was the only believable way to lead Arria to the temple without arousing her suspicion. Trajan was not in trouble, of course. He was simply bait: a cuddly, adorable kind of bait that would lure Arria right to where Cal wanted her.

'Come quickly, Arria!' Epona called behind her. She brought her horse to the temple stairs and Cal stepped briefly from the shadows to receive Epona's news.

'She is coming, then?' he asked.

Epona grinned. 'She nearly kept up with the horse.'

Cal flushed with happiness. Their ruse had worked: Arria was on her way.

'I owe you a debt,' he told Epona. He had been right about her. She had known of his presence all along and had been subtly trying to convince Clodius to accept him.

She had finally arranged a meeting between the two men the day before and they had agreed to put away the past for the sake of Arria.

Epona smiled, then gave Ephesia a little kick. 'Just make her happy,' she said and rode off deeper into the forest.

That is my greatest wish, thought Cal.

In moments Arria appeared at the temple steps and Cal moved back into the shadows. 'Epona?' she shouted and Cal watched her eyes grow wide as she beheld the crumbling temple he had chosen for their meeting.

Cal had discovered the structure the previous day. It was not large: perhaps three dozen persons might have once worshipped in its simple hall, which retained all three of its interior walls. The temple's columns had not fared as well—only half remained intact, but they were enough to hold up most of the roof, creating a kind of sacred cavern perched at the edge of a lovely river canyon.

'Trajan?' Arria muttered as she hurried up the stairs. Thankfully, Trajan responded to her call. His plaintive yelp echoed from inside the temple and Cal watched Arria hurry after the noise.

Cal could not have picked a better moment

for Arria to behold the space, for the sun burst out from between the clouds and shone down through the collapsed ceiling on to the bed Cal had fashioned in the temple's centre. Trajan stood tethered just beside the pillowy mound. He wagged his tail and barked, as if welcoming her.

'What is this?' Arria exclaimed. She rushed towards the centre of the temple, stepping among the stones and small grasses growing up between the cracks in the ancient floor.

It had taken Cal all morning to assemble the bed. He had first gathered the tallest grasses he could find—so many that the resulting pile had resembled a tower of hay. Around the soft mast he had piled dozens of heavy stones, then covered the mound with a deer hide he had been softening for weeks. Atop the soft white hide he had lain a bouquet of flowers; beside it, he had tethered the dog.

Arria bent to her knees and released Trajan from his tether, giving him a loving nuzzle, then stood and stared at the bed for a long while, as if trying to solve the riddle of it.

'Hello, my darling,' said Cal. She jumped at the sound of his voice, then turned and stifled a shriek. He was walking—no, running—towards her and she towards him. When they met, their bodies crashed together and he embraced her so tightly he feared for her very bones.

When she finally spoke, her voice was choked. 'I thought I lost you for ever.'

Her heart was exploding, her skin melting. Her fingers? They were bursting into flame. It was him, really him. His clean, warm skin, his stirring scent, his husky, resonant voice, filling the temple with its music. She could barely contain her joy, but she had to try. This was simply too good to be real.

Think, Arria.

For a moment, she was staring up at her would-be suitor, waiting for him to break her heart. 'How did you find us?'

'I have been with you all the while. I needed to know that you were safe.'

Ah, there it is, she thought, feeling the weight of truth settle upon her. *He has followed me in order to ensure my safety. He has acted out of his sense of duty, that is all.*

She pulled herself from his arms and stepped back. 'You are an honourable man,' she said carefully. 'My family owes you a debt.'

'You saved me from death,' he said. 'It is I who owes you a debt.'

She glanced at the bed, slowly piecing together

his intentions. He wished to give her the gift of pleasure in reciprocation for her bravery. How very kind of him.

'Please consider your debt paid,' she said. He had already declared where his real heart lay: with his wife, where it always had been. She did not want his charity—to share all of his body but none of his heart. She would rather live the rest of her life in a desert than taste a single drop of his pity upon her tongue. She pasted a friendly smile on her face. 'You do not need to worry. I understand.'

'Understand?'

'About your wife.'

'My wife?'

'That you love her, that nobody will ever take her place.'

'But someone already has,' said Cal.

He closed the space she had placed between them and pushed an errant curl behind her ear.

He wanted to remember her like this. Just like this. Staring at him in that cascade of golden sunlight, her cheeks flushed, her long braid a column of carved onyx. He wanted this memory and a thousand others, too. He wanted to fill the rest of his days with this woman.

'But...what you said to my brother...'

'I spoke in anger. I spoke without thought.'

'I do not wish to take your wife's place.'

'You cannot, for I have put her memory to rest in a small corner of my heart. Whereas your memory…' He gazed into her eyes. 'Your memory haunts me at every hour of the day. It colours my thoughts, controls my limbs and keeps my heart beating. Arria, you are all I want.'

A sheen of tears curtained her eyes. 'Trajan was not in trouble after all, I see.' She peered shyly at the dog, who had taken a seat at her feet.

'Trajan was not in trouble, but I fear that I have been since I met you.' He stepped forward, closing the distance between them. He took her hands in his. 'I have been waiting for you for so long, Arria. I do not think I can last another day.'

She squeezed his hands. 'I am so happy—'

But he did not let her finish.

He pressed his lips upon hers and was feeling sorry, so very sorry for interrupting her, but not nearly sorry enough to stop. He was a free man and he wished to kiss the woman he loved. *Really* kiss her.

He coaxed her mouth open and covered it with his lips, and his longing seemed to explode beneath his skin. He shuddered, pressing harder, feeling the sweet pressure of her response, which only made him shudder more.

How many miles had he walked imagining this moment? How many mountains climbed and streams forded, picturing her lips locked with his? Too damned many. Now, finally, the moment was here, and he could hardly breathe for wanting her.

He slid his arm around her waist and pulled her closer, and she gave no resistance as he took her lower lip in his and sucked, savouring her taste. He slid his tongue past her lips and let it languish, basking in his desire for her.

Her body folded into his. Her breasts pressed beneath the flanks of his chest like twin pillows. He slid his hand on to her buttocks and squeezed, then plunged his tongue into her mouth.

Dark rivers of Hades, she was not supposed to taste this good, or feel this good, or be this good. She arched up into him, pushing her body more firmly against his. In seconds she had met his tongue with hers and a maddening, erotic swordplay had begun.

They kissed with growing abandon, their tongues twining, their hot breaths mingling, their lust raging. They tasted and teased, biting and sucking, delighting in every second, as if these were their last moments on earth. Or, perhaps, he thought suddenly, their first.

Cal stopped to catch his breath. He gazed

down at her. 'I feared that I would never be able to get you alone.'

'I feared that you did not wish to get me alone,' she said.

The sunlight blanketed her face and it occurred to him that he had never seen her more clearly. Her big, brown eyes, wide with wonder, her shapely lips, crimson and chafed, her round cheeks and proud nose, the bold set of her gaze, how it seemed to be daring him.

Where had she come from, this raven-haired goddess? It was as if she had been sent to him with a message: that all his grave vows and dark certainties were but puffs of cloud in an endless sky.

'You rescued me from my death,' he said.

'I believe it was you who rescued me from *my* death,' she said.

He found a tendril of her hair and curled it around his thumb. 'Perhaps we saved each other, *fy nghariad.*'

'What does that mean, *fy nghariad*?'

'It means *my love.*'

'My love?'

'I love you, Arria.'

She blinked and two tears cut twin paths down her cheeks. 'I confess that I never thought I would ever hear anyone say that.'

He stroked his finger against her skin, wiping them. 'I thought you knew. I have loved you for so long. From the moment you cursed me.' He straightened himself before her. 'And now I cannot wait any longer for you. I give you my heart, Arria. Will you have it?'

She cocked her head and he saw her flush as the gravitas of his question overcame her. She straightened her shoulders. 'Of course I will have it,' she said, 'for I love you, too.'

He gathered the strip of hide with which he had tethered Trajan. 'Then take my hand.'

He took her hand in his and wrapped it with the hide, binding their hands together. 'Arria, you have not only rescued me from death, you have shown me what it means to live. I wish to be with you for all my days, to make myself worthy of you. I wish to show you all the colours of my love.'

Arria stared at their bound hands, then placed her own hand atop them. 'Cal, when I was invisible, you saw me. When I was helpless, you defended me. When I was hopeless, you inspired me. You tried to give your life to save mine. I wish to be with you for all my days so that I may pay homage to your beautiful heart.'

They kissed—a long, slow, tender kiss that

seemed to say everything their loving words could not.

When finally they pulled apart, they gazed into each other's eyes, and it was as if the chord that bound their hands together rose up and wrapped slowly about their arms, pulling them close enough for their hearts to meet, then winding about their heads so that their heads merged together, bound by the same knowing. It was Cal who broke the silence. 'We are married.'

Arria grinned. 'I believe that we are, though Roman tradition requires ten witnesses.'

Cal laughed. 'Fortunately Caledonii tradition requires only one.'

Arria glanced at Trajan, who was now balled in slumber at her feet.

'He will do,' said Cal.

'Do you think my brother will accept us?'

'He does not really have a choice. Especially if—' He took her hand and led her towards the bed. Her eyes glittered with excitement.

'Especially if…?'

Just the thought of her desire made him dizzy with lust. 'There is a certain debt I owe you. I do intend to pay it. Wife.'

'Well, I suppose we have a task ahead of us, then. Husband.' She ran her finger lightly down the length of his arm, then cocked her head in a kind of dare.

'You drive me mad when you do that.'

'Do what?'

'Tilt your head like that, *fy nghariad.*'

'And you drive me mad when you do that.'

'When I do what?'

She smiled, her cheeks reddening. She turned her attention to the bed. 'What beautiful flowers you have gathered,' she said. 'Gratitude.'

She would not evade his question so easily. 'When I do what, *hardd gwraig*? I must know.'

'*That,*' she said. Now the crimson was making fast progress down her neck. What could he possibly have done to have such an effect on her? More importantly, how could he do it again?

'I am begging you, *fy nghalon.* Tell me.'

'When you do that. When you speak in your tongue. It makes me feel…it makes me feel…'

Chapter Thirty

Oh, gods, what had she done? She had tried to avoid the admission. She had done her best to change the subject, to distract him from the truth inside her heart, but he had coaxed it from her like a snake from a basket.

He smiled at her wickedly now and she knew that the torture was about to begin. 'It makes you wild when I speak in my mother tongue. Is that it, *fy hyfryd*?'

Her skin began to itch. *'Rydw i dy eisiau di,'* he said. Hot, unbearable yearning churned within her. *'Nawr.'*

By the gods, she was doomed. 'Have mercy on me, please,' she begged.

He shook his head deviously and she could sense his wicked mind at work. He untied their hands and reached for the bunch of flowers, which he lifted to her nose. She closed her eyes and, as she breathed in their otherworldly scent, she felt a husky whisper in her ear. *'Mor dda.'*

Oh, no. It was too much. The words themselves were kisses—tiny, deeply erotic kisses that made her heart ache with yearning. If he said any more of them, she just might combust. As it was, she wanted to tear off both their tunics.

Fortunately, he was of the same mind. He tossed the bunch of flowers to the floor, then lifted her tunic over her head and undid her breast band. He did the same with his own tunic and then they were standing together, the sunlight pouring down on to their naked figures.

He wrapped his arms around her and she delighted in the feeling of his skin against hers. He held her for a long while, cradling her head against his chest and stroking her hair.

'May I undo your braid, Arria?'

She almost laughed. 'If you wish to brave such an endeavour, I will not stop you.' He gave a grateful smile, then pulled off her hair tie and glided his finger through her curly locks.

'Will you shake it for me?' he asked.

'Now I see that you are truly mad.'

'I have been wanting to untie that braid since the night we met.'

'Well, in that case...' She stepped backwards and shook out her hair. Her curls opened up and surrounded her head in a great twisting riot. She expected to see him grimace, but his expression was full of wonder.

'By the gods, you are beautiful,' he said.

She touched a round lock. 'This? Beautiful?'

'Yes, that. You.' His eyes slid down her naked chest. 'Beautiful.'

She gave him a doubting look. 'I think I would rather be bald than have this unruly nest atop my head.' She gazed at his shiny head. 'May I?'

He nodded and she moved her hands over the smooth surface of his head and said a prayer of gratitude, for it was as if she were touching a sacred object.

She did not wish to stop touching him, so she traced his thick eyebrows, then made a path down his cheeks and across his jaw. She let one of her fingers whisper across the contours of his lips.

When she moved to withdraw the digit, he closed his own lips around it and sucked softly, and a hot giggle bubbled out of her.

'Give me another kiss,' he demanded. He slid his fingers sensually into her hair and cradled her neck, then pressed his lips against hers.

This was wondrous. This was bliss. There was something so natural about kissing him. It was like eating or breathing. A foregone conclusion. The will of the Fates.

'You taste like heaven,' he said.

She glanced down. He was already fully aroused. His desire had emerged from beneath his loincloth. Still, she was not afraid. Experimentally, she pressed her stomach against his, trapping the huge pillar of flesh between them and rubbing her naked breasts against his chest. He gave a gratifying groan.

She stepped backwards in surprise. Was the beast so easily tamed? She smiled, but he did not return her grin. Instead he gave her a dangerous look. 'Take me in hand,' he said. He gripped her hand and pressed it against his fullness.

She could do nothing but obey as he guided her down the enormity of him.

'Now it is you who must have mercy on me,' he growled.

She began to stroke him, slowly at first, then with an increasing boldness. He was so very hard, yet his skin was soft and pliant. He groaned with pleasure as she gradually increased her speed. 'Do you know what you are doing to me?'

She did know. Or at least, she had an idea. When they had last lain together, he had rubbed his desire against her body until he was overcome with pleasure. She had thought of that moment so often afterwards that it had become something like a prayer inside her mind, or a beautifully painted fresco.

Though it was not piety that she felt when she thought of it. It was an odd kind of hunger—the kind that began not in the belly, but further down. Now that she was coaxing him towards his peak of pleasure once again, she was feeling that hunger again, too. It was growing inside her, like her own secret beast. It wanted to be fed.

He reached to the knot at her stomach and tugged it undone, then pulled her loincloth free.

She felt her body stiffen as his finger slipped into her hot folds. His breaths were raspy and short. 'I want you, Arria.' Sparks of sensation snapped and popped inside her, and she closed her eyes as his thick finger pushed slowly deeper. 'And you want me,' he said. 'I can feel that you do.'

'You can?'

He growled his assent and something seemed to squeeze deep in her core. It pulsed through her body, spreading the hunger. She stopped stroking him, the hunger growing so acute that she could do nothing but close her eyes. 'I can feel it,' he said.

He eased her down on to the soft bed and she settled herself on her back, yearning to feel the weight of him atop her. Instead she felt his warm lips on her stomach, kissing a path downwards.

Whenever she thought of the last time he had kissed that part of her, she became so restless that she could not concentrate on her work. Now there was no work—unless she counted the effort she was making to keep herself from going mad with yearning.

Then she felt his tongue slip beneath her folds.

Sweet merciful Artemis.

There was nothing to imagine now. There was only the soft wet forbidden sensation of his tongue making slow swirls inside her.

She slid her fingers on to his head, caressing it in rhythm with his tongue's soft movements. Her hips began to move of their own volition. His tongue continued its relentless mission, probing deeper until she was writhing against it with a lust so profound she had to cry out.

She felt as if she were perched on some terrible precipice and that any minute she might go tumbling off it into oblivion. 'Cal, please,' she begged, unsure of what exactly she needed, but knowing that whatever it was, he alone could give it.

He lifted his head from between her legs and swept over the top of her, bracing himself on his knees so that he straddled her waist without touching it, his obelisk of flesh suspended in the air above her stomach. 'Take me in hand,' he commanded once again and when she obeyed he moved downward, until she could feel the tip of him grazing against her soft curls.

'This is how we will join. Do you understand?'

She nodded. Oh, she understood. She had been dreaming of this moment for days, months, all her adult life. She could feel the heat emanating from the cleft between her legs, could sense her own wetness as he pressed himself gently against the folds of her flesh. He held himself there and the seconds stretched out.

'Do you want me?' he said.

'I want you,' she whispered.

'It may hurt a little at first,' he warned. 'But soon you will begin to feel pleasure.'

She nodded and gripped his shoulders as he thrust into her. He was staring down at her, his face obscured in shadow. But she could see the glint of his green eyes and the certainty reflected in them.

'Are you in pain?'

'No,' she lied, digging her fingernails so tightly into his shoulders that she feared she might draw blood.

But he only moaned with pleasure, pushing deeper. He must have sensed her discomfort, for he bent and whispered into her ear. '*Rwy'n dy garu di*, Arria.'

They were beautiful words, magical words, and in her heart she knew exactly what they meant: *I love you.* Her body relaxed as he thrust deeper. There was pain, yet she did not wish to be anywhere else.

He made a final thrust and she realised that they were as close as two people could be. 'The difficult part is over,' he said. 'The rest is only pleasure.'

He began to move inside her, his desire sliding in and out of her in a slow, enchanting rhythm. He was watching her closely, adjusting his movements as she sighed and gasped with each new sensation.

'You feel so good, Arria,' he moaned. He pinned her with a kiss so achingly gentle that she had to lift her chin to deepen it. 'That is it, my love,' he whispered into her mouth. His kiss became harder, greedier. With each thrust of his hips, his tongue plunged deeper into her mouth.

Her pleasure seemed to be building. His powerful limbs braced over her. His desire throbbed within her, plunging and thrusting and seeking something that it seemed she alone could give.

The heat. There was so much heat. And wetness. And sensation. It was as if he was chasing her up a steep cliff, tickling and daring and goading her as she stepped closer and closer towards the peak.

And then she was not walking, but running. And he was there beside her, straining with his limbs to run faster and faster until suddenly the ground disappeared from beneath their feet and they were running together in the air.

And then they were falling. The world around them blurred as they plummeted through space. They were convulsing with pleasure, moaning and gasping as the divine release hit them in slow, exquisite waves.

Gods, the sweetness of it. The pure joy. She was shocked, exhilarated, undone. She had wanted this for so long, not knowing exactly what it was. Now that she knew, she did not want it to end. This was pleasure, this was love, this was life.

This was *theirs*.

Cal lifted his head and let out a long, howling moan, then collapsed atop her. His voice echoed in the cavernous space, mixing with the warm spring breeze, and a collection of last season's leaves burst out from beneath the eaves of the ancient temple as if in celebration of their love. Arria watched in wonder as the leaves fluttered through the sunlight above them in a rainbow of whites and browns and greys.

Looking closer, Arria realised they were not leaves at all, but wings.

She gasped.

'What is it my love?' asked Cal, his face buried in her hair. 'Tell me, what do you see?'

'I can hardly believe it, Cal,' said Arria, her heart near bursting. 'Pigeons!'

* * * * *

COMING SOON!

We really hope you enjoyed reading this book. If you're looking for more romance, be sure to head to the shops when new books are available on

Thursday 27th December

To see which titles are coming soon, please visit
millsandboon.co.uk

MILLS & BOON

Coming next month

THE EARL'S IRRESISTIBLE CHALLENGE
Lara Temple

'And so we circle back to your agenda. Are you always this stubborn or do I bring out the worst in you?'

'Both,' Olivia said.

Lucas laughed, moving forward to raise her chin with the tips of his fingers.

'Do you know, if you want me to comply, you should try to be a little less demanding and a little more conciliating.'

'I don't know why I should bother. You will no doubt do precisely what you want in the end without regard for anyone. The only way so far I have found of getting you to concede anything is either by appealing to your curiosity or to your self-interest. I don't see what good begging would do.'

He slid his thumb gently over her chin, just brushing the line of her lip, and watched as her eyes dilated with what could as much be a sign of alarm as physical interest. He wished he knew which.

'It depends what you are begging for,' he said softly, pulling very slightly on her lower lip. Her breath caught, but she still didn't move. Stubborn *and* imprudent. Or did she possibly really trust him not to take advantage of the fact that they were alone in an empty house in a not-very-genteel part of London?

It really was a pity she was going to waste herself
on that dull and dependable young man. What on earth
did she think her life would be like with him? All that
leashed intensity would burn the poor fool to a crisp if
he ever set it loose, which was unlikely. A couple of
years of being tied to him and she would be chomping
at the bit and probably very ripe for a nice flirtation. He
shook his head at his thoughts. Whatever else he was,
he had never yet crossed the line with an inexperienced
young woman; they were too apt to confuse physical
pleasure with emotional connection. It wouldn't be smart
to indulge this temptation to see if those lips were as
soft and delectable as they looked. Not smart, but very
tempting…

Continue reading
THE EARL'S IRRESISTIBLE CHALLENGE
Lara Temple

Available next month
www.millsandboon.co.uk

LET'S TALK
Romance

For exclusive extracts, competitions
and special offers, find us online:

 facebook.com/millsandboon

 @MillsandBoon

 @MillsandBoonUK

Get in touch on 01413 063232

For all the latest titles coming soon, visit
millsandboon.co.uk/nextmonth